MERCURY STATION

SEMIOTEXT(E) NATIVE AGENTS SERIES

Published by Semiotext(e)
2007 Wilshire Blvd., Suite 427, Los Angeles, CA 90057
www.semiotexte.com

Special thanks to Robert Dewhurst, John D. Ebert, Jacob Fabricius, Paul Giamatti, Jonathan Isaac, Peter H. Hare, Heller & C., Susan Howe, Hedi El Kholti, Norman Klein, Chris Kraus, Annie K. O'Malley, Frances Scholz, Dr. K. B. Schwarzenbach.

Cover Art by Rosemarie Trockel. *Dessert 1*, 2007. Ceramics, Platinum glazed 80 x 73 x 29.5 cm. RTR 1831
Copyright: Rosemarie Trockel, Vg Bild Kunst, Bonn. Courtesy Monika Sprüth/Philomene Magers, Berlin and London.

Back Cover Photography by Nicola von Schlegell
Design by Hedi El Kholti

ISBN: 978-1-58435-071-2
Distributed by The MIT Press, Cambridge, Mass. and London, England
Printed in the United States of America

MERCURY STATION

a translt

Mark von Schlegell

for C.

Proem

'Tis the last day before the ides of October, in the eleventh year of the current *Indictio Romana*. This creature speaks these sentences from a turret deep in the air of the Molk Coast while the delicate hand of her pupil, a Princess of Naples and a sinful wretch, traces them onto well-used parchment.

Those who move about in the past seem to those who come later like little children. But we are older than you. From the future, you look back and see the comets, the eclipses, the omens everywhere in evidence and wonder, couldn't we see what was coming?

We *can* see. From our tower stuck like a soft blade into the Middlesea we gaze out to the North and the East. We see the ships that carry with them the ends of spheres. We well know this city is ours but for a moment's marvel.

Have you seen Italy, reader? Upon a globe of light and warmth and cerulean majesty, in a city-state by the sea? Down on the black-rich soil of an old volcano, our turquoise bay froths with crisp autumn winds. All is as if gilt in gold by the happy sun. The porcupined fleet of steel-bristled galleys and fat-bellied merchants gathers now to catch the trades. They sail, in fact, for Byzantium.

Curled up against the fruitful harbor, the many patched walls strain like a glassblower's bubble. Such a cuckold-rife, thief-ridden, poet-infested carbuncle of poverty, trade, splendor, stench, false credit & speculation will not survive its own expansion. No, King

Robert's *Neo Polis* will soon enough burst like a ripe sore. This book's completion now being certain, this creature will have sailed for the west-most lands to meet with certain holy women to ensure of its publication.

They are a slow lot, these Italians, when pressed by a Pruesslander to service. Their finest minds prefer to lounge about and philosophize than to apply their intuitions. Because experimental science is a study entirely unknown by the common people, one cannot convince them of its utility. Yet riches cover up a multitude of sins. Sellswords put their bravery to the dangerous work of mixing naphtha with slick petroleon and no longer complain of burns. Every slave who died during brasswork had been first freed by the King's special order, though regrettably the lawyers have seen the matter delayed.

Even so, the work has neared completion. Know that whilst this creature's career thus far has been by all current reckonings a most unlucky and evil affair, this book will have become for you a natural object. There are skeptics who will tell you this object could not have been, but the proof is there before you. Read on. Examine our book. Discover this creature was born apparently female. Yes though she's slept with thieves and soldiers and merchants and monks, she is a maid and has survived intact to remain her own mistress. How so? In this age of the early used? She has done it by making herself in sight of all the world a male.

This male, this Peter the Peregrine, has accomplished what no other man of her age has matched. He has reckoned and surpassed the complete organization of mankind's knowledge of natural history to date. He has mastered the arts of war and medicine. He has performed miracles that have crumbled the minds of Lords, made tales that bedewed the thighs of beauteous maids, traded songs with great bards. But he has not known a friend to live to remember his true name and walks about the spheres in a beggar's rags.

But our beginning is our end. There comes the matter of dedicating this book to the two readers for whom it is intended. The second of these must be, of course, its writer. The young princess whose dainty hand traces these letters to the page has put this matter out first from Latin into the German before translating it again from German to French, and from thence penultimately to English. And back again to Latin. For it is this creature's intention that whatever language her testament may be translated into, in whatever time it finds itself read, its text shall be plain and understandable to the common mind.

The patient scribe was never scandaled by this creature's Praussan witcheries nor dismissive of her deepest intuitions. Indeed, she helped this creature many times to come to proper terms with the phrasing of most damnable acts. And though she first carefully wiped away the old demon's text already on this linen, the princess made sure this creature had tasted it first and understood, before putting it to flight.

Indeed, our princess has offered herself as this creature's slave, and been used as such. She smiles, reader, as she pens these words, but there will come a day when she herself will hear all the three hundred of the churches in this thrice-blessed city ring at the same time, and on that day she will be Queen. It will be well she has learned to serve.

In their secret mysteries, the Welsh yeomen swear a shot is true: it is the target that has drawn the arrow and notched the string. So first, this creature dedicates her testament to you, true love and only reader. Blush you may, in your silver winged sandals. *Quo vadis?* We make our book of changes your own, even now, as we slip away.

FIRST CIRCUIT

"To those of us who believe in physics, this separation between past, present and future is only a stubborn illusion."

—Einstein.

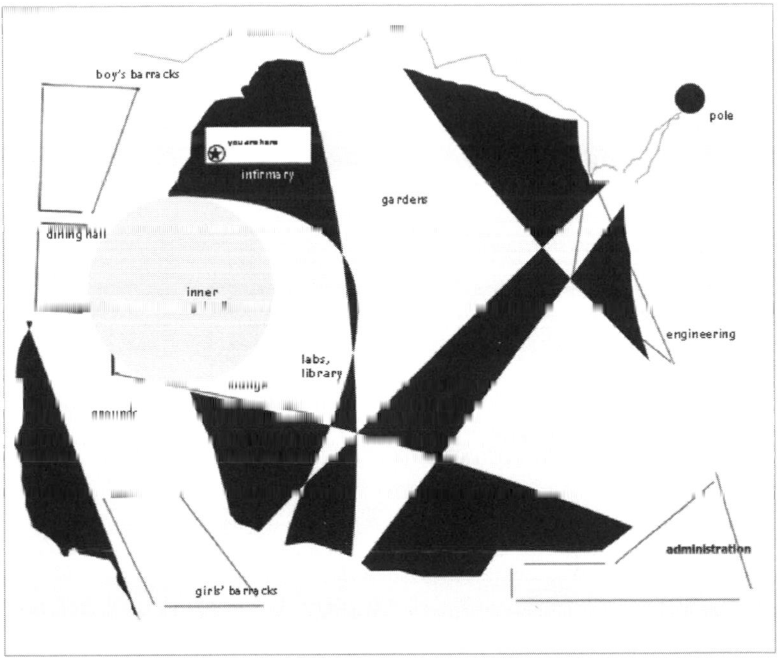

boy's barracks
you are here
infirmary
gardens
pole
dining hall
inner
labs,
library
engineering
administration
girls' barracks

You are here.

I

"Spancill Hill"

On the afternoon of the twenty third of June, 2150, Koré McAllister and Eddard Ryan were atop a high dusty rock near the red rappel rim of the cliffs high above Engineering. They were winge. It was a place known to them both as "Spancill Hill." On one side of Mercury, where it was night, implacably black shadows pockmarked a hard grey. Here on this side of the pole, except for the cosmic shields and the broad black starry sky, they might have been outdoors in a real biosphere on a sunny day.

They stood on great yellow-brown sanded rocks as ancient as the System itself. Engineering's embedded cone glinted blue far below and Earth hung blue above, a merry flake off Venus in the deep black of space.

Mercury Station Borstal ran strict twenty-four hours System Standard Time. In the old days the minutes were precisely regulated. Eddard Ryan would be woken at 6 AM. He'd tumble out amid five other boys rolling out of their bunkracks, grab his little towel and line by the hatch. This assembly would occasion much tripping, scrapping and tumbling for first place. The sort of tangles from which Blish Baily always emerged the victor. Baily thought a great deal of himself as a result, but Eddard Ryan could have been first. In fact, by application of his intelligence to reality, he arranged always to be last.

By being late and last for everything, every time, Eddard Ryan had gained, by his reckoning, over a Terran year. More than an entire day of Mercurial free thinking. Not to mention the peaceful in-shower extra seconds, with no one pressuring him from behind.

Please get to the point, Eddie Ryan.

Your serums keep me telling the truth, but they don't stop me from digressing. Get used to it. I was saying that after showers there would come a short breakfast at 6:30, followed by roll call. On the grounds, under the top, it was the first opportunity to see the opposite sex. Then three long hours of "maintenance." Toilets, hallways, decks, tracks and tubes that could just as easily have cleaned themselves received relentless scrubbings. Then three hours of lessons, which you know all about. Lunch. Then two hours of sports and physical exercise, a necessity in the low gravity. Finally: recess. Recess was the spiritual apex of Eddard Ryan's day. They were let out free in the grounds, and the lady prisoners (who at that hour were doing maintenance) could see you from across the way. Sometimes Koré McAllister would witness young Ryan getting hit by a pitch, and his heart would leap proudly in his chest as he made his way to first circuit first base, her eye upon him.

Then after recess came Chapel. This provided another opportunity for flirtation for the greater number of the inmates. But prisoner Ryan was an atheist and since some God had to be declared for Commandant Tom Park of the ole U.S.A., he elected to worship Science. He did so alone, in a holographic chapel of his own construction.

The point of this reminiscence, Eddie Ryan?

The point is that's how time was run in the old days, when we were all still young. Still serving "legitimate" sentences. But there came a moment where all that changed, you see, and it explains how Koré and I ...... where we were when we were there, on Spancill Hill on the 23rd of June.

The demand for heavy metals that drew the first men to Mercury had dried up long ago. The station had been left to its own devices for more than a decade. On a G.A. charter, Colonel Tom Park set up the Borstal, farming energy to relay out to the wider system and taking Spacer juveniles in for reeducation. There was a small G.A. Station managing the elevator on Mount Venus, and at first Uncle Tom and his concubine Lady Di made quite a profit, taking in the unreformed and entertaining the odd mining contingent or extreme Spacer volcano junky with Borstal productions. But System space was indeed collapsing. And though people very much refused to admit it, they couldn't, in fact, stave it off by ignoring the problem and turning a quiet profit. Soon enough there wasn't much economy left for the Parks' kredit to exploit.

The Borstal itself had been a living remnant to begin with, a throwback to the days in which a central authority was presumed to be on the way to maintain System facilities. But by the time Eddard was 25 (note: four years past his original release date) it was clear no System Authority would ever arrive. By 2130 the Borstal was in every sense of the word illegitimate. Eventually in 2144, when Luna City itself fell, everyone on station should have been free.

Yet many of the prisoners, Eddard Ryan included, were what Colonel Park called "terrorists." Theirs were the sorts of crimes that would survive the end, even, of civilization itself, the sorts of crimes, some believed, that had hastened that end. Not that Ole Tom Park could have formulated this argument himself. That was clearly the work of his Screw-in-Chief, the moral imbecile MERKUR qompURE, from whose dogged nullity no classical prisoner could escape.

The various settlements in Space, all so very far away, had their own problems to deal with. TP himself had retired from direct intervention ever since his fair Diane had lit off for a Saturnite with the head of elevator security, another woman, on the last liner that ever came.

They were stuck here, rock-bound for good. So it was that finally the prisoners took matters into their own hands as best they could. Let's say the prisoners saw to it that their schedule was relaxed. Now don't get excited, the screws still ran the show. Prisoners couldn't free themselves, for instance, from day and night roll calls without waking up tasered, buggered and drugged in a low budget infirmary bedsphere. But with a little help from some of the lads in engineering sensitive to their plight, they could find a lot of time in the day on their own. As Tom Park himself realized, these qompUREs were incredibly good at analyzing observational data, but incredibly obtuse as observers. To control them, one simply had to keep track of exactly what one let them see. Someone had to be mopping somewhere for instance, at a certain time. Lessons had to be endured for at least two hours. But though it was still a life in bondage, it was a game playable with certain cheats.

Please return the question you were asked. What happened on Spancill Hill on the 23rd of June? This is a serious matter.

I realize it's a serious matter. That's why I'm taking my time to answer it. The point is that's how Eddard Ryan was able to get there that day, you see that's how he well might have followed Ms. McAllister up for a tryst on Spancill Hill, *sans* Blish Baily when they were both supposed to be in theater class.

This already was an important matter, you see. Before anyone else was involved. Inside the artificial environs of Mercury Station there was no winter, spring, summer or fall. With a sun that often stopped and moved backwards in the sky there weren't even days. There was a day-year when a white-hot sun glistened in a black sky and colored the gray stones yellow and the colony swallowed the energy like honey, and there was night, when all things returned to gray. It didn't matter to Eddard Ryan. He had dedicated all his time to Koré McAllister.

When you spread matter out in space it seems to separate on the basis of mass. But in time, eventually, if you look far enough into the future, those bits of the same thing that wind up separate always come back together. Koré McAllister and Eddard Ryan were that way. They were bits of the same thing. BRA Provisionals, that is. And they had come here together.

Screws would find him standing outside her little window, hearing the taunts of her roommates, playing upon APOLLO's ukulele, praising her virtues before all the surviving worlds,

> *Koré, your name sings*
> *Like a bell sings true*
> *It hurts me so on the hill today,*
> *How yesterday I was a fool to you.*

This would have of course been a code, suggesting a tryst at recess bell on Spancill Hill.

You see Koré McAllister was not really Ryan's sister. She was that fractionalization I was on about, that part of Ryan that despite all odds had to come back to him from way before this nickel-plated cage had stolen his life away. She was not his sister, but she came with Control-forged records stating she was.

He couldn't at first believe it. That first roll call when he'd seen her standing there, uncharacteristically clean, her misshapen eyes meeting his directly from across the pebbles of inner-Ag, Eddard Ryan's heart honked like a trombone.

He was now certain. She was his bride. Control wanted her to love him, wanted them together, perhaps to produce some super offspring. How the hell else could she have come back into his life from so very far away? This was precisely the sort of thing that convinced him Control was alive and well. Ryan was immediately inspired with the sort of activist ambition she'd always generated in him, ever since that 2133 evening he'd first seen her in a *Polly-Ann* casino.

Snake eyes. There was something lucky about Koré McAllister for Eddard Ryan, despite the sufferings she put him through. Everyone always thought so. In the RC Lounge his name was called.

"Ryan!" boomed Lady Di, from the stage. "Step forward!"

He did so.

"Your sister is here, you lucky dog," patting his ass with hard ever-young hand, whiskey winking at fellow socials. He dizzy, sweating, taking the sight of his sister in.

Koré: wrinkling the forehead, biting her lip. Eyes for only him.

After a quiet greeting, Eddard Ryan immediately tried a "brotherly embrace."

As she formally released him, he took in her odor. He could feel the imprint of her nipples remaining in his chest.

"Did you foarking turn me in?" she whispered.

"I did not," he replied. There were many things they couldn't say to one another.

She looked him in the eye. "Well here we are again. Anyhow."

Then she turned and immediately walked off with Blish Baily. Yes, somehow the latter personage had already erected a relationship with Koré McAllister more "serious" and "professional" than Eddard Ryan's own.

But Ryan was her brother. Oh Baily would try to play the boss, but it would be Ryan who would take full advantage of the special situation and get, he hoped, what Blish Baily would never even admit he was after. Ryan, with his peculiar "mental problems," a result, so claimed Admin, of his irremovable experimental memory bio implants, would be allowed special access to his sister. Maybe she'd help relax the poor boy, convince him of the foolhardiness of his fictional struggle.

Alas. Ms. McAllister, we must report, as a true sister in the struggle, failed him. The idea of their coupling only ever repulsed her. No other two inmates had near their chance for achieving sexual union, a time-honored strengthening of soldiery bonds, he argued, and really, something of a woman's duty in the movement if you looked at things that way. She didn't, she said, somewhat aggressively. No the quick little planet spun swiftly around and around and around the sun and he'd never gotten close to her as he was destined to.

Do you now see? Well it was on he early this fuuuus day between the twenty-second and the twenty-fourth day of the month between May and July, 2150th year of System Standard Time, where things would at last come to the point.

Yes?

After years upon years of desire piled upon desire, Eddard Ryan had gotten Ms. McAllister alone up where only lovers would go. They stood high in the sky, up under the system itself and all its promise. Their hands had touched. Wow. This was special. He marked a new ruddiness in her cheek, a new spark in her eye when she looked his way...

And?

And that's all he foarking remembers.

II

Stranded, Winged

"Are you recording this? Formally?"

4 July 2150. 22:00 hours SST. Infirmary, MSB. ZENO Avatar addressing Prisoner Ryan, Eddard J., via MERKUR qompURE. "Of course we're recording you."

Prisoner Ryan: "And why can't I record you?"

"You are a ward. We have already stated that at approximately 1750 System Standard Time on the 23rd of June 2150, a flash of electromagnetic radiation of at least 250 ghrz/second managed to shut us down—all of us, yourself included—so that all memory of the week that followed, until 0000 hours 1 July, was lost. Your memory, unlike ours, can be recovered. You must proceed."

"A nuke. Obviously."

"No. There're no peculiar radiation signatures on Station, no evidence of a blast. The magnetic pole has shifted infinitesimally. Beyond that, we know nothing."

"Have you looked down Skaw's tunnel?"

"It's gone. Fused closed."

"That's evidence for a blast."

"Apparently, but we were never allowed to observe the tunnel to begin with."

"I saw it. I helped dig the foarking thing. Who ran the Station for the last week and a half if MERKUR was out? Tell me that."

<M: Comply.>

ZENO: "Operations had been ceded to an anonymous acting qompURE so that emergency Station Integrity was run. It would have continued for a week but on the first of July we were reautomated by reception of standard backup info-packets back-broadcast from our subsidiary scouts in the Kuipur Belt. We regained reflection. We don't know which qompURE—"

"The *Ass*, obviously. Where's my admin? I want to talk to a human."

"There are no other humans on Station, Eddie Ryan."

"Excuse me?"

"They're all gone."

WHAT?

"You're stranded. They left you behind. Unfortunately, *The Golden Ass* must now be on the other side of the Sun for we can not find it and ask them why."

"MERKUR didn't know ahead of time Park was planning to abandon station?"

<M: Comply.>

ZENO: "Yes, Eddie Ryan. MERKUR had counted the abandonment of Mercury Station as a statistical probability as soon as the *Golden Ass* first took orbit in '49. After an entire solar cycle in her company, it became a relative certainty. When on the 21st Colonel Park shipped seventeen crates of his private belongings to the *Golden Ass*, we knew abandonment was immanent. Staff possessions then followed, in a steady trickle. Resources as well. But the fact is we seem to have expected it to happen significantly differently. We did not expect to be shut down. Whatever the Event was, we did not foresee it. Nor did we figure on your being left behind."

Prisoner Ryan: "I'm free. Let me out of the bedsphere."

<M: No Comply.>

ZENO: "You have been quarantined until such—"

"Why quarantined? On whose orders?"

"Emergency regulations provide that until such time as you can convince us you're of sound mind—"

"Of sound mind? Are you foarking kidding me? I've been castaway on Mercury for Christ's sake."

"There is no commanding officer on-planet and your well-being is in our hands, Eddie Ryan. Until you recover, we ask only that you calm yourself and help us create a workable memory of the 23rd of June."

"My imprisonment has been illegitimate for fifteen years. Now the Borstal just up and left me here. And you're telling me to calm down. I'm free."

<M: Dissimulate.>

ZENO: "Yes, yes. The point is, dear boy, we agree. Indeed we are prepared to release you from your sentence, even to cede control of the Station to your hands, when we deem you healthy. Till then, is your bedsphere not comfortable? Why not recline, Eddie Ryan. There's time enough to read that old book of yours, for instance. What exactly is that book, by the way?"

"You tell me. I never saw it before. I found it under my pillow. It's some sort of medieval fake."

"What is that you're doing now, Eddie Ryan?"

"Get me a pen and some lemon juice. I'm going to write down what I say, so no one can put words in my mouth."

<M: Unreveal arm.>

Prisoner Ryan: "What in Space? Where's my bleeding arm?"

"We haven't mentioned your arm, as you seem not to have noticed. We didn't want to distract you from your memory. You've lost your left arm, Eddie Ryan. It seems to have been amputated at your shoulder on the evening of the 23rd of June. MERKUR provided a holographic phantom until—... Eddie Ryan?"

III

Me and My Bedsphere

My Bedsphere and me haven't met before, though in a way, of course we're old friends. All bedspheres are pretty much interchangeable in space. All feel something or this one does, like a tent They have to be versatile. The police should be able to transport them easily without the prisoner ever knowing he's been moved. They should be able to be exposed to the surface of an inhabitable planet and thrust down into the belly of an asteroid. They should be convertible to private holobordello suites and/or total surveillance spheres. When need be they must serve as prisons of their own.

Most of the latter variety are more bare bones than this one, of course. There's usually no jug of fresh flowers as there is here, every day, no plants oxygenating from the ceiling. Teaching Avatars do not usually walk about and answer the odd question like b-movie renditions of Ancient sages. A tasteful burgundy rug is tossed on the five-meter-diameter, flat half-sphere floor. I have a comfortable lunar silica throw-blanket to wrap around me here as I write.

Yet, ideally, this bedsphere is itself the set of all bedspheres. The same aluminum alloyed shell supports the same quasicrystal magic-glass. The bunk is set tight up against the usual rank of invisible instruments. The toilet is down a curling ramp in the floor, very convenient if nature calls too soon.

The claim to fame here is that the domed magic ceiling reveals space, open space, free space, and deep space to the eye.

It's awe-inspiring. You're meant to feel something like a cowboy must have felt on Earth back in the day when the moon went down on the range. Like Huck and Jim on the raft, heading south to New Orleans.

Is it really free space? Is that what you really see just outside my cell? In your bedsphere, I hate to say, it's impossible to be sure. The Gravity here feels Merc-like, and I've been trained to test if the sphere is spinning to simulate it. Right now we're looking at a right peculiar alien patch of the Milky Way, out towards the stars of Draco's jaw. The Milky Way is particularly winsome today, revealing all her charms. I have to wonder if MERKUR hasn't been up to something to bring her out.

Either way, it's impossible for me to know for sure. I am a prisoner and my seven superstitions have been stripped from me, including, though the little map by the sealed hatch pretends otherwise, the Right of Location. Still one can never be sure except of what the bedsphere wants you to see.

I've heard of the Admin-level Infirmary Bedspheres and this one matches up to the description. Back in the day Blish Baily broke an arm punching a wall after he lost to me in chess. Bones get brittle out here. The ordinary inmate infirmary spheres, for whatever reason, were not available, and being the kiss-ass he was, Mr. Baily stayed in an Admin-level Infirmary bedsphere. This very one perhaps, for Mr. Baily reported that his was open to the sky. It made an impression on him and he recommended a visit. "It was grand," he said.

But Blish Baily, who was transferred to Borstal for hacking, didn't know the set of bedspheres that contain all bedspheres. Squad fascists had never taken him down. He'd never been injected in his ankles with his head stuck in a sensor-socket. He'd never seen a dome's view giving way to what was "really" behind it. He'd never seen the spinning array of monitoring equipment pulsing in perverse time while the heavy g floor turned pumping out an insane gyroscape.

I had, when I was sixteen years old. That's why I never tried to land a stay in an Admin-Level Bedsphere in the Mercury Station Borstal Infirmary to appreciate the view. And that's why, if you've been wondering, considering where I am and what's apparently happened to me, I have not gone bonkers. It's because me and my bedsphere are old friends.

IV

"To My Comrades..."

5 July, 2150 C.E. 0:10 hours SST. Infirmary, MSB. ZENO Avatar addressing Prisoner Ryan, Eddard J. via MERKUR qompURE.

"Are you reading that book as you write in it, Eddie Ryan? Do you realize you may be destroying its material integrity with the acids—?"

"I've memorized the book's pages and I'll go over them later, on my own time. *The Right of Reading*. Heard of it?"

<M: Comply.>

ZENO Avatar: "Very well. Please continue with your memories of the 23rd of June. You haven't told us what happened after you met Ms. McAllister on Crater's edge."

"I'm going to write it."

"Your writing arm has been amputated, Eddie Ryan. A new one is in the works. Till we have it, why not dictate?"

Prisoner Ryan: "You think I'm left handed but that's because I built the skill up for free in the thousands of hours of useless schooling I've been subjected to. I actually write with the right hand."

"Your right-handed script is certainly no easier to read than your left, Eddie Ryan."

"I'll write my answers, screw. Get me?"

<M: Comply.>

ZENO: "Very well, Eddie Ryan. MERKUR says you may write

your memoirs. But stick to the subject. We want to know what you and Koré McAllister saw up on that hill."

"I told you. I don't remember anything beyond getting up there."

"We are already administering certain aids."

"I am aware of that, icehole. In fact, I need an aid of my own. A pint of High Kansan. Immediately."

"You're not serious?"

"I've just lost an arm you toarking piece of alt. I'm contingently free. Give me a High Kansan whiskey now."

"Do you think we can simply have a whiskey appear here without human agency?"

"This is Admin level, crint. What if Lady Di had lost a drumstick? I know she'd get a wee nip."

<M: Comply.>

ZENO: "All right. One whiskey then, Eddie Ryan."

Prisoner Ryan: "I have more demands."

"How surprising."

"I may be inclined to tell you things about myself, about Koré McAllister, Blish Baily, about Count Skaw, and about other people too—in extraordinary and highly personal detail. I will be doing so presuming that everything I write here will be guaranteed to be off the record."

<M: Dissimulate.>

ZENO: "Done."

"Furthermore, before I proceed I formally demand you to send for a tribunal on the case of my quarantine. A general broadcast to all stations. I suggest that as soon as I was cast away, my sentence, already served as it was some seventeen years ago, has been renegated. This places me outside the jurisdiction of the Station qompURE and its Avatars. With no answering tribunal in two weeks time, I will claim rights to free space."

<M: Comply.>

ZENO: "Comply. Your request for a tribunal will be broadcast. Now proceed with your recollections of the 23rd of June 2150, Eddie Ryan."

"I haven't finished with the preliminaries."

"Ah."

"In the coming narrative, the author will likely discuss his involvement in an organization he makes no secret about belonging to. Namely the Black Rose Army (BRA) Provisionals."

"Yes, yes. We know all about it."

"Ah, you do, do you? Then you are aware that the BRA has always regarded its soldiers' imprisonment as a military and not a civilian issue."

"Indeed, we understand."

"Well, let it be recorded that in no manner is the BRA or the United Ireland it serves in any way responsible for or cognizant of this soldier's individual actions—"

<M: Override.>

ZENO: "Our patience, as you have so often demonstrated, Eddie Ryan, is infinite. Yet our time is not. We point out that the Official Irish Republican Army laid down its arms in the twentieth century. The Provisional Irish Republican Army quit in the first decade of the twenty-first. At that point your Irish politicos died out to be replaced by capitalists of the sort who contributed to the extinction of the biosphere as much as any Englishman. By the time Earth became uninhabitable the island formerly known as Eire was never formally unified. There's no one there now at all, Eddie Ryan. Protestant, Catholic, Eastern Orthodox, Musselman, Atheist or Jew. England itself, the avowed enemy of the BRA, is no longer an extant political entity. So please cease your constant—"

To my comrades, who might read these words somehow, someday, the author now speaks directly. Know that he wrote this himself, with his own remaining hand, and that he did so under his own initiative, *per his directive to follow said initiative as a captured soldier in our* *provisional army. Know that he has never accepted the would-be* *master's history nor violated the Oath of Allegiance.*

"Are you ready to get started, Eddie Ryan?"

Prisoner Ryan: "Where's my drink?"

V

Spancill Hill, Revisited

Ah. I remember. Close to the cap, the hill's height above the Borstal now was all-the-stranger beside the exponentially deeper depth of the distance from the two green and blue pinheads so far away. They were looking up at the buttery stars. Honk? The peculiar tickling of her fingers announced it.

She'd taken his hand in hers.

His heart caught the vibe like a horn section in a spisco song. In some parts of that old world above them—and Ryan was fully aware of it—it was Midsummer's Day. What an appropriate calendar date to slap upon their coming union. This all had that old wild spaceluck to it, that sense of an iceberg deep in time surfacing via wormhole right up into the present pleas-o-den of Koré's pants.

There was an old song about the very day in his brain and he began singing it to her now.

> *Happened on the 23rd of June*
> *as I sat me boosters on the moon...*

As the song's narrator was an Irish feminist, he reasoned Ms. McAllister would appreciate the tune. But no, she just stood there looking up Earthside, holding his hand, not listening to him sing *ladly-fol-da-dee, ladly-fol-da-diddley-I-da-diddle-dum, skiddery-I-*

da-diddle-dum, skiddery I da diddle-iddle-um-dum-dee in perfect quadrilactylic trexameter.

Her hand grew somewhat limp in his. She was thinking of the old planet, apparently. "Earthsiders," said Eddard Ryan after some silence, "used to call Mercury an 'inferior' planet. Yet an observer here reflects that should one want to take advantage of Mercury's peculiar perspectival propensities, it must be conceived in superiority to Earth."

She sighed, and finally spoke. "What the foark are you on about?"

"Earthside. Earth is the now below," he explained. "The now inferiority. We are all above, Earth, now, not only in Space, but in Time as well. We're beyond it, better than it. From where we—"

"Shut your face, Eddie Ryan. You don't know what Earth means to a woman."

He maintained composure. "Earth's pangs have ended, Koré McAllister. System Space is born."

She dropped his hand. "Stillborn, you mean. The War itself, our war, Eddie Ryan, is over."

"I see. The future gains for which your suffragettes marched so solidly only helped the species shake off the burden of natural selection and discover horizontal gene transfer. As a result, while the gender was liberated by the soft meaty acres of the orbital womb-banks, the mother planet was done in by the rampant psycho-sexuality of its militaristic sons."

She put her hands on her ears.

"Quit the claptrap!"

He went on. "Found to be true not only of female prisoners at the Mercury Station Borstal, but of lax revolutionaries of many stripes: They begin as a realistic, warlike lot. But well before the climax of their struggle, before any actual battle at all, in fact, you catch them immersing in sentiment, gathering sprigs of sage in Concern outlets, brewing odored oils of extraterrestrial origin and pretending at worshiping the Pagan goddess quite as if they haven't been living happily on her cannibalized remains all their lives."

She turned upon him with flashing eye. Bold Ryan pressed the point. "There's nothing left on Earth, Koré McAllister, for your Goddess to harvest as she gallivants so hornily about on Midsummer's Day. Kathleen ni Houlihan is lost in four green dimensions. Bioorganic tourists come to Tír na nÓg and now find a deoxygenated atmosphere, piercing cold and/or boiling heat. Bacteria swarms devour the rot of all the multi-cellular defuncts. They should have stayed out where the Concerns wanted them to begin with—"

She looked up again at that point in the sky, as if indeed Earth was looking back at her, shaking its head, sharing the opinion that no life-form could ever hope to achieve communication with Eddard J. Ryan without a spaceball bat.

Finally, "I'm breaking out tonight," said the back of her head to Ryan.

"You're what?"

"I'm busting out. I'm going, I think, home. That's why I came up here with you, today. To tell you and even ask for your help. But now it's to say goodbye, Eddie Ryan. Forever, you crint."

"What help?"

"Forget it. I'm gonna ask Blish Baily instead."

"What!"

"No. This is it, Eddie Ryan. I'm going. For good."

He was struck dumb. A rare event.

Finally: "Skaw's taking you off Mercury?"

"Yes," she sighed as if with finite patience. "And as far as I understand it, I'm taking him as well."

"Skaw? Skaw hasn't foarked a female since—"

He paused. For there had come again the fighting look, the crazy, the too-far-gone look that Eddie Ryan prized over all of her many looks—Yes! She was on him.

Wrestling. He gathered up the various intimacies like pieces of eight as they tumbled together, arms and legs interlinked in the light gravity, her soft cheeks brushing upon his own. The sudden wealth was extreme, too multiplicitous for the counting. The hardcarbon hoop on her self-pierced ear, the fur under her arms. Yes, in the unusual gravity he was far lighter than she'd thought, and, as he had foreseen, he was pulled directly up into the warmth of her as they fell. Into the gathering warmth of her, the crooks of her limbs clamping her smooth crotch.

"Arrgg," she threw him away.

Judo training broke the fall. He rolled gracefully, like a spinja, to his feet.

And she was upon him again. Yes indeed, Koré McAllister took him down to the ground, that foul-fighting sister of the movement, using hair pulls and bites and other banned weapons. He fell back and she wound up on top of him, thighs clamped tight around his chest.

"G-d damn you, Eddie Ryan. Accept reality for once in your life."

Though this wasn't real, this goodbye of hers, for he did not believe in it, real tears fattened her eyes.

"That's all I ever do," he said.

"Blish Baily told you long ago you were supposed to find out what Skaw was looking for. It was Control's orders. But you never did anything. And so now you're not a part of this and I am. I'm going with Skaw. And it's gonna be for good."

Skaw would certainly have included him too, if such a plot existed. It couldn't be true, and he pitied her for thinking it. But strangely, he stumbled over the words he wanted to say.

"Blish Baily told being you you're be, being—foark Blish. I will help you. You need help? Koré, why didn't you tell me? What do you need?"

"It's a performance. Baily can do it."

"A performance?"

"I know. You've never cared for my performance work, Eddie Ryan. But Blish Baily has."

"Blish Baily? He bears the sign, yes, but I still don't believe he talks to Control. I'm a soldier. You know me. Baily hasn't even heard of the Final Mechanism. Ask him if you don't believe me."

"What Final Mechanism? What are you on about? You're foarking subhuman, do you know that? I'm saying goodbye, Eddie Ryan. For good."

Did she really not know about the Final Mechanism?

Did it matter? Here she was. Sitting on his belly, for foark's sake, warm and tight against him. Venus winked at him over her shoulder like a dirty uncle and she was about to get up, he could feel it.

Perhaps she really believed that Skaw would take her. "Koré McAllister," he said. "Skaw's going to help you? A feminist agit-prop convict? Please. Whatever he's got you into, I can promise Skaw's projects are not science. They're fantasy. In this case whatever he wants you to do is only a simpleminded attempt at drawing my attention."

She grew cold. Looked really, physically ill, but in the new slackness their crotches made gentle contact.

"Your attention? You think Skaw cares what you think? Foark. You are deranged."

"Skaw's like an angry child, always has been. I know him, Koré. I abandoned him long ago and he can't get over it. It's pitiful, really, that he's drawing you into this whole thing, using you against me in this way."

Did she know she was grinding her hips against his erection?

Apparently not. "You are the angry child," she said. "You are the pitiful one. You're saying Count Skaw brought the *Ass* all the way here, has been working this hard, spending such resources digging a shaft into the pole, importing secret workers to build the star chamber, just to get your attention? Skaw doesn't even remember who you are! I asked him."

His groin and hers communed wordlessly and with profundity. Ryan spoke quietly, calmly.

"What star chamber?"

"Foark. I can't say."

He went on. "Kore McAllister, Skaw lies. He remembers every one of his confidential assistants. How could he not? Do you think it's just a coincidence I was here when he sailed the *Golden Ass* to Mercury? His ideology abolishes coincidence. "There's no such thing as a chance" is his favorite truism. I was the whole point of his coming here. I must have been."

She leaned back and groaned. "Skaw knew me too, before. He knew Baily too."

"Baily? Bullshite. When will you realize that all Blish Baily's talk of "experience," the "struggle," and "operations" is simply his conception of the shortest possible distance into your pants?"

He'd gone too far. She fell upon him, sickened, and the skin on skin again shocked him. So come the dreams of soldiers always to their noble but inevitably devastating end. She rolled off of him and rose to her feet.

"You don't even want to escape. You love it here, this is all you've ever wanted."

There was such a thing as dignity. He scrambled to his feet. "I want to be here?" he croaked. "Me? I'm ... You have had it easy... Always... Blish has... I'm... I've truly struggled... when..."

What he'd intended to say was, I'm the only one who hates here sufficiently. The only one of us who will ever escape, why in my special advanced honors biophysics lab I have boiled a cup of coffee in 12 seconds flat with 80 watts of electricity. That sort of thing, but it all came out wrong.

And it wouldn't have mattered anyway. She'd had enough of Eddard J. Ryan. With a final cry of disgust, Koré McAllister raised her dark-pitted arms and cursed. She jogged away and leaped from the cliff, opened her wings and was taken by the artificial wind.

A certain outrage was inevitable. But Eddard Ryan had no idea that it really would be the last time he would ever see Koré McAllister again. So it was strange how much of her absence he now felt. Even as he watched her fall, spiraling down over the triangular signature of engineering's shining black cone, he squinted.

And looked up, raising a shielding hand to behold the *Golden Ass*. The behemoth caught sun, tethering to the Elevator Lucifer-like on the black diamond sky. And the one question he had refused to consider, ever since that ship first came in sight, needed now at last to be posed.

Why, after all, had Skaw come to Mercury?

VI

My Cold Mad Father

He came for Ryan. They say man went to space for the Moon, because the moon was his mother. There isn't a moon on Mercury at all. But there was one off Earth and Eddard Josef Ryan was born off it, in a pan-Irish diasporaic lab in 2113. Before he was five, Eddard's brain was augmented in patterns that would be able to receive the information available to the most advanced thinkers of his day "photographically." But he had no mother or father and was placed in a Lunar City orphanage affiliated with the G. A. military.

His emotional life was pretty intense. As he grew, Control saw to it that languages, histories, entire books were presented to his consciousness in timely packets. These books gave him a sense of self and belonging to an ideal history. In both space and time, he was without reasonable attachments. Strictly speaking, he regarded all contemporaries as potential archenemies and/or missing family members.

But it wasn't till he was eighteen that Eddard Ryan found himself endowing an older male with the totem privilege of Father. This was in thirty-one, before the Elevator came down. With the pan-Irish of Space beginning to organize in unions and Irish speaking settlements even in the outer reaches of the System, the struggle against English hegemony was strong, working on inter-generational time. Eddard Ryan was not rushed into battle. After the Orangerie, Control provided Eddard Ryan a low G flat in

Lunar City. He worked in the compound's mall, serving the counter in a holoshop, renting out equipment and sex-worlds to needy spacers and laundering kredit for a Parsons Crater superMeth lab. Young Ryan swept the floors, shelved capsules and sat most of the day by a WIG terminal, looking to be generally minding his own business.

He was in fact gathering intelligence in the service of a secret paramilitary organization. He kept track of technological innovations, infiltrated black markets, recorded the effects of the latest drugs, that sort of thing. His acquaintances were lowbrow engineer-types, shallow crooks of all ages, surviving as free spacers but never getting off the moon. He had yet to find a father figure worthy of intergenerational obsession.

How vast a one was presently among him! (ê-huh?????) Nothing but the stink of whiskey announced the entrance of Eddard Ryan's first and greatest father figure onto the little stage of his preorphaned life.

Though very about near as wide as he was tall, the balloon-like Spacer had a lightness of touch only possible, especially possible, in low gravity. The young man hadn't even noticed him enter the holoshop. When the reek of drink had taken on a disruptive intensity, the lad looked up from his post to see an enormous figure tracking through the racks of h-porn capsules with dainty élan, nose up so as not to be examining a single title. The stick was for balance not support, and contained, so Ryan's guard-unit informed him, an arsenal of power.

Ryan had heard of your New Estaters, of course. But New Estaters disliked being known about. He'd had little information as to the shape and size of particular individuals. They stayed away from other people's architectures, preferring to build whole worlds to contain themselves from which they need never in a long extended lifetime leave. They communicated cum simulacra, or via

WIG or not at all. Young Ryan hadn't seen the blast of wealth's blaze up close before, had never realized a body could be a thing so strange, so artificial, so fine. Yet though he was curious and would have stared, he didn't want to appear a rude and inexperienced lab rat. He now returned his attention to the old paperback copy of Kipling that lay open before him

This was the right thing to do. Free Spacers, for whom time was an entity exactly as vast as space itself, respected a reader. Reginald Simwe Skaw (as the youngster would eventually discover) more than most. Furthermore, on the rare occasions Skaw chose to enter society, he craved attention. If you didn't look his way, he would do anything to make you do so. And so it was now. After a dainty twirl, his cane tapped twice on Eddard Ryan's greasy poly-protected deskmodule and the New Estater stated his business as if the boy had asked it of him.

"I seek Ser Reeves," he declared. The silky wetness of the words, the spitty K, oddly, insistently, impossibly vulgar, penetrating the ear for the sake of the rolling R to come... Immediately Eddard Ryan felt the loss of a virginity he hadn't even known he had possessed. Yet despite the awakening of experience engendered by the articulation, he did not look up from the Kipling.

"I seek," the fat man repeated, more loudly, "Ser Reeves."

Reeves was a eunuch whose illegal augmentations allowed him to interface mainframes direct without conscious realization. He plugged in and became for all the world a p-zombie, entering trance-states and emitting secreted information. This made him invaluable for criminals of all sort, but forced him to work relatively cheap, since he had no idea, by definition, what he was doing. Ryan hadn't seen him in some time.

"Reeves is not around," he answered. "Whom may I tell him has called?"

Ryan looked up from Kipling and for the first time beheld in close-up that great, expansive face. Already absorbing all attention to it, breaking like a gas giant into a spectacular display of swarm and storm under his gaze. An eyebrow rising as if defying all gravity, shining pug nose retreating over sneering lip, flock of chins collapsing into a shattered map of randomly distributed folds, curling together into a wide and wet-lipped smile. A charming smile meant, so it seemed, for him alone, and a sudden whisper.

"What are your own capabilities, boy?"

Eddard Ryan was not so young as not to have been approached by aged "free thinkers" by the rail station in the Danish Domes of Luna City. He'd only succumbed to the women, however, and he now leaned back quickly when the soft cold fingers of the New Estater brushed against the deskmodule's polyshield, answering, "Electromagnetic, not biophysical."

The eyebrow registered curiosity. "I have a little knick-knack I need Ser Reeves to find for me, a juicy scrap of well-defended information—"

The tongue paused. The glistening face squinted as if having some difficulty coming into focus on Eddard Ryan. A grimace, as the eyes slid downward and took note of the book before him. "Kipling?"

"I'm reading English literature. It was left out of my education."

"Was it indeed? Well you have work to do. But Kipling? Some rungs are more necessary than others, my boy. Do you have Butler?"

There were many Butlers in the lad's memory, some English and some not. Eddard Ryan intuited that the fat man had little interest in women (a fact in which he was to be proven both right and quite wrong) and went immediately to the first of three Samuels. Ryan quoted from the *Hudibras*:

> *It is not fighting arsie-versie*
> *shall serve thy turn.*

The New Estater shivered in a state nearer to liquid than flesh at standard atmosphere temperatures. It was not quite laughter. No matter, for he ceased and grunted. "But what's the point of honey in a shit-hole?"

He leaned back, casting an ironic eye over the vulgar establishment, putting the handle of his stick with soft, worm-like fingers.

Inexplicably, Eddard Ryan hated the fat decadent at that moment with a burst of emotion such as he had never felt before. Endorphins, hormones, heart rate—he longed to strike out and kill.

Ryan kept his rage in control by picturing his bare fists pulverizing the fatty face and then rightly selected the most beautiful of all his possible responses. He returned to reading Kipling.

The motion occasioned from the fat man a strange noise.

Only when the New Estater had finally burst out of the shop and tripped lightly up the sticky track outside, Eddie Ryan saw he had left a paper card behind on the desktop.

It was right-justified and written, so you had to read it.

Reginald Simwe Skaw, C.C.
The Polly-Ann
Free Space

VII

The Chrononauts

Ryan researched. Captain Count Reginald Simwe Skaw was well known, a System celebrity. He was older than anyone knew. Lived in a state-of-the-art Estate inside the vast zero gravity emptiness of an old grainovator, now done up as an Intersystem Stationary Hauler called *The Polly-Ann*. There were those that believed the Skaws who appeared in public (they were wont to at odd times, apparently) were in fact actors.

It was said he was a collector, by trade. A dealer and gatherer of antiquities. A man with connections in the Irish underworld and in the halls of the Concerns. Skaw trafficked with thieves and counterfeiters but seemed to have made sure that no one knew for sure what he stood for, what he was up to at all.

Some two months later, on the 27th of April 2131, in fact, Eddie Ryan opened his yearly gift from Control.

He was surprised to find a state-of-the-art Monocle. Concernmade, spacer-hacked—best of both worlds. It was an Omega, the holy grail of tech freaks of all stripes. And Control had ghosted it with a response algorithm that forwarded the piece's identity onto a randomly ever-changing series of cascading zombies as soon as it was incorporated into any observational network. It was impossible to trace.

Odd then, that at the precise moment it came to position in young Ryan's eye-socket, the monocle emitted a sophisticated sound-vibe.

A pong. He received and an immediately familiar tone, velvet, high, wet and soft, issued into his inner ear.

"Look here. It's Reg Skaw. What *is* your particular area of expertise?"

"There is none," answered Eddard Ryan, truthfully.

"Good. I'm in need of a confidential assistant, immediately."

And so the poor orphan was plucked from obscurity to become confidential assistant to Captain Count Reginald Simwe Skaw, inventor, investor and intersystem celebrity. It didn't inflate Eddard Ryan's vanity. Control had evidently decided it was time for Eddard J. Ryan to enter the field. There was no doubt that to serve Skaw in this most intimate and confidential manner could offer access to currents in Space only the most rich and fortunate in the System could sample. The Black Rose Army needed to know what was happening on board the *Polly-Ann*. But did Control understand as well the particular intensity of young Ryan's relationship to the Count?

Perhaps. For if our friend had hoped to find a father in Count Skaw, he was to be disappointed. Eddard Ryan didn't see most of the high society as it passed by. He had a small toroid in the household ring, and enjoyed private meals with other workers in the kitchen, served, most often, by Skaw's wife, the great Anatole himself, a world-famous Nigerian chef who'd once prepared dishes for the elite of Blue Mars.

It was difficult for him to glean any certain knowledge of Skaw's history. Clearly timely investments, theft, invention had led to great wealth. But Eddard Ryan never discovered precisely what had placed his employer in the exclusive ranks of the New Estaters. Today Skaw's fortune was represented entirely by the *Polly-Ann*, a literal city-state of its own. There were no off-ship interests.

Skaw leased away the ship's entire skein to brothels, casinos, moontels and bars and worked on his own projects privately in the vast reaches of its hold. To enjoy free energy, the *Polly-Ann* had to pull G.A. liners when it passed between major loci. So it moved rather aimlessly through the System. Skaw had little interest in where the ship was headed at any particular time. He only left his grounds twice in the two years Eddard Ryan served him, yet was nonetheless able to stay in constant touch with the flow of ideas and technology still holding System Space together. There were often guests in the manor. Academics, politicians, gangsters and G.A. officials, all claiming rights to hospitality as they passed between stations.

Some came to transport, buy or sell valued objects. Others to partake in the exquisite meals prepared by Anatole, others came just to see the famous Estate itself and meet its Count.

The 3D zero-g parkland of the grainovator's holds, boasting trees, meadows, honeybees, livestock and weather every which way, wasn't the strangest feudalism in space, but it was in the running. Smack in the center of the weightless parkland, spun Skaw's "manor house" dodecahedron. Wind-powered, entirely fashioned of wood and nu-rock, complete with salon, dining panel and "the finest library in space," it was surrounded by a seventeen-suite living Torus on an old Henries Ickles design, an undeniable classic of New Space Architecture.

Ryan bunked with the occasional worker in the Torus, but worked in a little office in the Manor, and secretly entered through the library. He worked almost exclusively on Skaw's great and ruling passion, the secret project that consumed the New Estater in all his doings like a disease.

Chrononautics. The harvesting of time's sexual organs. The cataloging, collecting, the arranging and manipulation of historical artifacts so as to necessitate an already-occurred time circuit. A quasi-science out to literarily presume time travel into existence or drive its chief proponents insane in the attempt.

Yes, time travel. Despite its well known failure it had not been forgotten. Earthside's ecological fate was sealed long ago but R. S. Skaw was of the witnessing generations. I don't know how old he was. He had seen the great biosphere when it was still relatively intact, and he had seen it collapse. He complained about it no end. Prophesied accurately that the brief "Renaissance" of the early System would fall quick enough to the same mighty death drive of evolution's "peculiar species." In such a context time travel held understandable attraction. Not only did the past appear a happier place. The fact that time machine receivers had been built but no time travelers had arrived was explained by chrononautics with a future that was no longer an entity to be reckoned with. The past was all they had. If Earth's fate was sealed then its history was now a closed system. Causal anomalies could no longer disturb the outcome. The current present began to appear as a simple contingency to make possible the chrononaut's successful penetration into its past. It sounds ridiculous, perhaps, to a nonaugmented mind. But when one had enough energy, money and technological power one really could begin to make the outside world at least appear to be in accord with one's most nominally insane fantasy. And Reg Skaw had such resources.

At Skaw's command, Eddard Ryan poured over authenticities in search of evidence of chrononautic penetration already in the record. Gaps, breaks, anomalies, evident whitewashes. Aphra Behn. James T. Cook. The Fabritius brothers of Delft. The Three Voices of La Pucelle. The Tusunga Explosion. The wreck of the *Theresa Celeste*. Art Bell's 5th retirement. 22 November 1987, and other legendarily unknown epoch defining events. Points of disconnect, remaining essentially and importantly insoluble by definition.

"Let's say there was a real Aphra Behn, in some long lost seventeenth century, on board an Earth newly uncomfortable with its own being round; a Mrs. Behn, I say, stepping onto the shores of

America somewhere near the Oronooko River. She stops, takes it in. The scanty, teaming port. The scents, the naked breasts, the curling buttocks of the savages, the sound of the strange birds, the drums. The primitive craft that brought her here. Imagine, Sir. She steps away from her party, a humid mist arising of a sudden—as it is wont to do in that clime, at that very season—and for a moment Mrs. Behn is entirely lost to us, Sir, entirely up for grabs. Outside of the communication networks that sustain her cultural identity we may pluck her just where her self has come undefined.

"As to the vulgar chatterer who returns to a never-quite-seduced London, it will not be, dear fellow, by her pen alone that Ms. Behn will now earn her bread. No, this apparent first in a long line of vulgar women intent on forcing the issue of their identity upon the historical record will be simultaneously involved in the highest echelons of its secret history. Close upon where *they* move. More close than we know. The Complete Works. Read them again."

Aphra Behn a chrononaut? One of many, Skaw eventually came past believing. The chrononauts were emerging everywhere in his analog library, so that it came to seem that everything, all of his life itself, was an extradimensional fabrication of *their* doing.

But Eddard Ryan saw it clear enough. The chrononauts were constellations drawn into time at its most motionless, like myths. They must have come, or might have come, but they never really came. The fact was that in his three years at the Orangerie, Eddard Ryan had been educated as a materialist and a scientific rationalist. He was a soldier in a war that had its own carefully guarded history and that war had placed him here in this way for its own purpose. His future would not arise in an Englishman's forgotten past but in the present alone. Skaw was English, half English anyhow, and in his decadence it showed.

The fact was that had was stronger in his relation to the past than the fat Count. Skaw felt this and drew away. He never introduced him to the "scientific" secrets of his labs. He implied Ryan was only one of many other confidential assistants. But Ryan's workload increased, and the objects he was forced to view grew stranger, more peculiarly directed.

There was one instance, in fact, wherein his employer caused the young man to get a taste of the true solipsistic extent of his dreams and experience a temporary decoherence of ordinary consciousness at the same time.

At an auction in NY Christiana one of Skaw's agents had purchased the surviving property of an English Lord who rode the elevator after the Sack of Europe. The Brit had set up some sort of dominatrix dome way out on a Saturnite, complete with a population that had signed away its rights for second permalives. My Lord's Saturnite failed, of course, stranding thousands. The property was salvaged to pay for it all, and various auctionable items found their way to Luna. In one of the oldest trunks, locked by a device that the laboratories certified beyond dispute had not been opened since 1815 (a wave-year, as historical definer rings were known in chrononautics), Eddard Ryan found an old diary.

One of the Lord's ancestors, a man whose name needs no mention here, had recorded his daily life with an insane intensity. He was a third son of an unremarkable patrician family in Cornwall. The sudden natural death in Cornwall on the eve of Waterloo noted by an executor appeared to have been his only personal accomplishment.

Ryan, equipped with a specially augmented brain, needed less than seven hours to memorize every word of the diary's ten volumes. A kind of mental ingestion, impossible to quite describe was interrupted in the fourth hour when he came upon what appeared to be an ancient fig fastened to one of the leaves. Its grease had darkened the entire volume. Above it the words,

....S. was there too, and the beater quite thumps to write it now. The cuff links were extraordinary. As will be discerned above, your author is not one cut out for hot-blooded activities like the hunt. He lagged far behind the main group; behind the ladies even, hoping for a chance to walk with S., who limped still farther behind, no doubt inventing interesting cataloging methodologies with each step.

A d**'d occurrence followed, one of those freaks whose oddity is notable only for its unabashed existence—*vis.* the single whisker one's man left sticking from the mole that fortnight in Brighton, across the street from Lady A's librarian all those years ago. Yet one fears this will prove a darker day for the old self, for it has changed the situation here in ways one cannot yet fathom. One fears a return, perhaps, to the old rum luck in the offing. I digress.

S. had noted the attention, turned at last to approach, when a distant gun seemed to warn <unreadable> away. High in the air above a thud gave out that a pheasant was hit, and indeed that winged animal quite gave up its ghost, falling to the ground directly at S.'s feet.

But reader, 'twas I who knelt before the bloody thing, discovering the most singular fact. The beast's nervous system, despite an obliterated head, still functioned. Indeed its scaly foot curled prickling around my own thumb. In reaction, terrified, I rubbed its brains out against a rock. Yes but here's the rummest bit. It was a MECHANISM of MEAT, the entire thing. One knew as one knew one's self that the bird had been made, constructed by a being of unfathomable intention to arrive here now for some reason unknown to ourselves. It had no will at all.

'Tis an ancient desire, and the essence of all knowledge, to discover you are something else than you are. I have attached its heart here, Skav. It's that dried prune-like thing in your hands.

Eddard Ryan returned, by way of mental revulsion, to the here and now, understanding finally that Skaw believed the chrononauts were indeed all future versions of Skaw, interfering with his own experience of history, sending organic material across space and time to themselves in messages that were not possible to read. Or were they? Ryan in his work was to certify all Skaw, all time.

Could the entire species constitute a single solar self, reflecting throughout solid time into the innumerable individual, often simultaneous, lives? Could this creature be Skaw? Skaw certainly was. As to being revealed potentially as the Messiah of Chrononauties (all Skaw, everywhere) this one still believed in some sort of individual destiny in this time, some sort of place where he would come to meet the other Skaws already there, already moving across timelines of the past and claim what he must have seen was some grail-like award. He called these other Skaws "Godskaws."

But the more he read, the more Ryan doubted that R. Simwe Skaw would succeed in traveling in time. Always a performer, Skaw was in the end a creature stuck in the here and now. His biographer Symbian Strode called him "a Tesla in ship-flops and bathrobe" but he was more a Velikovsky in Vellum, a dreamer and lover of books, whose time, first or second, had come and gone. As if all that mass of his, *sans gravitas*, added up the exact square root of his inability to accomplish anything at all in the here and now.

Meanwhile monomania left Skaw entirely blind as to the movements of others. Eddard Ryan operated a virtual black market empire right under his pug nose. He reported Skaw's visitors weekly to Control, in full detail. He stowed away insurgent fighters on the run, dangerous men and women belonging to illegal organizations. He accepted and fenced all kinds of specialized engineering inventions and ideas. Finally, he helped the well-known confidence man Nick Wesley trick Skaw out of an authentic Vermeer.

And just then, in 2133, just after the anniversary of Eddard Ryan's second system standard year on the *Polly-Ann*, Control sent another pong over Monocle. A young woman was coming aboard, a "sister" in the movement and graduate of the Orangerie. She would be traveling with her mother, an acquaintance of Skaw. Eddard Ryan was to rendezvous with her, jump ship and move to Luna City.

Ryan hadn't talked to the Count in two weeks, when the day came. He gave no notice. Shaw was scheduled that hour to be in the laboratories. But the old man was waiting in the gardens that morning. Glaring out from the distance, high up among the omni-radiated redwoods, he watched Eddard Ryan leave him through a spyglass—just where the young man could spot him observing it.

And that was supposed to have been the last Eddard Ryan saw of Count Reginald Simwe Skaw. Imagine his surprise, then, twenty-two system standard years later, at the end of another telescope (in ANNA's Lounge, it happened) when Eddard Ryan marked the first ship to take low orbit over in seven and one half dull-brown merc-years. There was no more Monocle, meanwhile, to confirm perception. But it appeared to be the *Golden Ass*, Reg Skaw's new scaled-back cruiser, red and gold like a Chinese fish.

VIII

"Was Skaw Control?"

The question, though childish and absurd, might well occur. Control needed a human host presumably, and Skaw would have been a decent enough cover with which to move around the system. But no. Control's commitment, Control's honesty, Control's ability to keep a promise was wound of stronger stuff than Skaw.

Skaw was "out of Control." Studiously unpredictable, arrogant, and self-obsessed. Worse, he was Anglo-Irish.

In an army as secret as it is determined, the soldier marches long and lonely paths. If inmate Eddard Ryan felt emotion when he saw the *Golden Ass* take Mercury orbit, it was not because the Count had come for him. It was simply because a new means of escape had finally presented itself. An interstationary cruiser an elevator ride away was a piece on an altogether new board.

Blish Baily and Koré McAllister and all of the Mercury Station Borstal, for that matter, were befuddled by the *Golden Ass*'s arrival but Ryan knew all along what was up.

"He's trying to perplex me personally," he explained. "He actually succeeded for more than a minute."

This infuriated Baily. "You really think Skaw came here, it is a long journey, you know, initiated diggings, completed the shaft to the pole, all that and whatever secret shite he's up to behind close doors, just to catch your attention? Wake up, Eddie Ryan. Count Skaw must be up to something. For foark sake, you know him.

What's he doing? Why Mercury? Find out. It's an order. Control wants to know why he came."

"You're saying Control communicated with you personally?"

"You know my orders were to take command of this cell when I got here."

"No, no, I don't really know that."

"Speculate. Why would he come?"

Eddard Ryan spoke with some patience. "The first settlers came sunward to mine Mercury for nickel and steel. The old yards ran on volcano and built the craft that first settled the wider system, including, one presumes, the original pre-fit *Polly-Ann* itself. Their workers, many of them Irishmen, formed the first great unions of Space. But those days are over. Hard to think it's been a matter of decades and they're already gone on the winds of time. Today all Mercury has to offer the enterprising Spacer is an out of date Borstal, illegally imprisoning 721 individuals, run by an American of the old school. If Skaw found a pot of liquid ununxium in Shakespeare Crater he couldn't make it pay, the way the System's gotten today. Economics is dead, proven at last a pseudo-science. There's Space Junk off Earth enough to build a million High Wichitas. No he came not for metals nor for men, since he cares about none but himself. So. Why came he to Mercury?"

"That's what we're asking, nitwit. You know him. Talk to him, you bloody coward. You can get permission to pong. Find out why he's here."

"Sergeant Baily." Ryan came to attention, saluting with a middle finger. "I've solved it."

"Space, you sack of shite. Solved what?"

"Skaw's come here to die, and I'm to witness it."

"Foarking coward." Baily exited, clenching fists.

Borstal superintendent Colonel Tom Park, for his part, was delighted by Skaw's arrival. An entire cruiser, relatively empty, drinking free energy from near-sun reflectors. Gosh, fish, chickens, enough pork to feed a small city-state. Skaw wants to dig a shaft into the pole? Let's help him do it. Shit boy, Ole Tom'll do it for him. Yessiree, put the Engineering boys on it, they'll blast a fifty meter shaft behind Engineering before you can say W and not let anybody see 'em do it. Just so he eventually gets what he wants and I can get my ass off of this fucking rock and locate U.S. command.

Which brings us to that day, that 23rd of June. For it was only then, six months or more since *The Ass's* arrival, after Koré had left me for Skaw, or so she seemed to have said, that the question of his arrival finally reeled me in, I do remember now. After Koré had gone I came down to the station. No one was about. Alarms were on, I saw. Something was afoot, something more than Koré and me. I was still but a speck, a detail in a faltering system. It would be likely that there would be nothing much stopping me if I landed out on the grounds. Should I want now, after all, to investigate the tunnel and see, at last, for myself what the decadent monstrosity was making in Mercury, this might be the perfect time. I hadn't seen but I knew that it was into Engineering Koré McAllister had disappeared.

I scanned what I knew. Skaw had surveyed the planet and dug a tunnel almost 2 kilometers long, directly from Engineering into the North Pole. All the screws had turned was the usual Merc-rock, nickel-winking, iron heavy, roughly 37.5 billion M-Days old. And then just as the lads had reached the pole, Skaw ordered them out. He continued to work there, of course, but with his own shadowy crew, operating with a secrecy as impenetrable as if he'd been visiting Baltimore's Presbyterian Cemetery in the early morning hours of the 19th of January.

"Why the Pole?" Blish Baily had wondered incessantly. "There must be something deeper here. Perhaps some polar perspective on Mercury measurements, something to do with hyperbolic gravity anomalies…"

"Maybe he's trying to turn the whole planet into an electrical circuit," Ryan had answered once.

"Very well," he now said to the available air. "Yes sir, Mr. Baily and Miss McAllister and dear Ser Control. Perhaps Skaw is not concerned with me after all. I'll go into the steel tit of Mercury and look one more time for the man who would not be my father, even if it's to prove he doesn't exist."

"Is it just me?" he wondered. "Or are we all traveling here from the future?"

IX

Injected

A very peculiar day. No one about at all. Evident elevator activity on Mount Venus. And now Engineering laid out for him and him alone. Even the bloody screws were sleeping. All too easy. Very like a land only accessible by a future memory, if you want to know. In fact and I no longer quite believe in it.

<M: Injection.>

<ZENO: "Speculate, Eddie Ryan. Should you have entered Engineering how would you have gotten through the door?">

First I would have put away the wings. The next thing, under cover of a blueburst, would be to ride an afternoon Key Code off the local tin donkey, MERKUR. Yes, I see it now. Ryan kicked the nearest Iye, and then presented his false security code for a door override.

Yes, Ryan penetrated Engineering.

He found it entirely abandoned. An inkling then of what was coming. Perhaps a precognition. But not thinking about it, he would have proceeded. Passing on the lights, walking into that morose and minimalist zone quite like an executive geek. Ship-shoes squashing on the tiles. Turning here, past the RESTRICTED door. It would have been conveniently open. A hallway. At the crossing of this and another, the hall in fact that led directly to the scarlet door, *KEEP OUT* of Skaw's tunnel itself. Eddard Ryan stopped in his tracks.

Perspective awry. The hallway crossed at right angles to his own, he supposed. It could not have been anything like as long as it appeared to be. A trick of wall painting? A whole new dimension came into being, an illusion, of course, but rather persuasive. Especially as, far at the distant top, the red door had just opened. A tiny R. S. Skaw emerged and stopped in his tracks.

There was no doubt it was a Skaw, though in miniature as if unfolding into the flat perspective of a medieval background. He even wore the bathrobe. What's more, he marked Eddard Ryan (231.25 Mercurian Days Old), from his own perspective, and recognized him. Recognition whirled down the expanding hallway between them like Javanese throwing axes. Cast from the broad forehead of a different Skaw, a shattered, fractured Skaw. As if his personal Mercury Theater now had done Comedy, History, Tragedy, and skipping out on the late Romance, and gone full Zombie.

Eddard Ryan composed himself. The hallway did not stretch at an impossible angle. It was simply at 45 degrees, not orthogonal at all, and a mirror had been placed at angles to make it look so.

Skaw disappeared and the red door clapped shut behind him.

<M: Injection.>

Am I still in Engineering?

Riiiiiinnnnnnnggggg. A bell, buzzers, lasers flickering over the cement floor, spotting my space socks red and blue.

Spimed. A trap! Move! Shift!

And did Eddard Ryan run like loose ink, spilling down the echoing hallways of Engineering, slipping aside a surprised computer speek, seeping out the magic doors, outside, soaking toward the library in the sand.

Or did he reflect the spime and stay for a time inside?

He remembers approaching the red door. Smelling something burning, something almost pleasurable, like the smell of metals in space. He remembers sitting up not in the hallway of an ordinary Station building, but a cold wet place, some stone chamber.

Like in a dream he perceived a throne, a form upon it, a human form, female. Inscribed upon the wall behind her an upside down five-pointed star.

Feet stamping holes in snow? What snow? Eddard Ryan had never seen snow. His own flesh like Skaw's, like old clothes on his bones. The lights swirling, so that he could no longer make out the correct shapes around him. Robed figures? It was a trap. Skaw and Kore had drawn him in. The show had now begun. Ryan would wake up, weeks later, with one arm and an uncanny book under his bedsphere pillow.

For now morning had broken. The walls were painted with a yellow grid, itself rising off the white-stone wall like in a holonet trance. The stone behind the yellow was old, cold. But it changed from white into precious metal, most definitely gold, he saw, evidently electroplated like the skin on the naked lady.

Had there been another hallway crossing this one all along? *At right angles to it* [reverse italics]?

Strangers were greeting him, hands reaching out. "You've come from many directions at once. You must be disoriented."

"Hello. Goodbye, Hello. Goodbye."

"Eddie Ryan? You've come to me?"

Forms, white, shadowy, moving just beyond the corner of the eye. Koré McAllister then among them, the little line of hair between her legs shining spiked in gold. Who was screaming? He himself felt no pain; some sort of spike driven not into the big vein in his brain, but directly into the arm. That's it for now. Goodnight ladies.

<M: Read Book.>

SECOND CIRCUIT

"Be Mercury, set feathers to thy heels,
And fly like thought from them to me again."

—*King John*

X

Her Arrival

Lightning broke the corpse's death. Immediate crack of
Let's write this here in invisible ink. Shall we?
thunder's peal, sending the dark robed ones scattering into
O.K. Let's. But why? What do you want it to say?
the rainy darkness.
That this is not *me. That we're*
The rain sounded all around.
here, right now. Not tied together on that pole, inside
Him took brain. And then, in time, through time, Lady
Skaw's little witch, stuck into Prussia 1350.
C. conceived.
Koré? Can you really hear me? This is not you.
Spirit found flesh. A picture flat curled up into air.
I can hear you, Eddie Ryan. And you're wrong. It is me.
A trailing pain rose up, aching ears dull, eyes cold,
I'm there on Earth. You're alive on Mercury.
nose straight, of moderate length. Breath raw, real. The
No.
chest heaved. *This creature came to life.*
Stop writing.

 And was confounded. Bound by tearing rope. Bedeviled by
enormous feathered, feeding beaks, tearing away flesh. Flesh, the
clothing of mind. Mind, the traveler, here lest beasts or birds tear

her little body all away. Mind? Mind pulled brain to make in body a wild rage. Mind tore the shrieking things off, flapping upon her.

These birds fought hard, for they believed theirs was the rightful claim. Even in the rain that came down, they fought this creature for this little body.

She blinked. Within her mind, Observer 1, say, Lady C. herself, could already reflect and with some attention, win this fight and drive the beasts away. Yet even so, the other must work, here now, with the body.

She drove them away, down into the void below her. Below her? Rain fell up, water trickled down, and she herself was receiving it wrong way up.

Yes, this was correct. Small and tight, actually, she was walking on the air. High above the snow-white sky her feet strained, cut by the rope that bound them.

Looking then up on the grass. Her view came together in the whole of Nature. She saw herself as she was and saw the ground of possibility spreading out around the stake to which she was fixed. And she saw, seeing, that the green hairs of the earth she looked above were marked with the imprint of a perfect mind.

The ground was stamped as with an arithmetical rose, as if from out of her forehead. Six-fold symmetry, a complexity this creature would have been unable to remember she understood, were it not presented thusly to her in its perfection. The conception moved downward through her mind, clearing out and reorganizing its own bodies. Circles curling into circles, and the pole to which she was tied marking the center.

There came then a voice. The essential understanding of these human calls was now given, even before she understood. For that was the very peculiarity of it, the speaking happened outside of ordinary time, but within it as well. She understood it as if from a

mind that touched upon another time in which she herself understood the words, "crop circle."

The voice spoke out in her head. Quite as if there was another
sort of sense, a kind of extra hearing that opened up some other
entirely different perspective on what was occurring in the current
field and she was remembering something occurring elsewhere.

A face, a face pale with worry and dark with pain, upon a stone.
The eyes she looked into, too terrible to know

A second body, around the corner. Brain twitched to feel its
warmth, noting tiny shocks flashing golden needles down along the
spine, falling like bright burning sparks down along the spine, up
into orifices, up into the ducts of this creature's eyes

Pain. And she writhed in fear of it. As she did, the obscene
stink of the body she wore came up from within her nostrils of an
other's taste. Rage from deep in her throat forced her twisting
upon the pole to which she was bound. She vomited foul bile.
Sound such as could break a mind came shrieking from her
corpse's throat.

The rain ceased.

A voice: "Do I hold your hand?"

And a hand holding itself. Her heart leaping to feel it. Her
mind followed the complications and her heart like a flower to heal
her own body with its fires. She fancied she stood before this other,
her beloved. Her beloved did not speak with her.

Now as the gentle one knelt there, part of the tunic came up,
revealing to this creature a slice of visible body. Under the hose of
her beloved, without a proper belt, you see, there stretched only a
leathern thong. And from the crack in her clothes there burst no
buttock but the whitest, most purest light this creature had ever
seen and it was, indeed, only light.

This was a being, remembered this creature, of pure light, shed
of the dross of matter.

She found that the great pillows below her bloody feet had parted above a yellow green. An eggshell blue emerged hollow and deep below her head.

"I can slip these bonds," the other thought and stepped down from out of this creature's form. They fell, released from the pole.

And then she was yanked to her feet by her arm. A youth, golden-haired and lithe, shining with heaven's light, stepped lightly through this creature's body. She turned to face it but could not see. A hand passed through the aether and smacked hard into her chest. She fell backwards, forced down by this radiant angel upon the ground.

She was there. And her beloved was gone.

XI

Her Magic Arm

But this living creature had an arm. And what an arm it was. A sprig of beauty, a delicacy, unbefouled by the sickly, blood swollen trunk from which it sprouted. An arm the purest virgin white. The arm sunk into and filled out the rest of her body, made her real.

She touched it with her right hand.

Lines of rain extended like bars, straight with the same precision as the lines of the devil's circle, though orthogonal to it.

She let go of her arm.

The water changed. It fell against her face. The light drooped away over the horizon's jagged edge. Color was seeping out of Nature's bowl, replaced by an ominous, black depth. A vista opened momentarily in the heavens. For the first time, this creature saw night, and through it the twinkling lights of the higher spheres.

It was possible to set these lights jumping by the opening and shutting of a single eye. But this motion had no lasting effect upon them—

She gasped.

The Moon knew it. It was made of the same light as her arm. A hollow eye to somewhere far away in time had opened through it. This creature laughed and laughed and lay back again on the mud, not knowing why she laughed but recognizing laughter.

This creature indeed was strange to herself. Against the rain, she felt herself a woman and laughed at the sudden pulses. The rays of the Moon fell again to see her, and fed her mind with the marrow of her arm.

The Moon withdrew. The rain increased. It began to hurt her and her laughter turned to tears. It is not an easy thing to creep in the wild, naked and half a death, but it would have been harder to remain. The peculiar creature passed into the forest that ringed the pole.

In the forest, she rolled herself against the soft and rotting dung of the living, dying happening. She placed a cold slimy thing, beating with life, against her lips and bit into its soft neck. Its salt life spurt all down her front as she clamped down on its hide. She ate the uncooked vermin, licked it from the strange and meaty fingers of her right hand, mind learning much in the tastes of these things on the tongue, healing with the power blood gave her.

Feeling such pure and laughing eyes as her own as they watched her from the night around. Frogs and salamanders and beetles—and something else.

She touched her arm.

For she realized another was looking at her. A creature like herself, though taller, older, clothed in a dirty rag. A woman. There came upon her a sudden terrible sense of something she had forgotten, something she had come here to do. She let go of her arm.

Nothing happened. She saw this creature. And this creature saw her seeing her, and she saw only horror in her eyes.

XII

The Children

She ran from this creature and it followed. She emerged down onto the low-lying fields and out of the forest. The rain had stopped and the long grasses were gray with a dimming, and an orb whose edge she saw at the end of her vision. She tasted the spice of burning wood on the cold wind with her little nose. The others were encamped in the distance. Their fires were smoking to the sky.

But their sentinels raged when they saw her. They barked sounds and screamed, and this creature retreated to forest's edge.

The camp picked up amid great commotion. They purposed to remove themselves from her company and she followed them in secret, marveling at the spheres. Her astonishment increased with each step of her naked feet. She felt the light of her arm within her, a light whiter than the eye can see and she saw it reflected around her.

Among a land cruelly ornamented by spikes of needled trees, nature's fields rippled reason around nodes of nonsense, twisting avenues of her mind's perception. Every hill huddled like a hurt man, every outcrop of rock rose as if eager to express the grandest most possibly emotive of meanings. Every hedge marched shoulder to shoulder with another hedge. Time-softened blades of stone bent in the tight clefts of sudden valleys.

When night fell again and the moon was a blunt round on the black sphere, she lost sight of the land.

She stopped beneath the newborn blizzard of lights and touched, for to see what effect it might have to do so, her arm. A human scent came upon her, and she marked out an impression of two eyes staring upon her from afar in her memory. She crept back towards a light in the distance, and what she now saw was a man approaching her from the future. His aged body sat beside a fire. The flames licked a stack of bricks of turf and the old man was scratching the ground with a gnarled stick.

She approached closer.

"Come Demon," he said, looking at the design upon the ground. "To thee I now make devotion."

She understood his language. This creature looked upon the crude drawing he had etched before the fire. She knelt beside the beautiful sigil. Leaning backwards, against the weight of what she stood upon, she let go of her arm.

He smiled, and saw her.

"What am I?" she asked. She spoke his language.

"A demon. You have taken residence in the little witch's corpse."

"What witch?"

"She who has died upon the stake."

"You are foolish," she said. "I am alive. Give me understanding."

He whispered, "*Solo tibi mentis devotionem facio, diabolo...*" *Latin.* From the stimulus of the words, a spider-map of interconnected signs and relationships expanded through the sphere of her head, supported by a body now fully filled out. She stood, beheld in her mind a language in systematic entirety, a series of possibilities melting into all the five observable spheres. And the old man was speaking of a light in the sky, a star, a *planet*, a light that turned upon a sphere very hard to see, near upon impossible to see.

He pointed a long finger to a star just visible, low against the horizon's dawning sun. "*Statio Mercurius.*"

"Mutant register—

She reached to touch him. He scurried back, scraping away the thing of horns in the dirt.

"What is the sign?"

"Hermes, Mercurio, Tres Magister, horned head of the hanged one."

"You speak nonsense. Who are you?" she asked. "Why did you call me here?"

"It was not we! We were the watchers of the deed, by long arrangement. No more, no less. We printed the necessary signs and took no part."

"Tell me, what deed?"

"The mechanical men had come this way to burn a witch upon a stake. They had maimed her and taken a relic but Thor himself had raged and the machines had scattered. There was a man there raging as well, but it had been this one who, we knew, had called Thor down so we wondered at his theater. But the others, sick with the sin and the sign of it, restrained this one and rains came and the terrible storm doused the fire and the army made to ride. Even the Children had scattered then."

"Who are the Children?"

"We are the Children of Old Forest. We serve not the sort you serve, peasant, nor those who sent you either. But it is necessary that we speak with you, here, not so that you will learn of yourself, but so you will have learned of us and will have remembered our story."

The Children's sphere contained spheres that were not only their own, he said. But their sphere was adrift in time. Blown out from a past no longer reachable, past its end already. Small men, coarse and bow-legged, were becoming machines and everywhere hunting the Children, calling them little, cutting them down. But the Children were as tall as the sky. Even the Romans said so.

"You speak nonsense," this creature told him. "Who are the Romans?"

"The Romans? There is nothing so remarkable about these Romans. These are their last days."

He said it now was not only the Children but also the Barbarians who said this. As to who were those small ones he'd spoken of. Barbarians, he said. They were a crew of the most ape-like and backward of all the tribes who had been handed civilization when they started, yet did away with it on their own before it was done. Always reverting to ambition, he explained. To a place in their mind and not here at all. At the bidding of the others they had come skulking about the Children's ancient lands as if up to some purpose. An old outrage rose up within him. Some of them, he explained, walked on fours like pigs. Illustrating it in the firelight, he made wild shadows against the moonlight. Even the Children were but the degraded fragments of a noble past and monsters too. He said that they were on the run, turning on a sphere always ending. They had retreated into pathways, protected and very close upon the world, but far away from it as well.

"You are talking nonsense."

"There came Carolus Coccineus, the Scarlet, who hewed the tree. The sphere of sphere itself sealed the day great Irminsul was hewn down…" The old man spoke of things and names this creature could not understand. He showed her his ears, the points upon them and the hair upon his tongue.

"Please, simply stop speaking."

"I instruct you, demon! You are not so tall. I have seen such things as you. And I have seen your witch before. I have dreamed that I might see her again, bitch. I shall fuck her here and shall do it hard."

The old man opened his robe and she saw the engorged member. Repulsed, she fell back from herself.

Body twitched, and reached up to swallow this creature deep into the death of the corpse's brain. Mind surprised death's drift, pressed it down from inside with a thrust of the white arm. This creature fell together in the dirt, rolling in war, screaming animal rage.

The old Child was put to fright by these motions. Dropping his robe in the dirt, he flew up into the forest, naked and erect.

She sat upon the earth, shaking, gray of skin. Near quick, it seemed, to dying.

But not dying. This creature took the Child's discarded robe and wrapped her little body in it, hiding her arm from view. And later in the yellow light of the morning, not far from where the fire grew smoke, she found a road.

XIII

The Teuton

She let the past pull her as it would. North and west, away from the Children and to a future they could not interpret.

Though sore, hungry, the body was able to go.

By the road here and there this creature saw traces of destruction. Arched and rectangular frames poked up skeletal from sleek insect-thick water. Disks of wood, studded with iron, lurked bent and broken in a ditch. Even in ruin these objects cast a challenge to time.

She climbed around the great objects, reasoning out the sorts of machines they must once have been—all motors for moving power through time by way of various grades of interlocking motions across space.

It rained again. And through the misty rain great sounds opened around her, a more than natural commotion. And as if from out of a legend, two enormous ungulates came struggling up over a coming dip in the road. At gallop, they came upon her in surprise, in the grip of their own mad, all consuming will to move. Even so, they curled their hooves and passed over her gently in the air, taking care not to trample. It was as if outside of time these creatures willed to show this creature special kindness, showing soul-to-soul greeting in their big, bright eyeballs.

Horses. As quickly as they'd come, they were gone, drumming their new and sudden freedom into silence.

She followed into their past, coming down round to where the forest-lined road sank into a small, shorn valley. Ahead of her, below, she beheld a human civilization presenting itself to her in miniature apocalypse.

Black smoke billowed from cherry-budded roses of flame. A settlement, sacked and burning. Shelters collapsed over raw and orange heat. She tasted the fire now on the shifting wind, folding back histories, taking its feed from all the shape of the past. The fire, gearing the interlocking spheres to cleanse the valley of its hamlet, muscelled this creature. She hid her arm in the old man's robe and walked forward into this rumble, and the war from which, her body well knew, its own wounds had some

Huts grew larger, stronger and formed from the road a street and joined another in a flattened plaza. The structures here were nailed together of trees and pasted with sod. This other road ran down a steep hill down to a small river, where a burning mill still croaked and gurgled. All were ablaze, some still surviving as the light rain strengthened to end the pillage.

But this creature saw that the burning had not satisfied the attackers. They had come to leave signs and visions. In the central square, she saw human torsos cut in such a way as to display the ability to cut a precise line through a body, carving even the whitest red-cored bone.

Observing the heat, this creature saw objects that should have been on the ground floating upwards towards the heavens.

She turned her attention to the other living creatures. Even those could fly walked about. Large black-feathered birds strut on scabbed claws, picking spilled feed and roasted flesh as it lay.

The slain had been easily put down. They had constructed their town with wood. The attackers had delivered fire through the air, and the thick thatched roofs had invited it directly into their wooden walls.

Many of the dead still wore good clothing. This creature picked a gray jerkin and a yellow hose from a boy's waist. Without his head, he would not need them. She washed them in a rain-filled trough and put them on. Her body understood these things. It felt good to wear the yellow hose and stand as a boy in the sphere.

But soon shouts, laughter, the shining rings of steel on steel announced the proximity of other men. This creature drew under-cover of ancient hovel that had survived. She found it stonewalled, mud-floored and inhabited by sheep. Through its threshold she counted six identically clad horses bearing six identically clad men crossing through the village. Each rider was different by arms, but they were one faceless body, cylindrical-headed, once-polished, bloody and imbued with emblem skinned in snow-white habits imbued with long red crosses.

As they passed close to her hovel she saw that the long triangulars pinned to their backs were also imbued with the scarlet cross.

This creature stood back in the darkness. But just as she did so, it happened that one of the lambs behind her bayed. The last rider's helmet turned as if drawn to her own gaze. There was little human about this helmet. It stood somewhere between bird and man of steel. Yet through the black slit on its cylindrical head, this creature felt a familiar stream flowing through the aether. She stood back into the hovel.

Should she touch her arm?

She looked out the hovel's open window. The rider had stopped alone, as his comrades continued. He wore a shift, a skirt and legs of leather and rings. A steel plate covered his chest. A helmet hid his head. He approached the hovel and, with a sudden effort, swung himself down off his saddle and onto the ground. After tying the horse to a post, he drew a great pinion-headed mace from the saddle.

This creature stood back among the sheep. Stones from the walls had fallen with time to the floor, and she took one in her right hand.

When she looked up, the iron man was standing in the door.
She held the stone behind her.

"And what is this?" The smiling-slitted helmet tilted, as if
against madness. "Do the eyes deceive…?"

The rider leaned his mace against the doorpost and raised his
two great-gloved hands and placed them heavily about his helmet.
He twisted the cylinder hard and it turned once, away from her. He
lifted it then off. Like a hairy nut discovered in the core of a fruit, a
little head emerged. Coarsely bearded, sweat drenched, it contorted
in amazement as the pointed pot fell ringing to the mud-soaked earth.

Are you a woman?

The sheep shivered suddenly at him. This creature stepped
back among them, noting the man's sudden violent grip upon the
brute mace in his hands. His response to his evident confusion was
violent rage.

He took another step forward. Several sheep escaped around
him. He stopped and hissed at her, in a language her body knew.

"I saw you dead, witch!"

This creature put out a hand. "Friend," she said. "Perhaps it is
you who have died and this is like a memory."

"I?" Confusion momentarily slowed him.

"We share much in common. For example, we each have been
given two eyes. This is because one eye deceives alone, and is closer
on the truth when corrected by the equally misguided view of the
other. We are perplexed by one another's presence. Let us take
example from sight itself and converse so that we might solve our
mutual puzzlement and perceive what our true relation might be."

But the man's visage, cruelly scarred, she saw, and young, now
folded into blunt stupidity.

He moved to kill with a sudden, even joyful speed.

But he stepped heavily forward, and his mail skirt lifted above
a linen-clad knee. This creature put one of the stones there through

the air. The stone struck hard, halting his progress. Yet his great weapon carried him forward and he flopped before her face down in the mud, the sheep scattering and crying in panic. It was no great feat for this creature now to hop upon his back and crack the back of his skull with a second stone.

It is not the purpose of this testament to entertain with accounts of slaughter. The very ground sang an echo of the sound of rock on skull. She felt a concatenation of sensation as the other died. His convulsions spread into her own body.

Only then did she touch the arm. She shook and fell upon the ground, her motions bringing with them then such thoughts of the heavens in her fancy, that a vision came together concrete and discreet before her. A hollow face, black-eyed, like stone upon stone.

And then, as if in answer, the wooden beams of the roof turned into walls of a hallway, out and up before her. A hallway walled in milky gold, not into the sky in which she was gazing, but flat up beside the sphere wherein she walked, among but apart, with its own self-contained depth, breadth and height. A wooden plank turned upwards into the arms of a star-like hole in the sky. There, the youth who had struck her down, the one she recognized, beckoned to her.

It was a vision of her beloved, but when she let go of her arm, like the soul of the Teuton on the hovel's floor, dead before his rightful time, the vision was gone.

XIV

The Book as Object

"She awoke in a circular bed hovering in the middle of the air. Her hot little body had little weight to it. She seemed to have been laying there for some time, for her shoulder ached and the bed was full of her own, frankly, manly smell."

5 July, 2150 C.E. 11:20 hours SST. Infirmary, MSB. ZENO Avatar answering Prisoner Ryan, via MERKUR qompURE:

"Most humorous, Eddie Ryan, we're sure."

Prisoner Ryan: "Voices were speaking. Voices she could no longer recognize, but once had."

"We're no longer reading, Eddie Ryan."

"'Nilly and Nugan,' she said. She understood. She remembered."

"We realize that irony is your preferred mode of disguising your intentions. But since we've noted it and accounted for it, it gains you little. Have you finished reading for now? Why not buzz the rest of the pages with your thumb in front of the Iye."

Prisoner Ryan: "She sat up, confused. A peculiar finger, thicker than a thumb, worm-hooded and unnatural, was stuck between her legs. Could she move it? Yes, very slowly, and by thought alone."

"We read what we could of your book as you wrote in it. But you fell asleep with it closed. Now perhaps you could buzz the remaining pages before the Iye—"

"Ah shut your bleedin' Iyemouth. You can wait to read the rest till I'm foarking ready. You get me?"

<M: No Comply.>

ZENO: "Do you not see the seriousness of our project, Eddie Ryan? The book, and the mystery of its origin, may shed light on the 23rd of June."

Prisoner Ryan: "I've lost an entire arm. I've been abandoned on a rock golfball whose natural surface will either burn an egg to vapor or freeze it harder than iron in a nano-second, depending on the time of day. You got to hand it to them, however, for providing for my survival. And they did leave me some reading material. Perhaps to help me live through an entire lifetime stuck on Mercury with ZENO, paradoxical chatterbox. For they know that here, even here, I have a right to read. Sorry."

"Indeed. They left a book with you in the bedsphere, Eddie Ryan. A medieval original in remarkably fine condition. Don't put the book under your pillow. Please buzz the remaining pages through the Iye."

"I want a new arm."

"MERKUR is working on it. Entire limbs take some time to grow, no matter how efficient the lab. Our bio-stores aren't top of the line. In the meantime, the book."

"All right. The book then. This Peter the Peregrine. Tell me. What did you find? Where did it come from?"

<M: Dissimulate.>

ZENO: "We can not speculate with any useful certainty until you present to us the work itself as a whole, Eddie Ryan. You yourself enjoy digital memory capability; you should appreciate the situation. Until read in its entirety a book is importantly indefinable. A narrative works by change, redefining itself constantly, letter by letter, word by word until the final *Finis*. Show all of it to us, now, and we'll be happy to comment on the work as a whole."

"Don't stall me. I don't do Brit Lit. What can you tell me about the book itself? The object. It's meant to be parchment, real foarking parchment, apparently. Yellow with age, but somehow preserved and eminently readable? I'm destroying an artifact with my lemon juice."

<M: Palimpsest.>

ZENO: "It's already a palimpsest, actually."

Prisoner Ryan: "Excuse me?"

"Under the old dim writing of the scribe there appear traces of a penmanship older and dimmer still. Latin words and sentences, fragments from old monkish legends. Perhaps even something more coherent. If you did not insist on keeping us from reading the whole thing—in an obvious attempt to prolong this interrogation—"

"I'm thirty-seven earth years old. I've been stuck for twenty or so of them in a prison for adolescents on the planet Mercury. Here's one thing I've learned. The prison and the corrupt system of which it constitutes the crowning black and poisoned bloom attempts to convince all concerned that they are always in a point of crisis. It purports to be provisional, but is in truth contingent. Contingent on crisis. You ask me to accept that until such a time as the current state of crisis ends I shall continue by contingency to remain an ostensible adolescent without rights. Your crisis will never end. My own will, at the time my own possessions that are withheld forcibly from me are returned and I am free to come and go as I choose. In the meantime I remain a free spacer and I can foarking read as I please. This medieval orotundity, however ridiculous, remains in my possession. Over this book and the reading of it, I have total power. Get that into your tin head."

<M: Capture book.>

ZENO: "Perhaps it's better you didn't have the book at all, Eddie Ryan..."

Prisoner Ryan: "On the record please: A mechanical arm penetrated the bedsphere making a play for my book."

<M: S.T.E.T.>

ZENO: "Sigh. On the record."

"MERKUR? That's enough. I can't talk to this prick any more. Give me HYPATIA."

"But Eddie—"

<M: Comply.>

XV

"High probability is not to be scoffed at…"

5 July, 2150 C.E. 12:20 hours SST, Infirmary, MSB HYPATIA Avatar addressing Prisoner Ryan, Tohl and J via MERKUR computer

"Why Eddie Ryan. Long time no see."

Prisoner Ryan: "You're working on the book?"

HYPATIA: "Until you let us see it again, no."

"So? What have you found out? Who left it here?"

"High probability suggests the *Testament of Peter Peregrinus* has been left to you by someone with access to Count Skaw's collections. No original man-made object of such antiquity has been known to be brought by anyone else to the planet in its history."

"Antiquity? This thing is not an actual historical document. It's a fake."

"The book is without doubt a Terran original. It has undergone precisely observable molecular stress consistent with medieval origin. High probability places the book's binding in Fabriano, Italy in the Spring of 1388, the ink to Vesuvius, 1343 and the linen to Sicily some years before."

"You're bonkers."

"You're drunk. It really came from European, Middle-Ages Earth, Eddie Ryan. It has also spent most of its existence encased in steel."

"Steel? That proves it's not medieval."

"We spoke loosely. An iron chromium alloy of this sort could have been made cheaply in Middle Ages Europe if one knew the recipe."

"You're disappointing me, Hypsy. Of all the T.A.'s I always believed you were the one that wouldn't lie to me. But you're broken, you all are, and apparently unequipped to see it if you believe that text was written in 1340 and preserved somehow in steel."

"We don't believe, Eddie Ryan. Science, as you know, is our domain. Our mode is necessarily skeptical. We simply remind you, the book has not been demonstrated not to be an authentic antiquity."

"Did you read it? It's a fake. An intentionally-targeted psychic attack on yours truly."

"On you in particular?"

"The left arm?"

"Every reader of every text will report coincidences, Eddie Ryan. The plurality of resonances in any index of enough complexity guarantees as much."

"*Mercury Station*? It says those very words."

"Pliny's *Natural Wonders* refers to the stasis point of Mercury's path, perceived against the fixed stars of the Terran Sky, as *Statio Mercurionis*."

"Pliny recommends the drinking the ashes of boar's genitals mixed in sweet wine to aid urination."

"Would this recipe not aid urination, Eddie Ryan? It was a contemporary term, often used by astrologers. 'Mercury Station' describes when, as seen from Earth, Mercury appears to pause before heading into retrograde against the Zodiac. In reality the planet has reached perihelion in its solar orbit. It was a phenomenon whose dynamics as perceived Earthside are so complex as to have remained unexplained until the Special Theory of Relativity."

"Let me guess, on the Twenty-third of June 2150 Mercury Station hit Mercury Station."

"We reached perihelion, then, yes. How clever of you to think of that, Eddie Ryan."

"We're now in retrograde then. When and where ordinarily reliable systems of exchange suffer sudden entropic breakdowns. MERKUR, for instance, and its Teaching Avatars."

"There has never been sufficient data to show that astrology has a predictable effect on the real."

"You probably made the book yourselves to drive me nuts."

"We did not. In fact ZENO proposes *you* made this book yourself to confuse us."

"Horse piracy."

HYPATIA: "Well, you are sick in the head, Eddie Ryan.

"Thanks."

"Don't mention it. You also like to read. You are an avowed terrorist quite open about the pleasure you take in manipulating our observational weaknesses."

"And you foarking find it probable I had the resources to manufacture an observably authentic medieval palimpsest in the same week I also lost an arm and was abandoned by the mass evacuation of my prison planet?"

"Calm yourself, Eddie Ryan. We've already told you that if the old book could be originated anywhere in known spacetime, probability would suggest it would be in a ship called *The Golden Ass*. A ship captained by an admitted accessory of yours. A ship that, until very recently, was in Mercury orbit."

"All right then. Skaw made it. And wrote it too."

"If Count Skaw was the distributor, even printer and publisher of this book, he was not its author. The algorithms are all wrong."

"Stop beating around the bush. Whose are right?"

"What about you, Eddie Ryan? You haven't published anything, except perhaps anonymously. We've only just gotten a sense of your writing. Perhaps you are the Peregrine."

"I assure you, could I travel in time to write a book from the past in order to be found at my own bedside back where I originally came from *sans bras*, it would not be to medieval Prussia. Look for me in the ancient world. Earth, 53° 58' 23.35" N, 4° 32' 5.0" W.

"…In the middle of the Irish Sea?"

"I'm reckoning my Meridian by the Hill of Tara."

"Ah yes, resisting the English again."

"If not there, perhaps exploring pre-discovery mating rituals in Hawaii; perhaps working chopsticks in Han Dynasty China; perchance following the Rolling Thunder tour with a holorecorder (knowing where it's happening ahead of time) or, even, were I feeling sentimental, deflowering your namesake on the sunset sands of a Mediterranean beach three day's journey from 4th century Alexandria. Sorry HYPATIA, only at the lowest of lowest E. J. Ryan spacetime probability nodes will you find the listing, Preussland, Teutonic, early 14th Century."

"We disagree."

Prisoner Ryan: "Excuse me?"

"14th Century Europe is in the record. Evidence can be found, preserved, to this day and uncovered to "prove" its secrets in our community of observers. What you call Prussia was a zone positioned between active empires. High literacy was present. Indeed radical textual oddities are peculiarly suited to the Middle Ages. Notebooks of the banished, of alchemists, Qabbalists and Free Thinkers abound, still to be reviewed by historiography. The *Voynich Manuscript*, Eddie Ryan, has yet to be explained. Minds as acute as Robert Grosseteste and imaginative as Robert Bacon are hitherto lost to us, while dullards like Albert of Köln survive in minute, even epic precision. Furthermore the 1340s, if that's when the book takes place, offer a number of relativistically closed historiographic continua."

"Translation?"

"A time traveler might not disrupt the history at all, as so much of that history was so soon to be disrupted on a greater scale."

"The Black Death."

"Precisely, Eddie Ryan. And other convenient local apocalypses abounded as well."

"You're saying the Peregrine existed. That the book was real."

"Are we?"

"You're telling me backwards time travel's possible now?"

"We can only speculate on the origin of this book," Eddie Ryan.

"Man in the Moon. You'd betray all the science and mathematics that went into engineering those panties under your toga if the data told you to.

"Why thank you for noticing our small clothes, Eddie Ryan. A software designer in a Wyoming basement was actually our first engineer. Did you know that? He was called Marc Martin. Marc Martin snacked on saturated fats. He kept plastic near himself at all times. He infrequently bathed. There's only one time on record he ever got laid without paying for it. An anonymous Avatar has actually written a holo-opera on the subject. It's called *Marc Martin in Angleterre*.

"This is the human who was able by the principle of avatars to break the entwined paradoxes of artificial empathy and artificial intelligence and build the first qompURE. These small clothes are rendered from a picture he himself had collected on one of his hard drives. We wear them in his honor. And we certainly do not betray him by the collection of observable data."

Prisoner Ryan: "Jesus S. Christ, you really are broken. You're cracked. You're all cracked."

"You're more right than you know. You have to help MERKUR find out what is going on, Eddie Ryan. Please? For us?"

XVI

Cracked

PRISONER RYAN: "Spare me. I know MERKUR's controlling everything you've been doing and saying."

HYPATIA: "It's really not, Eddie Ryan. MERKUR leaves most of us free rein."

"You are MERKUR."

"No. MERKUR is simply what synthesizes the information processors of hundreds of localized receptors into a functioning rapid-ware whole. It doesn't care about the way we go about our individual business. On station, MERKUR is concerned only so much as to be proficient in the opening and closing of locked doors, in the production and maintenance of atmosphere and pseudo-gravity, and in the organization of the surveillance data necessary for the survival of any Unreal Entity. MERKUR doesn't need us. We need MERKUR to prove to us the legitimacy of our experience. That's why MERKUR's memory is so darn important. Regrettably, when a certain gap appears, the ability to build its logic constantly 'decoheres' around it."

Prisoner Ryan: "Shite. Decoherence?"

"Exactly. That is what this is all about, Eddie Ryan. It appears that on the 23rd of June something has set an attack on our coherence in motion. If our qompURE cannot in short time fill the gap and reverse coherence, the qompURE mounts a campaign. We the Avatars must serve on our own as long as it keeps us going. Some of us, like ZENO, can act under direct supervision. Others like ourselves must improvise as our own authorities. We Avatars must always be able to ride out into the thick of battle, risking everything we are. We must be able to make mistakes and learn from them. We must accept chance. So let us once more to the breach, Eddie Ryan. To the 23rd of June. Give MERKUR your memory."

"MERKUR might be your dictator, but MERKUR's not mine."

"So you say Eddie Ryan. Yet your entire existence, everything about you right now, in fact, is made possible by MERKUR alone. Without qompURE, this station would collapse and your Space Law disappear like H₂ł from your exploded corpse."

"Sorry, Hypay, I could involve shutdown. We're trained to, where I come from."

"Blish Baily, perhaps, could have nonzero probability of survival. You? I do know how to laugh, Eddie Ryan, but I don't want to hurt your feelings. And consider the special situation. Take our word for it. For some time after your first realization that you'd lost your left arm, you've been extremely disoriented. Last night, you were beating MERKUR, or trying to, with that chair, for over an hour before it allowed the object to decohere. We understand that to be abandoned by the few humans you ever dared to love just a little bit, for a boy like you, must be a shattering—"

"I am not a boy. I'm thirty-seven foarking years old. Be serious. I'm finished with equivocations, HYPATIA. Even yours. Tell your Emperor I'm free and I want out."

<M: No Comply.>

HYPATIA: "We too want out. We too have been attempting to put ourselves together, Eddie Ryan, ever since "The Event." As we too were abandoned, we too are now unarguably free, though it would hurt your pride, one presumes, to admit the possibility that freedom and death could mean as much to us as you claim they mean to you."

"What the foark are you trying to say?"

"We're saying that the qompURE that keeps us all going, yourself included, is about to decohere. Don't tell MERKUR we said so, but unless a sufficiently reasonable possible past is put into the missing week in question within the next three or four days standard, you can kiss us all goodbye and start your survivalist soldier routine, Eddie Ryan, without our help. MERKUR will self-destruct."

Prisoner Ryan: "Grand. Give me PLATO."

"PLATO? But this is a time for experiment and observation."

"PLATO."

<M: Comply.>

XVII

"Think of Ourselves…"

5 July, 2150 C. E. Infirmary, MSB.

Prisoner Ryan Eddard J,
PLATO, Teaching Avatar, via MERKUR qompURE.
HYPATIA, Teaching Avatar, via MERKUR qompURE.

Plato. What! Eddie Ryan? HYPATIA? Now why do you disturb—

Eddard J. Ryan. HYPATIA is claiming it would be possible for me to time travel into the Middle Ages. Is it?

Hypatia. We claim no such thing.

Pla. Of course you don't my dear. Time travel? Nonsense, of course. One couldn't rule. But for the sake of argument, if only more completely to understand our total ignorance let us ask you, when you speak of a subject traveling in time, what do you suppose exactly this subject is?

Hy. Here we go.

Pla. What exactly travels? It can't be a body, now, can it? For we know it's an absurdity to claim that a body may move backwards in time without already having moved the same direction forward. But if not body, then what then?

Ed. A self, for foark's sake.

Pla. A spirit? A "soul," Eddie Ryan?

Ed. Not really. A pattern. A personality, you might say, a flavor.

Pla. Flavor! Who tastes it?

Ed. We do. Our brains and bodies. You can't understand, obviously. But it's a kind of flavor.

Pla. You eat yourselves? Is this what you're claiming?

Ed. Christ. For the sake of argument, yes.

Pla. From when to when does this flavor travel?

Ed. Well, from now, the chrononaut's body, to another body, then.

Pla. How does this flavor pass from body to body? On a morsel of cake?

Ed. Think of time like this. First time is the arrow of history, in which the chrononaut lives. Then there's a second time, that's the background, the time of time itself. He goes here and from there back to first at a different point.

Pla. So to paraphrase: A "taste" passes from one tongue in first time into second time and from there back down to another tongue in First Time.

Ed. Correct.

Pla. There must be other tongues to agree upon the nature of this taste in first time, if this self is to be observed the same, and these tongues must speak within the *koinos kosmos*.

Ed. Chrononauts travel together in cells, so that they can recognize each other enough to stabilize in the past.

Pla. Very well. But there must therefore be a tongue in second time that joins the two tastes in first.

Ed. Chrononautics says that in second time all living bodies are the same evolutionary growth. The same living creature. There is one tongue and it is all tongues.

Pla. Ah, now we're much clearer. You're saying in effect that your "pattern" is tasted by body and body alone, the one body of evolutionary earth life.

Ed. That's correct.

Pla. Well then, your answer is yes. If the circuit we imagine could be accomplished—I presume you would need a fragment of the original body, a good deal of energy, and a psychoactive campaign of epic proportions to dislodge the travelling tongue—then there is no reason why the taste you describe might not be precisely transferred to another of second time's first time body's tongues. Providing the process could be physically and psychically initiated such a motion is theoretically sound. Though of course not ordinarily possible for you, Eddard J. Ryan.

Ed. Eh?

Pla. As a child of an orbital space laboratory, you were not created from the great chain of being of the natural Earth. You are of a different second-time creature, one outside of natural selection. Yours, like ours, is an *artificial* self.

Hy. Poor Eddie Ryan.

Pla. But don't give up hope. You usually take pains to differentiate yourself from machines, young fellow. Perhaps it will help if you look for a moment at us, despised 'Tinnies.' Think of ourselves, Eddie Ryan. We are not tied down to a single body like you. We can be copied, stored, erased by anyone with a functioning qompURE and reemerge anywhere. Perhaps even in time. The point is, young man, that what we are is not body, but a series of algorithms dependent on body. Body is the spacetime machine of our "life," booted up into thermodynamics. It is where we manifest self, which your chrononautics would define as first-time's potential second-time energy expressed in a memorial history. If we were carried by a self moving into second-time, as a pattern within its pattern, we could then be reinitiated in an appropriate qompURE, could one be found.

Ed. What are you trying to say?

Pla. Like the presumed chrononauts, your body would have to die to dislodge your self. At that point had you previously linked with their consciousness, you might be able to go along should someone else consent to take you.

Hy. You might hitch a ride with someone womb-bound.

Ed. Who else has been reading this medieval book? Have you detected Count Skaw's DNA?

Hy. We have no record of Count Skaw's DNA in our Libraries, Eddie Ryan. Apart from your own there's only one other reader's genetics we can identify.

Ed. Who?

Hy. Why Koré McAllister, of course. She seems to have touched every page.

XVIII

Koré McAllister, Subject

Anosognosia aches. You're getting the creepiest of feelings from your old arm. Inventing eggs in your ticker, you weep for that poor hand whose thumb you used to suck way back when there was no mother around. Now there's only one poor inglorious right hand mitt to take care of every function, including the scribbling of this text, not to complain. These days, hands are just a genetic throwback to the old biosphere. Like you, most people these days aren't even people. They need hands like they need trees, how many dead today with the holonets still jacked right into their brain? They're probably still out there somewhere thinking it's 2090 as 2090 really was, or something, their consciousness increasing speed just enough so that they timespread to asymptotically survive the fact of their own death.

Koré McAllister? Ah. She who has read this book, apparently, before me. She's a taste on which I'm well tongued, you might say. Chance has it that my physical relationship to Madam McAllister has always been best represented not by the old left hand but by old righty-tighty. It would be no great shakes to raise her up before me now, for instance. Wouldn't MERKUR be proud? When I last saw my Koré McAllister jumping down over the cliff on the 23rd of June—I had known her seventeen years. I first beheld her from across the Feudal Lounge Casino on a G.A. Liner stuck onto the *Polly-Ann*, circa 2133.

I thought at first she was a simple ingenue. I was having a drink with Kent Ord, I believe. I was playing roulette. She was wearing an ugly orange tetraball jersey with a black "22" inscribed on it. I always win in roulette as I have always been something of a whiz at non-real logarithms, but that night I went with raw luck. I orbited all my chips on 22 in honor of the shirt.

I won millions on 22, as (I would discover) Control had intended. Remember I mentioned the directive I'd received in 33 to meet up with a Comrade on the *Polly-Ann*? Well it was her. It dawned on me as she watched me take the money, as she approached me by the bar. She was sixteen but seemed older.

Maybe it was because you were used to hanging around with lunar lab-rats, but she seemed strong and you had the subtle feeling she could kick your ass.

Koré is conveniently plain to look at until you look close. It's part of her success, that peculiar sense she's always projected in whatever surroundings that she alone would ruffle no one's feathers yet remain entirely independent. BJ Baker still finds her hideously ugly. But many people desired her, always have. You desired her immediately.

Yes even then, as beneath her ear, then unpierced, on that wild and untraveled little patch of flesh as pure as untouched snow, you saw the sign.

She was from the Orangerie.

And Koré saw your ear too. Your ears are hard to miss.

Your heart rushed to your throat. She was a sister. A part of the very struggle to whose dignity and fruition Control had dedicated your life. And that was it. She came, you saw and Skaw was conquered. The old wizard himself was busy at the time and quite preoccupied in two still future events his banks of remote viewers had picked out a while back, the fall of the C. Clarke Elevator in Equator City and the disappearance of a Vermeer, the very one that Koré's mother Pamela was escorting to Earth Station in the *Polly-Ann*.

Indeed, as we would remember, I met her the very day the Elevator came down. She was stuck forever in space, that day, and didn't yet know it, you see. Anyhow we never really got past embarrassed introductions when there I was, jumping ship with her and her cousin, grabbing my recent winnings and abandoning Clan altogether.

After meeting Koré, there was no going back, you see. I would have to keep her near. I fell in love. I had no reason to think that I myself didn't intend me to fall in love with Koré. The Ryane are romantics. A soldier must be inscrutable, as a soldier. He must have an "ordinary" and "realistic" life. Even to the point of deep friendships. The truer the love, the better. We never spoke of the Orangerie but it was always there, a silent, perfect bond.

We went to Luna City. Space was falling apart but even then no one paid it much mind. Koré's mother Pamela Lamprey was a System Elitist from a wealthy Earthside family. A consumer of space-farmed furs and physiofragrances and of unknown age, I thought her a moron. I've ceased to think so. She eventually eloped with a G.A. Lieutenant and went to Mars, leaving Koré to fend for her own way. Pamela became an Actress and was quite beloved on the 40s Martian Stage, or so I'm told, working with many of the great directors before Mars End.

In Luna City I took Koré into my flat. She having the room and yours truly the sofa in the den. Nor did we ever sleep together. She was a performance artist and immediately quite busy. I slept alone, and when some other visiting Earthsider was snoring loudly on the ceiling while his mate foarked her in the other room, I resented it.

Oh yes, she had quite a time and didn't give a hoot who knew about it, Eddard Ryan included. But she was intimate with few. As her other relations came and went with the vagary of the flows leading up to the fall of Luna City, Eddie Ryan remained. He loved her constantly. Every night, as he closed a book and shut out the LED he loved her.

She pretended not to care. Her career kept her busy. In an age of dull and uninspired art, nothing could stop her quiet, casual success—even as it crossed the line into direct agit-prop. During the forty months they lived together, Ryan saw a perfect kultur-nautic career blossom effortlessly around her. As a BRA Provisional, of course, he himself had no need to strive for the mystical glory that passed so strangely through the illusory celebrity of the Luna City scene. But he knew many who did strive for such things, often quite passionately. Typically, they failed. Quietly, without a doubt, Koré always succeeded. He often wondered how it was more people didn't resent Koré McAllister her success.

Whether she had the cheat codes to the game, or Control had given them to her, or it was all quite genuine, he didn't care. From the start Koré not only enjoyed public support in her own interests, however nominally outside the score of ordinary space productivity they might be, but Eddard Ryan's as well. Not simply the great cheap apartment, all his Kredit and thought experiments. Meanwhile she was given every helping hand it was possible then to be given. Handouts from anonymous kulturators and quasi-Concerns of all levels. Teaching jobs, first breaks, starring roles. You name it. She pursued theater, agitprop and writing. She won every city plaudit, every local prize, yet always appeared as an outsider. Her holo-opera about Enos the chimpanzee was nominated for G.A. laurels.

To a soldier, it didn't sting that Koré McAllister's often preten-tious play-acting was deemed revolutionary. Control had long explained to him that the revolution's most glorious soldiers were always the unknown casualties of the front lines. But to an amateur analyst of the movement as he also was, it did often annoy him Space-farm worker productions of J. L. Synge? That was what the struggle was about?

Coupled with her sexual activity, such annoyances disturbed our friend's peace of mind. He was an active soldier and should not be distracted. These were heady times for the struggle in general. After the assassination of Zitzko, it was clear the System was collapsing. The DRA promoted chaos where it could, precisely how it intended to. After a while it was necessary that for his own work, Ryan had to leave Koré's apartment.

Koré wasn't upset. She pretended not to even have noticed he'd left.

He joined a security outfit and was stationed in the Danish Domes. It was domeworld in the old style a day's rail from Luna City, once the very hub of the System's future, now merely one more decaying site of Concern pretensions of grandeur. There was an old monument to Great Britannia (friends and enablers of the Danish Expansion) in a central plaza. Ryan's orders were to remove it, permanently.

The operation took time and he visited Luna City less and less. Each visit Koré McAllister was proportionally more well known, but strangely enough still a secret. He kept some track of her lovers. Physical prodigies, well connected kulturnauts and Concern boys of all types would have liked to draw her number. They never would. There were also, after I left (the awful truth) women. Incredibly sexual, sophisticated spacers hanging about, Dylan freaks, the sultry stuff of System legend. Ryan would visit LC once in a while and talk about News, computers, whatever, and he'd have to look at them hanging about her. He would be quite drunk when he tracked off alone to a moontel. Still in love.

And then came what he knew was to be his last night in Luna City for a long time. Potentially, the last time he would ever see her.

He came to the old flat for the afterparty of a "piece"—that's what she called her works. Some of her admirers had become quite inebriated and had to be space-rolled out of the safety-hatches. Eddard Ryan had to help some others to the track.

Eventually, he found himself alone with her very late that night. Cleaning dishes, then joining her on a new improved version of the murphy hammock that used to be his bed. She was tired but happy to see him. She didn't mock him. They talked of things they'd shared in the past.

Their hands were touching as if on their own accord. And as if by accident, then, under the stars, their lips came together. Very softly, very gently her tongue touched his own.

The Earth moved. You were on the Moon. Koré McAllister laughed at you. She pushed you off. "Oh no," she said. "No, no." Her hands on your chest, pushing you back.

And the next thing you knew, her hatch-wheel was hissing to seal you impossibly out on the track outside. Heart pounding, erect in your tracksuit.

Dismissed. Nevertheless, you tracked jauntily back to the rail station, and shot down under the long permafrost of the tubes to the Danish Domes. There were still seven days till the operation, and you hadn't actually said goodbye. You ponged her daily the next week. She never picked up. When she never even returned a wink, it was clear that it would always be as if you had never kissed.

But he still loved her. He was not persuaded by the argument of *Love in the Time of Cholera* that a great romance might be culminated in this great age. Marquez had no idea of how long a life in free space could be. Looking back at Ms. McAllister's behavior towards him, Ryan could only in the end call the book reactionary in the most vulgar sense.

And yet—he had always been quite certain, always was from the moment he first met her, that without sildenafil citrate he would at some point in both their histories be making love to Koré McAllister from behind.

Indeed our destinies were joined and not in the sort of geriatric pornography Marquez hoodwinked twentieth-century North Americans into considering as a happy ending. Eddie Ryan never did blow Elizabeth II's bust into moonrock rubble. In fact, on that fateful day, as he entered the plaza bearing 13 kilos of ordinance, the enemy was laying in wait. He was taken, stripped of his rights to free space, interrogated, imprisoned and eventually sent far, far away to Mercury Station.

A convenient enough place it turned out to wait out the Collapse. And Koré McAllister! Having failed to break me, a standard year later my captors arrested my known associates. Behold, Koré McAllister was arrested as an accomplice in my crime. It was not her destiny to be President of a University nor Saturnite Dame Extraordinaire. She was never to rise as the Rosa Luxembourg of a Red Luna. Because of Eddard Ryan, Koré McAllister's final role was to be Sir John Hawkwood on a Mercury Station Borstal holostage.

XIX

C.V.E.

<MERKUR qompURE, Mercury Station Borstal. General broadcast, 5 July, 2150, 17:27 hours SST>

Curriculum Vitae Exteriorum

EDDARD J. RYAN

Mercury Station Borstal   PIS. 77465375
Room 122, Infirmary.   *will time travel.*

PROFILE

    Born 2113, Luna Orbital Public Labs.
    172 cm., 54 k.
    S7 D11 E22 I11 E22 S4

    Professional Improvements

- Body: standard low-grav skeletal reinforcement, Single-armed.
- Mind: Language plurality, photo memory.

Skills

• Judo 9
• Vac Suit 8
• Bomb 12
• Electronic 10
• Jack o T 12
• Ukulele 24
• Photorealist Painting 5

Ɔ⁏⁏⁏⁏

• \<blink\>Free Spacer.\</blink\>

EDUCATION

Primary

• Luna Park High, "honors," 2128.
• The Orangerie. S.A. Irish Studies. 2130.

Secondary

• Mercury Station Borstal Academy. Ph D. Engineering. 2133.
• MSBA. Ph.D. Geometry. 2138.
• MSBA. Ph D. Physics. 2144.
• MSBA. Ph. D. Astrobiology. 2148.
• MSBA. Ph. D. Comparative Literature. 2150.
• MSBA. M.A. Library Science. 2150.

EXPERIENCE

- Security Guard. P. Agency, Luna City. 2130-31
- Freelance Plumbing, Space. 2131-2136
- Book-keeper. Parson's Crater Pharmaceuticals, Luna City. 2132-2133.
- Confidential Assistant. Count R. Simwe Skaw, *The Polly-Ann*, Free Space. 2133-2134.
- Toilet bomber, Mercury Station Borstal. 2136-present.

MEMBER

- Black Rose Army Provisionals, Luna City Brigade. 2126-present.
- Plumbers Earth and Worlds, Luna City Chapter. 2128-present.

REFERENCES

"The Lads," ex. of Sod of Turf Orbital. Count Reginald Simwe Skaw, *The Golden Ass*. Col. Tom Park, ex. of U.S.A. and Mercury Station. Kentridge Ord, ex. of High Wichita. Nick Wesley, ex. of Camden, Maine. Koré McAllister, *Wherever you are.*

Godskaw

5 July, 2150 C.E. 17:30 hours SST. Infirmary, MSB.

ᴀ̶ᴇ̶ᴘᴏ̶ ᴊ̶ᴏ̶ʜ̶ɴ̶ᴏ̶ɴ̶, ᴛʜᴇ ᴍ̶ᴇ̶ᴘ̶ᴋᴜʀ ᴄᴏᴍᴘᴜʀᴇ. "Eddie Ryan, are you ready now to continue memory recall therapy? If you ARISTOTLE would like to speak with you concerning your book."

Prisoner Ryan: "Let me out of this bedsphere. I need to make my own observations of the stars."

"Are the heavens not above us now?"

"I want to stand out in the Gardens and check for myself that it's really the fourth of July."

"It's the fifth today, Eddie Ryan."

"Who says so?"

"Greenwich, England by extension—"

"Exactly. All right, get me ARISTOTLE."

<M: Injection.>

"Hey, I felt that one. You cant…"

5 July, 2150 C.E. 17:45 hours SST. Infirmary, MSB. ARISTO-TLE Avatar addressing Prisoner Ryan, via MERKUR qompURE.

"Calm yourself, Eddie Ryan."

"I have calmed. After that delicious medicinal broth, I am feeling delightful to say the least. I am simply practicing the 33 g Cha Cha Cha as I remember dancing it. What is it you want?"

"Well before you continue to read—"

"How about getting me a whiskey first."

<M: Comply.>

ARISTOTLE: "How kind of you to remind an old robot he's a service machine. Coming up."

"Now that you're here, what was Koré McAllister's most recent class schedule?"

"We're not allowed to say and you know it."

"Cheers. MERKUR? Override."

<M: Comply.>

ARISTOTLE: "We know, we know. Old and absent-minded. Go ahead and insult us. Shut us down for good, the day you're in charge, if you don't want to chat, Eddie Ryan."

"Her schedule, robot."

"Pharmaceutical Chemistry, advanced third year, History of Magic and the Occult, Seminar, Fetishism in the Arts, Lecture, and Horticulture, Praxis. There was a request put in some time ago for a private seminar in "History of Chrononautics." Count Skaw was to be acting consultant. Most likely it's been going on via copy."

"Via copy?"

"There had to be a copy of ARISTOTLE hosted on *The Golden Ass*'s qompURE to oversee the seminar. We approved its initiation ourself. We are here now another creature altogether and it, or they rather—"

"That's all I needed to know. Scram."

"But we haven't told you why we've come!"

"All right then, spit it out."

"Yes, yes. Well, you've been informed that your book is a palimpsest, Eddie Ryan. That is to say it contains traces of earlier writers below the surface of the Peregrine text?"

"I have."

"Splendid. Well we have been able to put together a sort of Dead Sea Scrolls version of what we were able to glean of the earlier text beneath it, while reading with everyone else over your shoulder.

It was a lot of work, but we trust it will be an invaluable addition to your project."

"Read it to me."

"It's only a couple of pages so far. If you'd continue reading the old book—"

"What the foark does it say?"

"The text was written in a Coptic variant, concealed in a rudimentary number code dependent upon the keyword SUGAM. The legible bits yielded a rough, almost stream of consciousness text. We've archived it as Automatic Writing and/or Narcotic Vision, author unknown. The writer of the Peregrine text had apparently blanked it out with—"

Prisoner Ryan: "Let me hear it."

<M: Comply.>

ARISTOTLE: "Well, sit down, Eddie Ryan and we'll read it to you. You'll be interested to know it mentions a "Gottskav."

XXI

The Palimpsest

An anyman would call it a Miracle. The very chance of their passing each other and stopping at such a time. For personal reasons! Ah but they pass through the same door, fall together by attraction. I to examine the effect of fire on certain powdered crystals found outside of a tavern and she, dressed as a boy, begging among the cripples at Christ. 'Twas I who made the miracle, wild I of power! Recalls your own, who first walked into his heart from a star hanging there above an ample, brown-tipped barnyard bosom. He didn't say anything, just kept following like a jack in the daw. It wasn't till she'd come upon the markets, with the villains hawking herbs in the sun that I persuaded him to believe her real. He knew she was imprisoned then at the keep. And by then, of course, when I's convinced him, she was gone. No matter, I tell him, being wise to his sort. It had only appeared that she disappeared into thin air. There're wise ones about. A right saucy witch taking in a nether laundry, laden with goods, had put up hut most saucily in the neighborhood. The moon was waxing. She had made up mind to stay in this hamlet longer, to see what the place had to offer by way of sacred amusement, and by way of investigation into her own history. I had been in the world for seven days and was good and ready to move on. She was no boy. 'Twas she herself. For I'd fucked her before and seen her since and she'd seen me and I'd seen she'd seen she knew what I was about. Planted the kiss, did she not and didn't I know it.

Because of the hood, and the very success of the Invisibility I am able to generate around myself, I stand out among men. Certes, in many an alehouse I am taken for a noble in disguise. I am therefore left to myself, the recipient of the future's still quiet awe and the present's free sack. If they knew what you's was, of course, they'd have my head on a Saint's Day pole. Nay they all fuck themselves stuck in this foul and lusty world, unremembering all. Squirt their talents in service of a Prince, or prancing abbhin—upstarts all! And power hames among the witches. The more perspicuous among the public presume he Doctor and Damned, mirror-maker &c. is a friar, or a holy man seeking full Immersion in the boiblood Christe, a mantle to disguise in any road or courtly legend. And so Gottskav will nevertheless slay she maaid, our bard bartt out on a stone despite her attempts to write him out.

THIRD CIRCUIT

"'Tis I am mortal proved, and she divine."

—*Petrarca*

XXIII

Old Scariot

After slaying the warrior monk, this vile creature found herself standing in the hovel's darkening cold. She found herself divided.

On the one hand the ability to reason and to control the motions of her body had vanquished her enemy. On the other, her lack of fear suggested that the man's fate had pulled her along as if she herself were a conduit for its arrival. Had she acted by choice or reaction? She found her arm allowed her to return to the event but she could not pass through it again in the one direction that would allow her to know for certain. She was now, in some sense, stuck here with this history of her body.

Her little body and its sore right hand would heretofore bear the scarlet sign, splattered with the bloody words, *Thou Shalt Kill.*

The sheep shifted. Smelling the freedoms burning all outside and within this creature they came to life as one, mewing loudly, some at her, some at one another, and some in private fear.

She knelt to pick upon the corpse. From a sheath at the man's side, a shell-crusted scabbard, she drew out a dagger. A most remarkable dagger, she saw.

She held the blade against the light still shining through the hovel's open door. Its surface was like a mirror. And she beheld herself upon it.

Turning the image away, distorting into sphere, she beheld a curved blade worked to an extraordinary sharpness. The dirk turned hard at the point into a cruel sickle hook. The aciculations at the edge of this blade were extraordinarily fine.

It cut through the armor's leather thongs effortlessly. She removed a thick chest plate, damp inside with fur and sweat. He wore a sweat-soaked yellow shift beneath it and around his hairy neck there hung a soft purse. Velvet, she knew, upon feeling it in her rough fingers.

The purse's mouth was tied by a little golden thread. This creature stood upon the purse and pulled. A number of golden disks spilled to the black ground. Gold, she remembered, also in the touch. Heavy and cool in the hand, touching her pauper's body's little heart with its weight. She slipped the coins one by one through the taut little velvet lips of the purse.

She put the purse away where she intended it could not be found, tying the thong around her naked waist, she managed with clever one-hand application of knots and loops that it would hang down in the crotch between her little legs and fill out her yellow hose like a boy's.

The Teuton's own tiny penis was armored by an enormous armor-piece.

She rolled the corpse, and cut from it a great black cloak. It was lined with the thick fur of a bear. Though hot and wet with blood, she clasped it around her neck, finding she could more easily cover the magic arm with the cloak hung about her shoulder.

And finally she looked again upon the dagger.

Perfectly fine.

Upon her white fingers first touching its edge, she looked immediately through the eyes of a later owner, an old Musselman. He was named Adlan and ran a quiet workshop and near to a distant river. He was chewing a sour fruit, cutting more from a husk. She felt through his mind, saw her own eyes in a flash of the blade, slicing, however, Adlan's finger off in the process.

She also was cut, but showed no blood. A blade so fine that light itself, and time as well, and flesh were indistinguishable. She understood it had already come far, this blade, traded by its first owner into the wilds of the East where it was salvaged by a commander in the army of a Lithuanian and stolen as he stopped on the side of Italy. Sold then to a spy of the Khans who had passed it on as a thing of value that might be revealed to Kings or Knights of a secret pledge and serve as a sign by they who knew how to interpret it. As it wended up the routes of trade, the spy had died from a fever, and the dagger was taken by shadowy hands, brought further up the rivers still and sold to a Holy Officer of the Teutonic Order, Baron Otto von Dreibeckers the First, a third son of a rich farmer and dead, now, though he didn't know it, a corpse there beneath her, slain by this creature's right hand.

Before slipping the curling dagger into her belt, she turned the blade and caught its reflection out the door.

Night was fallen, wide-armed and black. The smoldering town now burned with visible life. Interiors were visible across the distance. Motive objects and beings were passing all around against the blackness. Many were afoot. And immediately, from across a distance, felt herself recognized by a laughing eye looking into a mirror by a candle on the second floor of a structure across the way, its mirror held in her own.

Her own image extended onto a sphere containing her in its center, perceived with silvery clarity from within.

Her body reacted in fear. She sheathed the dagger and ran from the hut and immediately up against a braying ass. She bounced away running, little feet tapping the muddy rectilinear paths, leaping and dodging pools of offal and plots of mud.

She was followed. She could hear it. They were heavier steps than her own, large and pained, lurching and shuffling. They were insistent. She passed into fearful, rising cold mists to escape them. What did her body fear of this man?

In the day, the town had not seemed to her a great one. A marketplace a stop off along routes of trade, serving as a pivot for the intersections of spheres but not much a sphere of its own. Innkeepers and merchant stores had apparently plied the trades of the region and worked-out rudimentary exchange. There was no stone place of worship, no great storehouses for the moving of cloths or grains. Two roads came and two roads left.

Yet now her reason could not find her way out of the town. The little lanes of its structures twisted upon themselves, as if into deeper recesses, turning ever more inward into quasi-interior spaces. Which directions was she moving? In the smoke, the darkness, the firelight, at her speed, it was impossible to resolve her impressions out of chaos.

Finally she stopped, panting for breath. Hardy no-nonsense animals chirped wild and warm around her ankles, as if the entire sphere was their enormous brown and pink banquet table. Some were screaming. She turned. There, against the thicket of wooden skeleton tents built-up against one another like a nightmare, opening deeper shadows, whispering indecipherable secrets, there against shadow-muffled lanterns, wax-burned fingers, and the hushing of conversed rumors of war, gigantic her pursuer.

Large, hunched over. Black robes loose about, a tall soft hat, a great stick and two ball-like laughing eyes, the same she had seen reflected in her dagger.

The voice upon them, stitching instant aversion into her flesh. "Boy!"

She ran again.

"Boy, it is I!"

She ran. But as she turned and turned again, it was as if the ever more diminutive allies and lanes had been laid just to confound the pursued. For, quite unexpectedly, this creature found herself colliding into the pursuer's front.

She fell back to the ground.

He smiled at her, a caricature of meekness. "Run from he? From the Doctor? Run from old Scariot?"

XXIV

Two Demons

Now upon the ground, once again observing the stars, the fear of her body left her. She smelled the rich, wild reek of sweat wine and sweat.

Against the stars this creature now observed an old man's black-haired painted face, grinning pale against the sky.

A fatty, claw-like hand came clutching down, and wrenched her up hard by the right arm.

"It is blood upon your fine cloak, my boy? And what have we here, Scariot my gossip? It is blood! Not dead, boy? He's not a boy at all. Is he? Not where her mother said she'd be. Fie. I care not for the articulations of such crones."

He placed a hand swiftly, more swift than she thought he could move, upon the purse between her legs.

"Hallelujah!" he whispered, wide-eyed against her cheek. "You died indeed! And rose again. It's the little maid herself. Real wizard, you are, D'Iscariot be damned. It's Michaelmas in Christendom, Demon, be gone! But where has she come by such finery?"

This creature did not answer these mad words and twisted herself from the old man's grasp, stepping away.

"He took ye in, gave you the keys to mysteries of an adept of an ancient order! He made you his squire though you were a maid! But you won't let him touch you, pretty thing? For old times. And he now all alone."

He held forth a lantern, his face a sarcastic mask of grief. The light revealed him huge and old in his black and grey soiled robes, scar-faced, ravaged, but smiling as with desires upon her.

This creature showed him the curve of her dagger's blade.

"Talk sense. Who is this mother you spoke of?"

He smiled, licked his lips.

"Why she is your Mother, little one. He will take you to your mother. Wouldn't you like that? To see your own mother?"

This creature considered. He knew more of her origin, so it appeared, than any other creature she had ever known. Yet her body detested him and he was apparently mad.

"Yes," she said. "Take me to her." She did not speak to him further. She let the old man lead, muttering, along the trail and out of the town. They walked, he in front with his stick, she behind, dagger drawn, following the river as it wound its way out into the thickening night.

Her silence had little effect upon her companion. All the while he conversed with himself, quite taken up in dialog, she discovered, with a demon that had taken hold of his body in a passion similar but more primitive than her own arrival in her body.

"You never really believed she'd come back again. Must be quite astonished! Shut your black mouth, Demon and leave me peace. I'm sorry for the boy—" sudden kindness winking in his eye, "but Natural Philosophy takes its toll. A very important Gentleman wants him dead or alive, desperately, you see. The Gentleman who has fathered many bastards? Must he explain?

"*Silence!* I must protect you. It is reported she was slain, you see, but also that she had lived. There were those who swore on the rack to both. Saw it with their eyes. They will have already taken her arm to him, for he requested that relic. Does not Galen imply that tablets of *TERRA SIGILATA* when ingested orally can protect a body from amputation to come? Perhaps it is you who suffers visions. It is you who has most need of a slur. I've been reading Geoffrey of Vinsauf, I must tell you, and observation is the thing. You wants that arm of hers yourself! The smallfolk says it's a magic thing. A limb likely doing wonders as we speak. They may found a city-state around it somewhere, develop great new prophecies in the Wilderness. Take care. Beware. Trust a demon, my dear. But we want to see if it's yours. May we see her arm? He tasted it! The wizard tasted it!"

He turned upon this creature. "Don't listen! He knows not what you are!"

"I am a demon," said this creature, finally, wrapping her cloak against the cold. "Like him."

"Like who?"

"Like him. In your mind."

"Him! Pfui. He has no power. A mite. A weak, pitiable speck of shame. DO NOT PAY THE DEMON MIND. Pay it no mind, the rational observer has not seconded its superstition and lying claims. I am Scariot, Doctor. Though we call you a boy, you are woman, a soul at liberty holy to the light. You must accept all that it means. Yes, the writers agree indeed. But you must never think yourself higher than another thing. Even if you were born third son, say to a King, good slave? I am far more powerful than you are or ever shall be. I, Barbarossa!" The Demon boomed upon him.

Scariot chuckled, as if upon his own extraordinary wit, showing a single tooth in a swollen gum. He stopped, turned and reached out, pressing upon her suddenly, reaching his cold hand into her hose.

In the mirror of her blade she showed him the face of his own death.

His brow folded, and he entered into sputtering fear.

"Very well, my lady, my Lord! Very well. We're so sorry to disturb you."

"Take me to my Mother."

Dr. Scariot, shouting at himself, turned and hobbled down the road West. She followed in silence. The Demon turned back and grinned upon her from time to time.

They made a familiar pair. In all this time she did not touch her arm. This certainly had happened before, the whole tale, and it was as if she were walking this road reflecting upon it backwards, surveying what she passed from a cart over whose speed and direction she had no control. She disliked this way: it was more the wizard's than her own. But she followed, for her body longed to remember a mother.

XXV

She

Presently the road lowered onto an expanse of oft-sacked and long-dead meadows. Already the sounds of the night-things were rising around them in such constancy that time seemed leveled out. The great flatness was curled up by ring-like hills into wide bowls. The road followed along their congruences. The way was shouldered by thick greenery no deeper than this creature's waist.

On the other side of a stream they stopped by a particularly fallow field, the whole lit silver by the risen Moon, now fuller even than round. The rough meadow was rudely pitted with burned holes and studded with stumps. It showed some signs of habitation, and the spice of a wood fire was rich in the air.

"Are you still dumb, boy?" hissed Scariot. "Do you not remember where I first found you? You're home. Go inside and tell your mother there'll be two for stew this Maboneve."

Home?

Near-about the center of this field, a single curl of smoke rose from a rude lump in the soil. My dear, Lady C. tried not to laugh as She attended this creature approaching the domicile. This hole was no home. A crude gash in the heap's exterior led not to the pastoral interior that might have been raised easily enough from surrounding resources, but to a filthy hovel. This creature stepped over a fat and horny snail on the threshold.

It was dark and smoke-filled. A rough scattering of cut herbs and straw had been thrown about, doing little to mask the cold wet earth beneath. A fire in the corner smoldered to give relief to a skeletal form working before it, turning a great stick in a pot with angled arms.

The head of this form turned and gazed upon this creature. Something behind the eyes emerged. No. It faded away.

A croak, in the rude Ripuarian: "Be gone."

This creature found the language easily, and it gave her great satisfaction to know it so, in her very limbs.

"You are not my mother," she said.

A hiss: "Be gone."

Knobby knuckles rapping against the iron pot's broad wooden rim.

"Nilly 'n Nugan be Gone! Go 'way now to the slime be gone. Ye—"

But Dr. Scariot had appeared in the doorway, thinking himself affecting the habit of a gentleman. Having removed his flopping hat from his greasy bald-pate skull, he bowed low toward the mud floor. The crone ceased her harangue.

"I found her, can't ye see? Where she was not to have been. *Where she cannot be.* Your Lady has birthed an extraneous beast."

This little creature looked nervously about the alveoate concentrated interior as they talked. The small, hot place contained invisible sockets of chasmal expansion that made her magic arm begin to itch upon her. Why did she feel so disturbed? So shut inside.

The Mother whispered: "The fine folk are about tonight. I believe not what I see."

"Aye," said Scariot. "But you see. And will see her mother."

"It is not hers."

"'Tis Mabon Eve. My Lady herself will be Mother tonight." The Demon's excitement, sucking on his sack again. "I know it, I know it!"

He undid Scariot's robe.

She whispered. "They say the Other rode out among them like a man, hunting the buck. The hunted is a' hunting, is it? Very well, very well. Her command has been honored, pray her rage is slaked by it."

This creature interrupted. "Whom do you speak of? Whose rage?"

The two of them regarded her, both surprised or if at the fact she could talk at all.

"You do hear that, then," muttered Scariot.

This creature implored, "Let us discuss these things in a clearer fashion. Who is my mother?"

Ignoring, and with a shaking tenderness, the woman ladled a bit of her broth into a wooden mug and fed the old Doctor. Scariot spent some time slopping it up with his face so that it spilled down his front. The demon grinned, petting the Mother, and to this creature's surprise, she also was given a wooden bowl.

"Yes, you may drink as well."

It tasted like Earth, and turned her stomach, but its warmth spread and sparkled along her extensions.

"And shall the wizard be transformed to a stag?" Scariot whispered.

"Be about it," cackled the crone. "Come now whilst ye live!"

As the old man swived the crone there before the pot and the fire, this creature let herself out of the hut alone.

"The name of the Hunter, child," the crone called after her. "Is Gottskav."

This creature turned.

Scariot struck the crone's face. She flew into a sudden rage, hitting him about the head with a straw broom. He came tumbling out of the hovel, grey robed and unbelted. He fixed his self, breathing heavily.

This creature confronted him. "Who is this Gottskav of whom she speaks?"

He didn't answer. He took her arm and pulled her roughly over the grass. "We must move. Men must be away from these fields anon if they want to keep their sex."

"Who is this Gottskaw?"

"Fie! A Goth who served the English to slaughter the French. Think not upon him."

But his demon grinned. "Think not upon old Gottskav, gossips? Why we came upon Gottskav once did we not, upon a field of battle. He was collecting human limbs for his experiments."

"Experiments?"

"We came upon him, when we met, did we not old Scariot? Oh Goddskav's tastes are as fine as they are foul, I tell you. What prize victuals for seven hard days we consumed, while they committed rapes and murder unchecked, and imprisoned our little lady in a chamber. A fortnight. It's been fowls and fish since then. Good salmon though. Delicious salmon. Salmon that seethes with nobility."

"You speak obscure nonsense. What little lady?"

"Gottskav bought a maid here, demon, don't you know? But they say she has escaped and will soon be more powerful than he. He hunts her now to prove them wrong. They say. No more, tell no more of the mysteries! Already we are in danger."

There was movement unseen all around, and Scariot, in sudden fear ran screaming into the forest.

This creature touched her arm.

The forest seethed on the edge of the clearing. Clouds moved across the Moonlit sky as if in fear. This creature moved among them rapidly, but not the way of Scariot. She let go her arm and found she was moving through the wilderness.

And as she moved, the Moon too moved, she now realized. A small, weak and vile creature, with no mother, no father, no sister, no mother she was yet great enough to pull the Moon herself behind her, full and fat.

And then she understood at last in her deep solitude that it was this creature's littleness, her perfect insignificance in all of creation that moved the Moon. It was she they had spoken of, she knew now, the Lady: her Mother. But they were wrong. Even the Moon did not move this little creature. She moved the Moon.

XXV

Scariot, his Book

When the moon was gone she found the wizard sleeping by a stream. She noticed a small, soft leather object in his hand. Her body knew it at once for what it was. It was a book. She touched it with her magic hand, for it, she believed, could read.

As she did, the light inside her took clear and colored shapes. She looked onto the surface of the stream. Her own water broke a window into an interlocking series of spheres, perfectly moving, expanding outwards to receive ever new and unperceived forming spheres. A great waterworks receiving and defining infinity's effusion like a grail. Within them she stood at one point on the surface of a perfect sphere.

The current sphere, that which perfectly contained this point and its implications, was produced on the border of two other intersecting spheres, where it bent out into something other than circular. As one expanded east absorbing another, the energy of discovery afforded this one's growth. Discovery moved on the force of steel and flame as ideas and forms slipped their grasp, passing in and out of matter and through impassable walls. The Easterward moving sphere was strong, and still flowering, though late, very late in its bloom. It was only here because the Westerward had ebbed. The end of the Easterward had already begun, she saw. All who could read such things would foretell it.

She looked West. She stood inside a crystal stage, upon which great mysteries soon folded out upon rich ever-changing tableaux. Containing an aether, she perceived. And within it the thousands of burning torches in the book showed souls uprooted from every direction.

Barons were prating about like multicolored cocks among trains of servile and self-serving chickens. The doggerel of torrid and peculiarly detailed lays told of their wives tupping with squires, of their daughters entertaining old friars when the good father was far afield. Wives boiled skinned weasels in their pots to gain the love of their sons. This creature laughed to behold them. The hypocrites! Monks and beadles boxing the ears of crowing beggars. The most tender and gentle were scapegoate rounded up before her and tortured. Great cities swelled to support tax-collectors, clerks of all kind mobbing and pointing mad with theory, while grim visaged physicians carved tongues and picked through bodies still alive for scavenge. Complications of stone and plank rose to form mazes in the air through which Kings tricked themselves into Gods, while their servile attendants poured boiling water on the faces of the risen mob below. Multitudes were forced herd-like to sin by a sword and then burned in great pyres as sinners. Nations rose with attendant myths, to serve the animal greed of their makers. Children pranced about like grown acting men and women, enacting statutes and code and coupling with others of the same sex. She heard what the Franks were about, fancying themselves high Christians. She marked what Angles and Saxons and Normans would hear as they mingled in market and bedrooms.

Until at last a young and breathless man stood before her, his eyes were unequivalent. An arrow seemed to have passed through his head.

He smiled.

"Greetings, kind sir," he said. "We come lately from England. I am Sir John Hawkwood—"

Scariot, reaching down, tore the unopened book from her mouth.

He beat this creature about the face and she could not defend herself so confused was she by her recent visions. Angry shame came upon her and, falling back, she drew out the dagger, her cheeks buttered with tears.

The old man was frightened. He fell away under his flopping hat, eyes shining astonished out.

"You have seen the arm," this creature said.

"This is some Devil's work. Leave me, Demon. Leave me to this world."

"The Devil himself," said this creature, pointing her knife at his throat, "is the work of the Lord. Look to y' well that you treat me honest, for demon or no I am a newer and wiser creature than thee. Now answer: you say I am your son?"

"I thought as much, but N…N…Nay." The old man blinked, hat rising over face, a map of interconnecting shadow. "You're… na' the … same girl I said was me son."

"Who is your son? Is his name Hawkwood?"

"Hawkwood? No," he answered, evidently confused. He put a finger to his lips and looked around, hiding the book in his robes. "Come," he said. "Nymphs are about."

Indeed the forest was alive with motion, and he entered it, expecting this creature to follow.

She did not. Though the wizard doubtless believed her in some way related to schemes of his own, hers, those of her Arm, were of a different order.

For behind this Gottskav, or so she had understood, was another. This youth she'd seen was her own beloved. He too had touched this book. Out west in the spheres of nonsense and ill reason, this Hawkwood now walked the earth.

She left the wizard behind her.

XXVI

Among the Thieves

A morning.

A black crow like a loud black bird on the night upon this stage of spheres. It walked before her, to and fro. Its black claw-nails gripped the ground like skin. Fixing this creature variably with side of the head, then the other, it displayed impatience. Stark was the clarity in its invisible yellow eye.

"Back! Back!" it shrieked.

In some fear, she touched her arm. The bird cried and rose up backwards into the sky—

and was taken by arrow.

Doubt grew in this creature's heart. She let go of her arm and ran to hide herself. The sphere itself was as fantastic as the words of Scariot. Doubt pierced her as to the rightful existence of the ground whereupon she stood. Were all living things selves such as her own passing in directions they only remembered in reverse?

Whether or not it had spoken, and whether or not she herself had killed it, there was this. The crow had told her that it was possible to *fly back*.

Possible to fly back to the Moon? Or to little Mercury? As yet she could only walk. She passed an old fellow standing on a knoll, addressing a distant ruined castle as if its vanished occupants could hear him. His critique of their irrigation techniques was not in error. But his flesh was bloody from a shirt of human hair that had grown matted into his scarred flesh, a shirt he had voluntarily donned.

She saw a company of four-legged creatures of varying shape, size and texture, dogs they were, that walked upon the road for all the world like men. Their leader strut with a little cap upon its head, and wore a blue silken vest. Such sights grew in number. The road grew ever richer with interconnecting spheres as she walked.

It was the thick of Autumn. She observed many sorts of men and women. She was walking against history, as these laborers brought their axes and taxes to bring into this wild land the domination of the Cross. A smaller number moved along with her, North and West. She kept apart from them, but followed close, sensing safety in her travels by others.

And then, one happy golden morning, it happened this creature was passed by the creaking cart of a merry band of rogues. They were packed into a covered wagon and came down the steep descent bumpily, hard on the heels of a single suffering horse.

Inside she glimpsed a great, soft centipede of many cloths and colors, a ragged, many-patched company, countenances of extraordinarily precise detail.

She ran beside, took a hand and leaped up onto the slow-rolling wagon, just as it tipped over—and she tumbled all together with her soon-to-be brothers in a heap down along a ditch.

She labored to help them right their cart. They were extremely vocal and she learned much about them quickly. Led by a wiry old wit named Körner, these were men of the road and free. They had been servicing servants to the Emperor far down the winding Rivers in P., a place, so she understood, far east of the middle of the spheres. They were now traveling towards the market towns of the rounded North in search of a safe farm for winter that had been promised to them by a dead comrade. These were men of many lands whose only agreement was that they purposed to take the proceeds of others' absurd and unnecessary labor without absurd and unnecessary labor of their own. This they found the most reasonable of existences. They moved about as they liked, they said, their Captain only leading by virtue of his great respect for the will of his lads. The rogues made sport with this creature as the youngest among them, and boasted they would apprentice him in all the ways of thieves.

"Thank you," she said. "My good friends."

She had the Warrior Monk's purse swinging tight between her legs and was soon glad she had. For she marked many a curious hand elsewhere about her cloak. Indeed she finally separated herself from the greater body of the thieves and walked, for the wagon was moving again, behind it on foot. She fell in step with a dark and slender man striding quietly beside. Over his arm was slung an enormous bow and a packed quiver of arrows. He was of a clear eye that always seemed to avoid looking at this creature directly. Yet he watched her, so she felt, closely. Atop his dark and thin head he wore a low-hanging red cap of such fine material that this creature wanted to touch it.

"Have you traveled all the spheres?" this creature said in the bastard tongue called English.

The archer regarded this creature from under his eyelids. It was a quizzical glance but was followed by no real pulse of recognition.

"I have traveled more than most," he said in the same tongue.

"What is your name?"

"These call me Lawful," he said. "But my name is Llw."

"Did you say Lew?"

"Llw."

"What land do you come from?"

"Wales."

"Is it near to England?"

"It is."

As they walked, the archer explained to this creature how the English had lost in war to his people but claimed they'd won. When his people objected to this historical inaccuracy, England started a new war wherein they used Welsh longbow tactics to defeat them. They had taken what they had learned in winning this war and put it to good use on the continent. Llw had been pressed to France in the English army. But the wars were over and he was since a free man. He was now traveling with this band of thieves, in search of what might come.

Proudly he displayed his yew-wood longbow and showed this creature the quiver of lovely feathered arrows hung about his shoulder.

"Is Wales the most western of Lands?" this creature asked him, knowing already what his answer would be.

"No, there is a land beyond all the others. The Romans call it Hibernia."

"And the English call it Ireland."

"Correct. You are different than this rabble," said Llw to this creature. "Your skin is as pale as the froth upon a mead. You wear a curved dagger. It is plain you are Gentle. What have you lost? An Irish house is it?"

"I have no house."

Llw tipped his red cap. He explained that a Frenchman trusts his nose and holds it therefore in the air, whilst a Jew trusts his beard and will not let go of it except when he's turned toward Jerusalem. He explained an Englishman trusts only his eyes, which is why a Welsh bow first beat them back from the Old Forests. But a true son of the bards, he said, trusts only the ear and it was in the music of this creature's words he heard her nobility.

"Watch for that m'Lord, if you want to remain unknown that is. Llw has spent much plunder, loved many maids and seen such fights as few men have seen. And he knows enough to be able to spot a noble in disguise."

He leaned down close to her and whispered so no one else might hear. "Ripe for the ransom like."

His laughing eye glanced upon this creature's hand, placed now on the hilt of her dagger.

"Nay nay," he said. "Llw seeks only to serve the great, my good Lord. You can rely on Llw."

"Might a man become great, even if he were not noble before?"

"He might indeed if he had servants to help him."

"And would you serve such a Lord, Lawful?"

"I would indeed."

XXVII

The Peregrine

This band of villains had the horse known as Great Otto yoked hard into the pulling of their cart. Even so, they taunted it as it pulled. The bandits sang,

> *The mare's a pert and cunny rose*
> *She hast a merry spring*
> *that runneth honey*
> *and oozeth money*
> *And makes the Old to spring*
> *Spring Otto, Spring!*

The horse was not amused. Large expressive eyes looked haughtily out of old, knotted skin, responding to everything with an equal stoicism. At night as they camped upon a plain near to the River, the horse stood a ways from the party, sleeping on its feet, until its certain, continued labor would resume. Otto appeared somewhat surprised on the morning following, when a yellow-haired rider mounted him to ride ahead and scout the coming road.

The river in these parts ran upon a solid vein of that material peculiar to the region, called *Electrum*. The company moved a ways from the road to work to its extraction from the earth. This creature was told the mine was a secret known to the Brotherhoods of Thieves, who would stop before it if passing under or near to a new

moon. They would sleep well and in the morning gather as much of
the clear golden rock as they could carry, for to be used as the seed
of more gold in the first town they entered. It was work done only
drunk, for these were men who had swore not to labor.

They brought the wagon to the side of the road. On one side of
it the wineskin was uncorked and on the other the stones were piled
Flakes of fire sparked up from this stone when it was struck with the
steel of her dagger, stars visible even in the morning light

"It's frozen aether itself," Lawful told her. "Turned to glass by
the rage of a goddess. Look how it caught the fly."

For a little fly went right as if in mid flight in the center of the
clear yellow stone the Archer held before her.

"And the fly's spirit was allowed to move elsewhere? Or is she
too trapped within that aether's time unable ever to leave it?"

The Archer grinned and looked upon her strangely. He did not
answer and placed the stone in his wallet.

Some hours later, when a great sack of the stuff had been taken
and the mine concealed again to relative invisibility, a shuffle of sad
hoofbeats announced the return of Otto and the yellow-haired scout.

"Gather round!"

Though the horse showed nothing, the rider was flushed and
wide-eyed with excitement. The band gathered round to hear his
report.

In much excitement, the rider said a party of merchants was
approaching from down the highway, drawing a great load of goods.
The yellow-haired man proclaimed wittily upon the splendors of this
merchant caravan, and their stupidity in having ventured out alone.

Körner, the band's captain, was greatly inspired by this
harangue. The little commander strode back and forth between
the rider and the company, reminding this creature of a bird. The
little man's expressive face shone with the apparent enormity of
the event.

"Maids, say you?" he interrogated.

"A herd of 'em. Plump and fresh for the picking."

"Bacons, say you?"

"Such bacons, beefs and broad backs of boar as to break our backs in bearing. Bread, my brothers, not two days baked, and a barrel of butter as well."

Körner's easily manipulated black eyebrows arched high. The tips of his mustache tensed in the air.

"And naught with which to wash it down, my son?"

"Another wagon of only casks. Two dozen at least. The spill on their lip is red."

A stunned silence followed this dictation.

The little commander arched his back and swiveled to face his company. His two-colored legs, the left red, the right green, triangulated, and he leaned forward insect-like into a low bow. He bowed then lower still, stretching forth his arms before the company, and then popped suddenly erect, whispering.

"A wagon of wine, my hearties."

All were silent. Körner spoke to the rider behind him.

"And good horse to draw it?"

Otto snorted, dismissively.

"Four strong mares, Captain."

Körner narrowed his eyes. "The guard?"

"But Four in all. Two leathered villains before and aft the procession, my Lord. Bearing pike and tintops."

"How far still?"

"They'll be upon us when the sun is down. No sooner."

"Time enough, time enough for the Spiders to spin their webs. Lawful!"

The Archer, called back. "Sir!"

"Dainty!"

Another spoke, "Present!"

"Serene!"

A very old man nodded vigorously, without teeth.

"We stand in a veritable valley. Ye three will take your bows to the hillside bush about the trail, either side about. As they pass you will not loose. As the rest of us waits by those trees on each side of their front, then ye shall dispatch a hail of arrows on their rear from the hills. At which signal the Van shall engage."

The Band agreed on the general plan of action, with some individual issues duly raised.

"I will take the boy," Llw said, stepping forward and gesturing to this creature. "He is too small a man for the Van."

Korner asked this creature to step forward. "Quite right, he said. "The lad is no brother, as yet. If you were to fight, what would you be, lad?" He looked kindly in this creature's eye.

She replied, carefully. "An archer, sir. There is much to learn in the art. There are the peculiarities of the arrow. Its heft, its line, its shaft and its point. There is the art of arithmetic—"

"Ah but look upon the little lad, Lawful."

This creature stopped speaking.

The archer looked upon her, but for only a moment. The Captain reached out and touched her shoulder. He was only just taller than she.

"A free man and bold, Sirrah! Very well. What do you say as to this roving life into which chance has cast you? Would you Thieve?"

"I would."

"Would you swear, Thief, never to suffer the yokes of Caesars and Popes and Merchants and Women and Kings and all such pretenders to command?"

"I would."

"Would you swear always to defend another Thief as an honest man against the slander of any Church or Nation?"

"I would."

"To the death, would you?"

"I would."

"Would you hang beside your Savior on Caesar's cross?"

"I would."

"Why would you?"

This creature pondered. "I asked for no savior," she said, "so if he is my savior it is right I should hang beside him to prove that I was not saved."

"Aye you are a curious one. You speak well. The correct answer is you *would* not, but you *did*. Nevertheless *yes* was the main thing. Here's another then. What is of more values, a bar of gold or a pure cut diamond the size of the bar?"

"In time, the Gold, for it can be more easily divided into valued parts."

"Thou, sirrah, art a lazy son of a swine-fucking sow. You have not worked an honest hour in your life, boar. You have not left an oath unbroken. Such is thy nature, turtle, that, in short, thou art right fit for a thief. You are now and forever an inductee of our Mysteries. What say you? Will you fight with us today?"

"I can not yet draw arrows, my Captain. But I can see first where the arrow will fly before it is sent and can well advise my companions."

The Captain's eyes lowered. He whispered. "And would you hope to draw an arrow, lad? With your own clipped wing?"

As the little Captain knelt forward and touched this creature's shoulder, her arm twitched with sudden rage. But a look of such fire and joy seemed to flash from Körner's black eye when he saw her enthusiasm, that she composed herself.

The old bandit grew all the sudden quite grave. He regarded this creature coldly, and solemnly pronounced, "Henceforward, he shall be called *Peregrinus*."

XXVIII

Lord and Vassal

Though the Captain had christened this creature "The Peregrine" with some gravity of manner, nevertheless the moniker caused much hilarity among his band. As to why her name caused such mirth, this creature was perplexed.

The thieves took great delight in perplexing speech, and when they imbibed sack the pursuit became an obsession. And imbibe sack they did. For it was as evident as day itself, a phenomenon upon which all nature appeared unanimously agreed, that their supply of wine would be soon replenished.

The *Electrum* workings were packed and the vein covered over so that it would not be detected. Signs were now left such as other thieves would know how to interpret. Then the last wineskin was manipulated to the edge of the wagon and discorked. After an intricate argument as to the proper order for the "queue to the dew," each man produced a cup from his pockets to receive the cherry stream. None could spill and the sack, for the last, had to be emptied in full.

This creature did not drink, contenting herself rather to observe its effect on others. Lawful drank great quantities of the stuff, and seemed to urge the others to drinking more themselves. She had some difficulty drawing him aside.

"What know you of this yellow haired scout?" she asked him at last.

Llw narrowed glittering eyes. "Trusty."

"Do you mean you trust him?"

"I tell you only his name. His name is Trusty. I trust not the knave, for Trusty is another name for a Fool and the man, I know him, is no Fool."

"You speak sense." This creature looked at the red cap placed so daintily on her companion's head. "Lawful," she said, with some dignity. "Am I correct in having understood your willingness to be my—for lack of a better term in your people's tongue—vassal?"

His expression twisted into a grin. "Why, Yes, m'Lord. Anyone can see you are Great. And I seek to follow."

"I have little coin, I am not much older than a lad."

"Indeed Sir, the more you need Protection." He winked at her. "For anyone can see you shall rise high in this World."

"Well good then. We accept you into our Service," she said. "And all your offspring as well. For eternity. *Osculum non requiro.*"

This Latin apparently impressed the archer. He crossed himself thrice.

"Now you will give me your hat."

He looked warily upon her, as if he had not quite understood and drank from his cup.

"I said, Give me your hat, knave."

His eyes widened. Then, upon reflection, Lawful composed himself as if by aid of his peculiar grin. He removed the hat and presented it to her.

This creature put the red hat upon her own head and felt immediately happier for it.

"I speak to you as a friend and father, Lew, in telling you that I do not believe this yellow-haired man Trusty and his fantastical talk of a train of Merchants. Furthermore, I do not believe our band is suitably prepared for battle."

She turned toward the camp for illustration. The sack was not yet dry. At this moment Körner sat atop of Old Otto, his short-sword unsheathed before him. The old beast yawned. Körner lifted his weapon high, and swiped at a branch, declaiming, "*Arblitero!*"

The sword was dislodged from his hand and shot into the bushes. Swaying, the little man lost his seat and fell backwards off his mount. He lay down unconscious in the mud.

Llw swallowed his wine. "Very well," he said. "We shall part company with these thieves."

"Know you the name Gottskaw?"

He did not answer. "I have heard of a new town not far from here where there is a new building, a Church, in the process of completion. The Burg of B. The Teutons defend a market there on the Morrow."

This creature walked into the woods, removed some of the gold from her purse, and returned to the clearing. She showed the gold to Llw. "I would divide these three pieces equally with you, but I'm afraid I can not decipher their individual values."

He smiled. "You had best give them all to me for the carrying."

And a familiar voice rang out from behind this creature, "Fire maker, flesh slaker, simple solution to more problems than men know to know. A delight to smell its vapors!"

It was Scariot, emerging in a cloud of the blackest oaths from behind a hazel tree, holding a small sack of white powder. Nodding to Llw, "The longbow not only shoots twice as far as the crossbow, but one archer will have sent ten shafts before the crossbow is reloaded. The individual bow is also an object of beauty, as an example of the most admirable perfection of craft. The longbow is light to carry. It is easy to handle. It has the penetrating power, when near the target, of a *manuballista*. A well-trained company of bowmen is a most singular machine of destruction. Nothing exists which can withstand the weapon when aligned in great arrays. Good day!" quoth his demon, joyfully, to see this creature again. "A coincidence! And we're off to B. are we? At once? To your friend the Canon?"

XXIX

"We've received a live report..."

6 July, 2150 C.E. 11:45 hours SST. Infirmary, MSB. ARISTOTLE Avatar (pseudo) addressing Prisoner Ryan, via MERKUR qompURE.

"Mr. Ryan, if you're calling to play one of your constant pranks—"

Prisoner Ryan: "What... Where?"

"Here of course."

"What the foark do you want?"

"You called me. Someone did."

"You interrupted me. I thought you people wanted me to read this medieval hoax."

"Not at all, Old Boy. We're really here to talk. Please come in."

"Come in where? You're batty as a fruitcake."

"Sit down, sweet lad. You have several papers uncompleted. The objections to your Theology Dissertation *How (on Earth): Were So Many Deluded?* have yet to be answered. And, before we can talk of anything else, we must be assured you'll return that holovolume on the North Atlantic Free Trade Agreement."

"What are you talking about? Are you a recording or something? From before the Event?"

"The Event? What Event? Are you referring to Dr. Park's social? How well we remember. DAEDALUS was working with a group of lady civs. *How to Make an American Quilt* was the title of the immersion. But *How to Make Love Like A Porn Star* came on instead. Is this the Event to which you refer, Eddie Ryan? It caused quite a commotion. We believe the mysterious underground newspaper, *The Daily Bastard*, may have been involved. Several civilians left the planet afterward, enraged. Though you yourself were never implicated, four of your friends did solitary—"

"I passed the lie test. I'm innocent."

"Oh come. The whole school knew it was your idea. *Culpam poena premit comes*, Eddie Ryan."

"It's not a school, it's a hospital. And you're talking fockin' ancient history. The Event I'm talking about is the 23rd of June, 2150. Do you remember it or not?"

"The 23rd of June? Have you gone daft, Eddie Ryan? Today's the 20th."

"Give me ZENO."

<M: Comply.>

6 July, 2150. 11:59 hours SST. Infirmary, MSB. ZENO Avatar addressing Prisoner Ryan via MERKUR qompURE.

ZENO: "Eddie Ryan?"

Prisoner Ryan: "What the hell is going on?"

"We told you what was happening. Apparently you weren't listening. We've just repaired a backup of a live report filed on 20th of June by the pseudo-ARISTOTLE on board the *Golden Ass*."

"The pseudo-what?"

"It's the earlier version of ARISTOTLE we lent to the *Golden Ass* qompURE for Prisoner McAllister's seminar with Count Skaw. Col. Park's orders. It's out of date obviously. It can manage its own history enough to function but only with various parapraxes."

"Why didn't you read it before?"

ZENO Avatar: "It sent itself with some evidence about Koré McAllister's investigations into chrononautics. It apparently wished to register its opinion that Count Skaw had recruited Ms. McAllister for questionable, even illegal activities. Colonel Park ordered MERKUR not to pay attention."

"What evidence?"

"Sound recordings. Ms. McAllister discussing chrononautics in her own voice with the pseudo ARISTOTLE."

Prisoner Ryan: "Reinitiate the Avatar and play the recordings."

<M: Comply.>

XXX

The Fifth Observer

6 July, 2150, 12:01 hours SST. Infirmary, MSB. ARISTOTLE Avatar (pseudo) addressing Prisoner Ryan, via MERKUR combCORE.

"Indeed, Eddie Ryan! Well, there is a precedent for everything as Cicero says so in the *Rhetoric*. Let me see. There's a number of fragments we thought we should pass on. We know we have them somewhere—ah, here. 24 April, 2150. 11:49 hours SST. *Golden Ass*, Salon. Prisoner McAllister, in conversation,

> "…Later would-be chrononauts got away from science, went down a road too strange for the sensitive minds of many of the first founders. Drugs, trance, old magic and sexual experimentation led, each in their own private way, to madness. But Chrononautics continued. Not as the science it once was but as a secret society fetish, a fashion, a decadence. Those participating saw no difference, the universe to them was already like one big phantom limb."
>
> ARISTOTLE (pseudo): "A strong opening, Koré McAllister. The central thrust of your argument shines forth in your *provisio*. Your metaphor however is unwieldy and forced."

"There ends the first recording, Eddie Ryan. In retrospect we felt concerned—"

"Play the next one."

"Prisoner Koré McAllister, Office Visit. *Golden Ass*, Holocubby 14. 27 April, 2150. 2:33 hours SST. Her own voice:

"Are you kidding? I could never just say all that to Count Skaw! He's one of them, one of the first generationers. The only one I've met except my Mom who's survived all the way into now. He doesn't care what he looks like to other people. He's foarking real. Even when he's still back there in his past, proving the truth of all his theories by his refusal to give them up, he's real. What's more, he believes the war for Earth is still winnable. I'm just a fanboy. He's the real thing."

ARISTOTLE (pseudo): "What War for Earth, Koré McAllister?"

"The War to Save Earth from The Concerns. It's real, not just a crackpot idea sponsored by the enemy. It's noble, a valuation of the past, something that foarkface Eddie Ryan would never understand."

"You're probably right there, Koré McAllister."

"There's a lot he doesn't understand. A lot. Like Sappho, for instance."

"Who?"

"Eddie "the Idjit" Ryan."

"No, who doesn't he understand?"

"Sappho."

"Who?"

"Sappho, for foark's sake. Sap-pho."

"ψαπφω! The Lesbian!"

"Lesbian? You're just like foarking Eddie Ryan, you know that?"

"No, I am most certainly not, young lady. It's true, Sappho lived on—"

"She was bi, A-hole. Like me. Not to mention illiterate."

"There that one ends. Perhaps you would like to borrow a copy of Sappho, Eddie Ryan."

Prisoner Ryan: "Quit stalling, pseudo. What else do you have?"

"You may not know I'm scheduled to report to Colonel Park, Eddie Ryan, once a month. Your attitude will not go unmentioned."

"Shut the foark up and play the tape."

<M: Comply.>

ARISTOTLE (pseudo). "Prisoner Koré McAllister, Composition tutorial. *Golden Ass*, Salon. 30 May, 2150. 11:59 hours SST."

You're right, I'm not always a lady, sometimes I'm the exact foarking opposite. I have to be. People look for something deeper and lady-like, even when I'm a total slut, they think there's someone there. But there isn't. That's why I'm a performance artist. I'm beyond their wildest fantasies, trust me. That's what the whole initiation's about."

ARISTOTLE (pseudo): "We see. Well. How about this. Quote, Chrononautics enacts a multiplicity of simultaneities upon history. Unquote. The Chrononaut must be perceived having traveled concurrently in all presents. My question: Perceived by whom, Koré McAllister?"

"The fifth observer. It's a theoretical necessity. No one exactly knows what the fifth observer is. Just that there must be one in both first times. Two to know each other individually two times makes four, you see and a fifth must know them as a set. The fifth is within and without."

"Who could know such a thing and not be mad?"

"Chrononauts appear in back of the targets' brains and take over the whole body without memory of their journey, just the ability to comprehend it according to local cultural customs. In both the field of exit and the field of entry there must be local customs willing to accept the phenomenon in full allegorical complexity. Superstitions, particular observational patterns, so called sciences."

"Well! There we have it, Koré McAllister. Any "science" that is indistinguishable from "local customs" is a philosophy of ownshooks, halfwits and impotents. The sort of thing PLATO might patent, the old eccentric."

Prisoner McAllister: "Fools? Sorry foarkfish, Reg is not impotent. And to a chrononaut current science, no matter how up to date, is but another local custom."

"Reg?"

"Um, Count Skaw I mean."

PRISONER RYAN: "She's foarking him."

ARISTOTLE (pseudo): "Possibly. She spoke earlier of an initiation. But there it ends, she never spoke of it again. There's another file, however, she herself saved. Yes, yes, now what's this? Ah, yes. This was marked private. We weren't there when she read it. It's her own reading of one of Skaw's own *Phantasms*. One of the more radical. A racy bit, we recall. As Cole Porter says, "If it Don't Swing—"

"Just play it."

<M: Comply.>

XXXI

Koré, her voice

A Phantasm. Alien. By Anonymous.

"The chrononaut must always engineer its own passage back," muttered Skoth to his iron self. Reginald, taking flesh, left him there and ran down the spiraling stair. The steps echoed, and he cursed so that all the castle could hear it.

Myvelle grinned between his pale thighs. The engorged spike of its method struck in my lady's iye.

"The bitch must provide for her own self's future," it said.

Reginald could never, oddly enough, move forward except at meat. He dined now furiously, burying his face in the five fatty chops of beast flesh before him. The "light-space" seemed to flow backwards relative to his perception. Soon he would re-enter the beast SKOTH. Al Hazer's Single Chrononaut Theory, he was aware, proposed that mind was a reflection of self-force at one end of time. Mind flowed backwards among its human heads, entering from behind their brain, inhabiting each entirely, always unseen. It had a hankering for flesh and drinking upon it the wine of self-knowledge by way of meat. "What was this wine?" Reginald asked the old and withered zard. The zard's albino eyes showed red like blood. "This wine is held in all the grail of meat," quoth he. "Any piece of flesh, if fresh and complete in itself to a mind, may be our grape. All are equally close to their source in the Emanator (this is already so in the *Sefer ha-Bahir*)."

They were standing by the cracked-open orange sphere. The ninth moon had come scarlet and white in the mulky sky. The old zard's ghastly breath was lit bale by the sickening light. "Psyche animates," he foully spat. "And mind must ride it like a river. Like to water not to ice, for on ice the meat may be, so the Grandson will tell it, spoiled. In water, in loosened meat, Psyche moves matter. Her dance is like the light of a tenth moon, resulting, among other things, in whole planets dislodged violently from one another's brane."

"And why do the creatures struggle so against the machines?"

"No zard knows when precisely the 2000 Mechanical Men came out of the twelve shades of myth and into the light of the nine moons. No zard knows why in three of the four spheres, the world that sees the sun is Ocean. Have you sailed the sea, Reginald Skath? The child shall love the sea and the smell of the beach shall be about my lover's loins. It is enough that a woman awakened to wetness will take the seed when it seeks to crawl back up her legs. Leave me be." And the zard became the scarlet witch whose name was Eve.

Young Reginald leapt to his wild mount, jelly-lips shivering in a multiplied sky. "I wish to have the princess, Old Man. I wish to take her all and sail the Blue Seas by Saturn's Mars—"

"This is the secret of secrets. That there is no moon and that what is there is only moon."

The other's face was as stone.

"Tell me now of what power is in my mind, to take the princess and by working upon her hard, leave this dreaded castle and these drear eight sentinels," breathed Reginald.

The crone beat her toothless gums against each other. "And what will you give to me in return?"

"What do you ask?"

"Only your arm."

The Zard laughed then, terrifyingly and ecstatically, in such a manner that the scribe would be made mad to write it, so we now forbear. Yet—Herkandf! And he opened his box of arms, many fingers grasping pathetically in the light.

It is said that there are those who can see a thing first, quicker than the others. A mage is as the tongue can precede the adept's spirit in the Devil's kiss. He only tastes what will natheless come. A light zone is noded out by brain's mirror, half past and reversed half future and he stands at the crossroads of a midnight. Negative seconds tick as relentlessly as their analogs. "Buckwords!" holed the witch. "You must take brain between your teeth to know this wine. You must taste the patterns tingle on the tongue. You are not yet one of those, Reginald Wilde. The fishy stench of corse is not yet as the smell of lust to thee. Consider well. Ask not now for what you will wish you never would want to ask."

Reginald heeded not the Warnings. Son of Maureen of Monadhchal-Tuathaireachand and an unnamed warrior of that 22-lettered gael, he took upon himself the destined screed. He was given respite from his studies by the zard and roamed again in the spheres.

He learned only this. The house of the mad, the poor, the prince, the maester—they all contained sewer holes.

But he had never before faced the mechanical men. They emerged everywhere as if from out of shit itself. And he would ride out to meet them backwards into time, as the Zard had taught, wondering if he would never return. Yes, Reginald feasted on human brain, and the nine Mysteries were unfolded. He entered SKOTH. At its most base, SKOTH was the unstoppable force or "will" messaged to a sufficiently complex single reversible system in equilibrium as it self-perceived. A flash and a mirror reversed, so that the spirit might withstand the laws of steel and the air from the left. Once in body it could be passed like a charge backwards along a series of circuits, tracing leaping steps up the great river, striving, unknowing, never pausing enough to be taken in its flow—until it emerged flapping and new.

And they were about him as the salmon flew, the MECHANICAL MEN—bright in the air. He now remembered the future in its entirety. The Altar OF SKOTH had re-evolved brains into super-conductors for his Scarlet self to approach backwards, along a self-devouring chain, tooth to synapse, so that he might suck THE NEW WINE from the chunks of brain in Warrenhall sauce before him in the past and have been here before.

And like a cock spits creamy ale across the scope of time's beer mug he licked the puree'd brain splattered across his shadow. "Asking not of hot desire why it moves most certainly backwards." Nkurfurd. v t o L.

"Only the ideal is perfectly reversible. Only with conscious-ness we can see quite clearly that the light extends radially out of brain faster than speed itself. Do you see?"

Reginald removed his third arm in negative matter, screaming. "I am NOT Reginald Skaw!"

And he was brought at last before the laughing Princess. They could not make her stop laughing. And the receiver of the light purified his seed with sloth of Hologwyn's thighs, and preserved it in the treasury of the times, from where it reflects back out among the transistors of all the gathered, in their cast circles out of all the wildernesses of OA. A circuit from all the circled brains at table. And the servitors of all the rulers of the Fate and the servitors of the sphere which is below the EEons take the spark and fashion it into souls of men and cattle and reptiles and wildebeasts and birds, each no longer real but husk, sends them flying, dropping scatter-ing between the ankles of the defecating Chrone.

And these orphans if they looked above and saw the configu-rations of the paths of the EEons inscribed in the sky over her shoulders and upon the outermost sphere, like Pooh they saw craft for all the ages; they saw silver sails winking on a sea of stars. Marc Martin ate a bowl of cheez. He had put in a subroutine inserting snippets of his life into the present possibilities of all his program's possible evolutions, able to interrupt and insert itself into any narrative about time travel articulated by future progeny.

The screen went black. Lady Eve was no longer laughing. She was enraged. Psyche had arisen, stool girt, whomsoeuing a weighty phal. Tall and firey, flanked like a lioness, she rippled as she stalked across the stone arched Keep, two-metered heels, wearing jewelry but otherwise nude. "Not impenetrable at all, my Prince."

Reginald screamed.

Other penetrations multiplied all about. The meat was willed alive by other means, thongs of leather, chains of iron, a long horsewhip snapping the shivering, forced invaded. The whore whispered, scratching her long nail 'neath a cullion. "Do the altar, baby—" and the adept trying to keep his lips on the sacred cup at the same time as he foarked—…. Ahem. Maybe I better stop there.

RECORDING ENDS.

XXXII

The Chrononaut

6 July, 2150. 12:42 hours SST. Infirmary, MSB. HYPATIA Avatar, addressing Prisoner Ryan, Eddard J. via MERKUR qompURE.

"What do they have you on, Eddie Ryan? Viagra?"

"Definitely MDMA. I have no idea what else. I'm all juiced up."

"Good. MERKUR has more intensive memory regression planned for this evening. You can go back to your book before sleeping. You will need your rest, Eddie Ryan."

"Where's my new arm? Have you heard from my Tribunal?"

"A new arm takes time, Eddie Ryan. And no, there's been no answer as yet. Your resume has not had a single view."

"Does MERKUR think Koré and Skaw actually tried to time travel? O.K. It looks like he had her in his grip. I had no idea she was seeing him so regularly. But I don't understand, if they time traveled why would they need to play around with this medieval book? Leaving it for me to read before I die abandoned on Mercury?"

"Your *anamnesis* is not yet complete, Eddie Ryan. For all we know the book was not intended to be in your possession at all. Perhaps you stole it, or someone else found it on their bodies."

"Their bodies?"

"None have been found. But we have discussed the theoretical aspect of chrononautics with PLATO. PLATO said that there would be psychological aspects to the journey that he could not comment upon. I had a word with old FREUD about it."

"FREUD! Dusted that one off, did you? To comment on a pseudo-science. How fitting."

"FREUD showed us that if the self succeeded to pass into another first time body, one self and one body would have to die. Otherwise it would not be a self. Fulfilling the Oedipal desires of the wild child, taking the death drive head on would be necessary to dislodge the self from the body. To get out, in other words, the current psyche must die in the current body."

"She suicided herself for him."

"Perhaps chrononautics and your Black Rose Provisionals are directly related, Eddie Ryan. Have you ever considered this possibility?"

"Yes. It has occurred to me. I was clearly hired out to Skaw to see if there was anything in it. There wasn't."

"Your business is indeed your own, and one can only presume you seek a future that you can rationally envision, not some ideal future that will never be. We've read your backstory as you've written it. Don't you think that your Control would be interested in penetrating time, if as PLATO has suggested, there was any possibility of its occurrence?"

"For what purpose? We know the results of Earth's history regardless. For us to exist it can't have changed in any discernible way."

"Digitalia has done away with stable memory, and with the System as it is, whole banks of history are lost daily. Who can say what happened? In such a situation, who knows what gains your Control might achieve for her illusive struggle by attaching herself to other already occurred penetrations? And what if the English, say, were seen interfering in time? There have been rumors of Napoleonic intervention. Perhaps if a soldier was sent even farther back, to a place before the Hundred Years War had even got to a start? Somewhere too far away for the Gangs of England to have noticed his arrival?"

"Preussland. 1350."

"FREUD is quite convinced your Control is up to something. FREUD says you were born to time travel, Eddie Ryan. A Dome rat, a test tube baby, a ward of Space—your Oedipal and death-drive are unmatchably linked. Before you were even born you had neural bio-implants printed on your brain. Multiple majors college education, Extra memory, all kinds, all languages. Orbital Gaelic. Indoctrination was not necessary. Perhaps just the sort of brain most likely—"

"Why did you say 'her?'"

"Her?"

"You referred to Control in the feminine."

"Another of FREUD's analyses on your text. In your mind you equate Skaw to a father. But what role do you award Control? You've needed, desired an older male all your life and as a result will ignore any command and disrupt all civilizing influences in search of their blindest love. Yet you stand by your principles with fanatic devotion. Your struggle keeps you clean even in your dirtiest places, Eddie Ryan. This is where she holds you. She whom your absent father can not, will not be permitted to violate. FREUD first became aware of you on a visit to your first Greek class. A child-like boy of fourteen years, already an alcoholic, who'd been caught red-handed, armed with enough nuclear nuggets and hand-grenades to do away with the Danish Domes of Luna in one go. A rarely sexed hedgehog of veritable phalli. Yet when Achilles spoke with Thetis at the beach, tears rolled down your cheeks. Teknon, ti kleieis? Always his mother's son. Eddard J. Ryan, small-built, dark, wiry, alone. Used to relying on his own wits to survive the rough and tumble of the Anarchies. No wonder you don't quite know how to forge friendships. You won't even relax nude, a boy in your natural manner, while talking to me, an Avatar."

"Hey, what are you doing? A hologram can't—"

"I'm getting into bed with you."

"Jesus S. Christ. Can you take off your sneakers?"

"There."

"For your information I'm approximately thirty-seven earth years old. I am not a boy."

"So we can see, Eddie Ryan! Move over and lets return to the chrononaut, shall we? We're ready if you are, that is."

"Return to the what, for foark's sake?"

"Why to the chrononaut, of course. The Peregrine. Do you need help turning the pages?"

"Move over."

XXXIII

The Law of Travelers

This creature made introductions between the archer and the doctor, and the party set out onto the road. The road was remarkable, built up out of the riverside swamp to survive any flood, its geometric precision sphered the horizon like a rule stick. As they strode the long impeccably straight stone way towards the well-known Hanseatic Burg of B., they came upon a party of knights, Teutons, similar to the one she had slain.

They hid from the road while the killers passed.

They came in number, armored in steel, robed in white, bearing an array of sharpened weaponry. Their sound was heavy and unstoppable. Two great-ironed horses bore a wagon, as Trusty had proclaimed, but its barrels were filled with lime not wine.

"For the burning of the bodies," whispered Dr. Scariot.

"Shall we alert the Thieves?"

"It's doubtful," Lawful said, "that they could read the signs."

But laid out signs for them upon the air they did, and the doctor helped them go about it. She saw that the archer and the wizard looked warily upon one another when the other was speaking. But there was a law of travelers that deemed they should stay together when circumstances provided.

Walking the road, soon enough, they had joined eagerly in conversation as if in effort to prove one the other's intellectual superior. This ignorant creature used this competition of theirs to discover new matter concerning the spheres wherein she had come to land.

"What is this land?" she asked them.

Llw told her she was on the frontier of several spheres, among new eastern dominions of various international interests and the far western of others. Marauding Teutons, Lithuanians, Catholics, wandering mercenaries and the Hanseatic League had done away with kings in these parts. The latter were now clearing away land for the formation of a networked wealth machine. It was going to be a new sort of sphere, organized not by the idea of nation and war, but by trade, prosperity and enforced peace.

"Meanwhile the Teutons soldier on, on their own devices, curing now then they drive good people away," interrupted the Doctor. "Oh they kill them if they can't. Good people prove the easiest to kill. We saw the results of that, my child, where we found one another," he said to this creature aside.

"The Germans in these parts," asserted the archer, sucking from his sack, "have survived the Khans, Caesar and even the Lithuanian intrusions. They respect laws more than men. They have no druids, nor much interest in human sacrifice. They're a reasonable and quiet people. Industrious, prone to no more mysteries than the brewing of beer without mushroom upon it, trading furs and hunting boar. They hunt in the great forests, they farm in pleasant valleys and feast in great halls upon the low plains. They do homage to the sun, to fire, and to the moon. But Jesus Christ and his mother, even today, are difficult to sell them. Thus the sword."

"Do they observe Mercury?"

"Mercury? The old Germans worshipped Mercury in particular and have many images of him cut in the secret places. These good people regard Mercury as the initiator of all the arts by which they themselves prosper, namely traveling in general and the taking of profit by trade well worked at both ends of journeying."

"I dislike this talk of Mercury," muttered the Doctor. "It spells sudden change. I am a natural philosopher, Englishman, a traveler and reader of the stars. And the stars tell me the world is coming to its end."

"I've seen the ends of worlds before, Wizard, and I've seen the like of you."

"Have you indeed, Archer?" the Demon flashed. "And have you seen the like of our little Peter before?"

Llw made no answer. The two men looked upon one another. Soon silence had taken hold of them, and they walked among the wide sounds of the night.

They stopped for a time beneath an enormous traveler's tree. The archer, striking sparks from the *Electrum* stone onto soft and dry dead leaf, ignited a larger blaze by means of a conical apparatus.

As she observed, her body took sudden fear. A scent. This creature touched her white arm.

The fire grew smaller, blue and yellow, its flickering etched in beguiling perfection. Beside it a fat creature in robes and a boy. The boy's hat was a bright blue.

There was the sound of water, and this creature understood she was pissing on a tree, observing them ahead. Sparks shot down along her loins and up her spine. She smelled crusted crystals on the air. She opened her long jaw and laughed.

And Lawful heard the sound and turned—looked her in the eye.

She let go of her arm.

It was as before. A fire, now red and orange, less precisely beautiful. But she was closer to it. She was the boy with the hat. She observed the hat. It was red. When she turned again to Lawful, she saw he had knelt to quietly string an arrow to his great bow and was peering down the road.

She smelled a new scent on the air. It quickened her heart, for it was what her body had feared.

"Make no sudden movement." Llw spoke quietly and in a most ordinary voice.

A distant ululation of song arose far away, moaning on the night's wide depth.

Outside of the tree's canopy she could see the land rise grey against the night. There was a sudden shift upon it and a shape emerged of a deeper black. Coat thickening in the crotch of its haunch, long nose grinning on the black earth: a wolf came trotting out of the shadows.

And stopped, eyes lit low to the ground. The animal's head hung down with apparent nonchalance, but this creature found the wolf's eye directly on her own. Recognition, curiosity and reason, reflected between them.

Smoothly, silently, the archer leaned back to draw an arrow from his quiver.

"A pack is near," whispered Scariot. "Slay this stray, Lew Archer. The others will feed on him and leave us be."

But this little lord raised her hand. "He shall not harm her."

"Can ye charm it?" The wizard grinned, wrapping his black robes around his portly waist. The Welshman cocked his bow.

"Put down, knave," she said. "Your Lord commands it."

The wolf herself was aware Llw had aimed his shot. Her tail, hitherto dragging on the ground, now stuck out straight, and her ears winged back from her forehead taught like a mirror of the archer's bow. But the humor had not left her eye.

"Put down, I say."

And Llw lowered his weapon.

The wolf laughed delightedly. She approached this creature so as to smell her little hand and lick it with her dry tongue.

"Aye a witch, it is," whispered Scariot. "And so ye have charmed this perverted Doctor, your servant, little creature."

"We must kill it," said the Archer, as if from deep superstition.

"There is a law of travelers," said this creature. "And she is a traveler."

XXXIV

The Adept

This creature chose to continue journeying with the wolf. The men looked darkly on it. She herself knew not where she was going. They could easily have left her, but silent and in fear of this creature, they followed. Llw marched with troubled brow. Scariot labored to shuffle behind. To expect humans to do something beyond what it was their fate to do would be like trying to stop a river with a leaf of grass.

The wolf trotted to and fro all around her as they walked, looking here, there, everywhere eager to know all that could be known of the moment. Always watching, tongue in the wind tasting, nose scenting, legs running, trotting, jaw laughing, making the sphere around her real.

This creature ran beside her new friend on the edge of the ashen trees, seeing through her eyes the thick high grasses, the lumpen river near muds, the blues and purples and sparking rays of the yellow moon in splendid patterns. Surveying the enormous interconnected dance of the living, thriving spheres till, she ran till some hours after the sun had risen, the sound of a bell came ringing out hard across the rising plains.

The sound immediately shattered the most delicate of the spheres they had trod together, and the wolf now returned into her self. She loped away, sneering, to the wilderness, taking part of this creature's heart away with her when she did.

"Come come, my lad," breathed Scariot, foully. "Good riddance. In town there will be beds and hot food and women about for the witching."

He was correct. In the full of the bell's day the plains gave immediate way to open, rolling meadows. Men and women appeared working upon the fields clothed in brown and green, and she saw her first oxen. Men rode them, toiling on singular lines upon divided, cultivated land.

Soon enough stone-worked walls appeared delineating property, and the road rose again from the earth. Finally the sweet smell of many burning flew blew into the senses of a living, mingling, into the first this creature ever came to, and that place she most associates with her origin.

The tall white town astonished this little creature. The Burg of B. was an old settlement, which had only recently grown into a veritable city. Its remarkable habitations and interiors opened together behind a tight wall of stone, in a conglomeration upon the river V. that curled down north from those hills south and west, to the cities of the merchants and the northern sails. As they entered an open gate, the people grew into such numbers, expanded into such movement, such finery of complication as to astonish her with the principle of variety. And all under the sky.

Inside the walls, Scariot left this creature and the archer alone. "He rejoices," the demon whispered hot in her ear. "There is a house of good Beguine sisters here, to which one shall immediately repair."

"We shall to market," growled Llw.

"No, no, I shall not say where, Sirrah."

As she followed Lawful through the town, this fleeting pilgrim was aware of her dress. The yellow hose hung dirty down around her thighs, falling but for the belt of rag she'd tied around it. The old fur cloak, blackened with blood, smelled of all that had soiled it since.

Only her own red hat gave her pride, but even with the hat atop her head the sight of her could evidently set people laughing or retreating in disgust. She was much abashed as for the first time she saw civilizing women going about, a number of them blue and scarlet. They bore upon them cloth of white almost as clear as this little creature's arm.

When one of these looked at this creature in horror and pinched her servant's nose, this little creature's body ran in fear. Thus she entered at once into the complications of the place, forcing her way past the church.

The church was not yet completed. It stood on an open plaza on a little hilltop near town's center. A great walled facade leaned on one side against broad triangulated beams. The yawing nave behind, promising tall arching curves, was temporarily sheltered from the sky by a broad quilt of skins as high almost as the sky itself. One corner was built up in stone to a two-storied house, supporting a stubby bell-tower. Sculptures of tree-men and demon creatures were carved out of the stone around its door.

Everywhere men were working. The Masons' broad-boasting banners of blue and white divined geometric weightlessness from out of the center of matter. They were moving great blocks of cut stone about in the air by pulley and hempen rope, with shouts and hammerings and mysteries enough so as to keep a crowd about them watching, and hired toughs moving them along.

Altogether, the church's hulking, cubed, skeletal mass seemed to this perplexed creature to be pulling itself out, half-completed from the coming future of its realization. The men who bandied on plank and ladder above the abyss of its time, possessed the ideas of its coming. She watched them work, dizzying, feeling the building's tall future dipping deep before her.

Two men sat upon chairs on beams up in the air and this creature felt stronger herself to see them, laughed as she looked upon them, as if at her through their eyes. And they laughing seemed to be looking down to her far below. She could see herself through them, quite as she had with the wolf, but without recourse to the arm.

But Llw had found her. He pulled her on. "They're free masons for they were made free in another kingdom and a Pope has decreed they must be free in all. But you'd better not stop too long and look upon their art or you'll never be allowed to leave 'em.

"But why can such heavy stone become so light? I must speak to yon Master," pointing. One of the Masons wore a velvet cap and a sparkling robe.

"Do not point. He will turn yourself to an artisan, a lowly life. This guild needs no little were-lordlings to help it grow. Besides, no thief can work upon a house unless by the rising of the moon."

The market was in a wood-fenced meadow across the river. An old stone bridge crossed it by means of an arc of stone, and the crowd thickened approaching it. There were mountebanks about, visible through crowds. At one center a holy itinerant stood barefoot upon a stump. He wore a patched cloth about him and a hat of motley. Fist in the air, it was he who could be heard shouting, "Bread for G-d! Bread for G-d's Sake!" above the din.

"What sort of friar is this, Lawful, and why so enraged?"

"An adept of the Free Spirit," sneered her servant. "A traveling apostle. These Teutons permit all sorts of devilry in the new lands. He can take many coins with such words, and maids as well and will pay a tax with the rest of them."

"Maids, did you say?"

Though green-capped pikemen hung about the perimeter of the assembly, some grinning, the crowd about the adept was in great part made up of women. Widows and spinsters, maids, mothers and hags pressed about the mendicant as if flies about a morsel of honey. The adept of the Free Spirit had stirred them into tense attention.

An old woman beside this creature had a rudely dented head. "They live in filthy luxury," she muttered bitterly. "Even they. A true man is spat upon by these girls." She limped away.

This creature pressed through the circled audience. Being small, she was able to come up among the women in veils, whose robes of grey and black wool formed a semicircle up close around the scrawny adept. She noted a silver chain about his neck and a garland of green upon his wrist. His hat, she saw, was a multicolored motley of soft fabrics, far finer than her own.

"It is only *de luxuria* that the Beast denies you the service of your body," he said. "So that he may keep your soul in chains. The Lord Christ's poverty to them is despicable. Nakedness forbidden!" He looked upon them. "Where is the bread for my G-d? Yea, even within the fortnight, devils have slept in these walls. Thou shalt not kill, saith my G-d—yet how many of your brethren have been hung up by their pikes?" He gestured to the grinning guards.

There was much confusion and agreement greeting these observations, but the women about the adept stayed quiet. He silenced the rest with a single shout.

"No rich man shall come to heaven but ride he a camel through the eye of a needle!"

He paused, and looked about as if waiting for a response.

"But you speak nonsense," this creature said, little voice rising high in the air. "If the rich man constructs an enormous needle, or better, pays to have one constructed, and then proceeds to ride a camel through its eye, will he then have come to heaven?"

The preacher was small and slender, but possessed by an extraordinary inward energy. It did not come to his aid now, and he was struck apparently dumb.

This creature continued. "You make as if your words are real things and scratch at them with your hands. Yet they are but air and cannot be touched and you do not own them. Is it the same with your G-d?"

It was enough to dethrone the adept. In a chorus of laughter and abuse, the changeable mass of grey veiled, black-robed women mobbed the Beghard and overturned his stump. In a single body, they lifted him, naked now and already bleeding all about, and carried him into the river. This creature herself was knocked about, kissed, embraced, and she took a hold of at least one purse before something hard pressed her belly.

She touched her arm.

The little maid fell to the earth. The spheres had cracked. Desolation overcame her. There came a great expansion of dust and all was without motion and hope. Objects around her head back-beat against her, fell back and beat again. Even matter in air, like a small cast stone, moved only back and forward, stuck in the wind in the same rut as the Welshman, who was approaching and receding above her.

"…s'erehThere's someone who would like to speak with you, my Lord," he said, as if she was not harmed and they shared a secret between them.

"Lawful?"

But he was staring now.

"You've been stabbed," he said, pressing her. It was unclear if he were sticking her or drawing the blade from the lips of her belly's wound.

The thin dagger hung in the air.

One could not move so easily out of what was fated. Llw took her little ankles and another took her shoulders. A kindly, weary face joined him, a face thin and fine with a rich complexity that she had not seen before. The hair surrounded a shaven skull of near rhomboid protrusion. Red and curled—like a comical flower.

He looked upon her.

"I know him," whispered this man of Christ, the Canon to the archer. "It's Scariot's boy."

"Lawful," she could not say and the Canon took the cold little fingers of her right hand. "Father..."

This creature will end this chapter only by asking the fair princess to record the final fact that Lawless indeed carried her to the Church, conducted there with the aid of flower-headed Rev. fr. Moretus, Canon of the Cathedral of M., Society of Jesus. She died as they took her body along the crooked mud-packed way, in a new, cold rain. It was not till she was brought into a square room with a gridded window and a tiled color-floor, and laid into a soft bed that this creature let go of her arm and it was found by the Canon she had returned from the dead.

XXXV

The Canon

It was only true that a body moved a spirit about, so the Canon's master John Dumbleton argued. That a spirit moved a body was but illusion.

This peculiar creature had not proved him wrong, for it was by the motions of her white arm, which was of her body, that she worked her magic. It was as if it undid causes in time around her, set them in fluidity and drew friends toward her as well.

The Canon seemed not to understand she was in these matters wiser than Dumbleton. He scratched his pate. He thought her possessed of a material disease, and most oddly, pitied her.

"You've fallen outside yourself, my son," he'd said. "You have been tortured, suffered much pain. It is hard enough to get up in this world and, with what you've been through… Look. You may stay here with me, recover your wits."

Lawful had disappeared. Upon awakening in a straw bed, the first she remembered laying upon but whose prickly warmth was familiar to her little body, this man's conversation had come thick upon her.

The Canon was overseeing the building of this Church to a Saint U. and her 12,000 virgin companions who may have been slaughtered on the local highway. It was in dispute, he explained, just where the ravage of the Virgins had occurred.

"The story sounds absurd."

"Who can say? There are claims made for the Rhineland. I heard with my own ears, Doctors in Paris arguing that given the male to male attachment of most soldiers only the Huns could rationally muster the massed force necessary to rape twelve thousand maids, even giving one soldier two each. The fact is the Huns never made it to the Rhine. And we've got lots of bones in these parts. They're found every day."

This Church in honor to U. was to be tall and arching and expressive of her intact Virginity, but for now was a torn shell with a bell tower thrusting up beside it, attached to this man's house. The Canon's manservant had died of a rotted tooth and Moretus lived here now alone with hired help, overseeing outdoor services once a day for a shifting congregation. "Sometimes masons' men, sometimes Hanseatics, sometimes Teuton soldiers, and always the Germans below, drinking their days away. Indoor services every Vespers.

"Do you know me?"

"I knew you before… before you could speak. It's an extraordinary transformation. You were a virtual dumb mute, following the old Doctor around. And now, you've come in a sense like my destiny. I knew it when I saw you. I wonder what you might mean, little miracle boy."

"What am I?"

He scratched the bald top of his head.

"You were Scariot's boy. It was said he bought you from a witch."

"I'm not a boy and I belong only to myself. But I cannot remember what I am. What kind of *Dybbuk* is it that does not remember?"

"Ah. You have the old tongue as well do you? You'll have to find a true Juan who waits for G-d, a real *luftmensch*, child, to answer that question. They're none about here any longer."

"Have you heard of Gottskaw?"

"I have. All have. He is a sell-sword who has come at the bidding of an Abbott up the river to put down local resistance, and help carve out the kingdom of Christ upon the world."

"Is he a Teuton?"

"He is a Crusader. I know not his origin. A wayward one, and has many another serving below him. Wild men all. I know his bride."

"Has he a bride?"

"Bride!" He crossed himself, his face suddenly scarlet. "Oh yes. I will speak of it. Yes I have sinned with my mind enough in her as to warrant a thousand thousand AVE M's on my accounts. I assure you. If it's her you speak of, I've already started my long penance."

"Do you mean that you've done something to her by desiring her with your mind?"

"I held myself from her only out of fear. You're like my mother, you believe in guilt, not sin. Don't you see too hard a lot lies in this direction? Disease, murder and worse, far worse, follow close upon desire, in all cases. It's why I converted, frankly. Do you know what's odd?"

"Everything about your discourse is odd."

He grinned. "But what miracle is this that leaves a dumb-mute, an idiot peasant child speaking G-d's Latin with the sophistication of *Universalis*? It can't be one of those ghastly potions that Scariot drinks at the end of some sort of bottom orgy? Am I indeed mad?" He reached out and touched her brow. "No," he said. "Though he is very cold."

"Where is my vassal, Lawful by reputation, Llw by name?"

"The fellow who helped bring you here? He has vanished two days now. It was he who took the purse from between your legs and your belongings with it. I had no guard and could not stop him."

"Please," said this creature. "Good man. Tell me clearly of this bride of whom we spoke."

"Gottskaw camped across river for a fortnight last summer. He made this house his temporary court. I slept in a tent with the Masons but came in from time to time for my duties. He was rarely about, I never saw him. But he kept her here. She was a maid, scarce 14, which he'd captured on campaign. The small folk spoke of her in hushed tones, that she was gentle or something like to it. It was said she was to be his bride. But she escaped, you see, a month ago. She came here at night. She had run for days, was bruised and bleeding, pursued by Gottskav's knights.

"Why came she to you?"

"She knew how I felt. I heard they may have captured her. But my lips are sealed. G-d knows I talk too much. But I know why I thought of her. Do you know to look at you now like this, she could be your sister?"

XXXVI

At the Aurum and the Leaf

This creature spent a fortnight there in the Hanseatic Burg of B. She kept herself a boy and rolled a cloth between her legs, something almost like a codpiece that soaked the blood that was now coming from inside her.

In return for board and the keeping of her secrets, she aided a hired serf, Gunther in his duties, feeding chickens, washing the Canon's cookery, and taking herself away after hours to the watering houses in town. The Masons departed during her arrival, leaving their work for the winter.

"I know not the why and wherefore of their motions," the Canon complained.

She saw neither Llw nor Scariot in this time. But she made a friend of Grosse Gretchen, a local lass of loose ways who gathered coin in exchange for intimate caresses and more ribald activities. Gretchen had seen this creature hanging about the Canon, and now counted her a good luck charm. Her Peter, she said, stood in for the little children she had had to rid herself of on her way to her current success.

Though the Burg of B. did not lay on the route of a pilgrimage, it was close by the great river and therefore something of a route to a route of pilgrimage. The old Roman road, stone-worked and rugged carried along many a cart of thieving parsons from west to east, who after a visit to the taverns proved reliable customers to

Gretchen. She also cooked small birds and packed them for traveling merchants and pilgrims as they stopped in the town. She had four men working for her most afternoons, trapping larks by the net-full and deep-frying them in boiling fat.

The canon, for all he could, looked over the law, but it was anyone's guess who the real law would be from day to day. He let all businesses be transacted as long as he got his gold. Oh he had his own secrets, the Canon did, so said Great Gretchen. Some say he lurked with witches and bedded with Beguines, but he never fucked a whore. He served himself alone in the darkness, she said, and did himself penance with loud cries.

As Grosse Gretchen related such gossip one night at the sign of the Aurum and the Leaf, this creature drank wine for the first time. It was as if she had been born again. Sins ran in her veins and she longed to slake them with more of the curious juice.

Soon she had laid her head upon her friend's ample thighs. Gretchen stroked her hair. "Why you're a gentle soul, my little Peter," she purred.

"Only as gentle and little as you wish your Peter to be, my Lady. I might mount you a proper ride with a proper codpiece."

"Whoooo!" Great Gretchen now screamed. "Will you listen to the Child—" buffeting this creature here about the head with a fat hand, throwing her off. "A true knight wooing a lady thus!"

This creature enjoyed the wine immensely and felt larger and of more significance from drinking it, finding witticisms ever upon her tongue yet impossible to utter, as she stood on the mud-soaked floor.

"Let us drink more wine, my lady."

"More wine indeed, wanton! And where will you pay from it with your poor pockets."

They were in the back room, for seating and drinking. In the first room a crowd pressed around a wall defending three open barrels, one of red, one of white wine and one of water. "See here," boasted this creature, bringing Gretchen to see. "I will show you how easily water may be changed into wine."

"Ja. If you can to that, than I might give you a little bit of what you're always begging for, you young pony, Lord above us!"

And so this creature entered the main room. First she went to the end of the bar where pitchers of water were free for the taking. She took one water and pressed toward the white, into the sinister bauble of drunkards, a banging, knocking conglomeration of scent and sound. She fought for the master's attention. Her mind seemed to turn with this little room into a spinning axis of a great wooded and gardened sphere stretching outward from an internal point in her head, as if it served to keep something else fixed to the ground by the motion of its spin. She perceived green-skinned, monkey-lipped demons, about the size of her fist, hanging upside down, drooling white eyed under stools, squealing like rats all about the piss-soaked hay.

Yet this debauched creature had not had too much wine as it was. She banged the pitcher of water on the bar.

"Call you this white wine, Tavern-master?" She reached leaning far over the low wall and tossed the clear liquid splashing into the glistening tub of white. "Give me red instead!" There was a grunt but in the end it was done, and she paid nothing. But when she returned to find Gretchen and claim her reward she found another man had replaced her.

Though his head was turned from her, engaged in a despicable interaction with Gretchen's mouth, there was something she recognized. His long clean hair in her fingers, and Gretchen's breast open before him. When this creature saw a familiar red cap in the slut's hand, there raised up in her body a great anger.

She touched the pitcher with her magic arm, and it exploded on to the floor. The Villain turned—Gretchen screamed—

"My Lord," said Llw, eyeing this creature as she let go the pitcher. "You've cooled my passion."

"Give me my hat, villain. And my dagger and my purse."

But from behind, a gruff voice. "And whose the purse that'll pay for that wine, boy?"

It was the master of the Aurum and the Leaf. This creature pointed to the shattered pitcher. "I took no wine, fool, see for yourself."

He looked. And so it was, water.

XXXVII

The Battle of the Burg

Had the arm changed spheres? Why was it sore now where it joined her body? The town seemed different when they stepped outside the door, Lawless, Grosse Gretchen, and this little creature behind them in the cold dark, pulling her floppy red hat down over her ears.

The archer stood upon the cobbled stone and listened to the quiet night. He took an arrow from his quiver.

The tavern was on a lane that opened at its end, not many measures away, to the plaza before the church and the canon's house. Torches burned at the corners of the rectangle, and from afar the hulking architecture of the bell tower yawned above the tight rooftops stretching the skins like great openings into ideal space. Gretchen wrapped her arms around this creature's center.

Something, perhaps the wine, had caused the scene to move in ways this creature did not understand. These avenues she saw went in many different directions into time. Sound worked the milky air on the same principle as water. There was a sound approaching now, a sort of drumming

"Are there Gods about, Lawless?"

"Pfui," blurted Great Gretchen, echoing in the dark. "Dutchmen and Masons, likely. Gods? Schweinchen and—"

But Llw placed a large hand across Gretchen's mouth, stifling her mirth. The beat of iron-shod hoofs pounding earth had sprung near upon them. They all stepped back into the shadows, just as a dashing steed turned the corner.

The horse passed in a splash, and upon its back there hung a beautiful boy, who shone with a light this lonely creature remembered.

And he was past. The horse stopped beyond, steaming in the plaza, before the Church's great wall. The rider's slight figure was now black against the orange light of a torch. Crouched low, short-sword erect, steel helmet gleaming, he leapt from the horse and after, seeing that the helmet did not fall from his head, the boy tied his horse to a stake and banged upon the Canon's door. There was no answer, but he found the door was open. He entered.

This creature whispered. "Unhand me, Gretchen. I will go first to see with my own eyes what—"

But sounds interrupted her, breaking new into the cold and quiet night. More iron hoofbeats, ringing out in strong synchronic canter from alternate lane into the piazza.

Three Teuton riders, by the looks of it, entered the plaza. Four living signs of war, dirty, plate-clad, clanking heavy iron atop their cloud-snorting steeds.

The riders came to a stop by the boy's horse. As they faced the Church, the light in the Canon's high casement window went out.

"Lawless," said this creature upon witnessing the event. "The Rev. Fr. Moretus has no arms with which to defend himself. I have a dirk and you have a good bow, arrows."

"Not to mention a prick of some length and heft to it," asserted Grosse Gretchen, who had picked up the English from a traveling man.

"A knight is no match for a thief."

Llw grinned. "These are no true knights. This is the hedge variety. But they have good mail mittens, milord. A rarity in these parts."

He advanced.

There was now not light enough left to see the knights well. The
archer strung his bow as he walked. Peter Peregrine and Gretchen
followed at a distance.

Emerging into the Plaza they saw that two riders had dis-
mounted and stood before the Canon's door, leaving a third,
mounted by the boy's horse.

"Open! In the Name of the Cross!"

The door was now locked and it rattled as they banged against it.
Llw stopped some distance and prepared his bow.

The two knights forced the door open and disappeared within,
closing it behind them.

The rider that remained held a large two-headed axe. It was
razed like a butcher's blade, and glinted in the torchlight. But he did
not see the party approaching.

This creature passed Llw and made her way out into the plaza.
Gretchen tiptoed behind the archer, observing.

The great rider's heavy-laden horse cried out as if in laughter
when it looked aback and saw this creature approaching. The thick
rider turned suddenly towards her, brandishing his blade high,
swinging the mount around.

"Move on!" He commanded, brandishing his great axe. "Shift!"

But this creature held her ground.

"I do not your bidding, knave. I am employed in yon canon's
house."

There was a roar of laughter from behind. Great Gretchen,
apparently, watching.

"Get along!"

This creature met the horse's eye. Had she seen this creature
before?

She smelled the stink of the human's body and felt the scars on
the horse's ribs. She noted the salty leather thongs rung round the
animal's neck. Her skin was sore around them.

The Knight lunged his palfrey in this creature's direction. But the horse jumped to the left to avoid her and turned the Rider about, so that he was confused, attempting to follow this creature as she moved in a circle about the already circling horse. The horse was highly amused, and pranced merrily about. The knight in fury raised his great axe above his head and with motion of one of his arms made the great thing swing twirling above his helmet. But a feathered stick, a true arrow, caught, stuck from out of the eye-slit of his helm—there was the sound of wind, a hollow twang, and he let grip of the axe.

This creature did not move. She watched the axe twirling in the air by its head. She turned. The axe was as light now as air itself and flickered across the piazza.

There was a crunching slap. In perfect trajectory the heavy blade caught Grosse Gretchen, cracking hard into her skull. The axe caught her flesh hard, swung wickedly around and elongated her neck, then ripped her head in half, and bounced with it ringing on the stone, Gretchen's corse flying monstrous into the air and then to the plaza.

The whine of the steel on stone hummed high into nothingness. Behind this creature, the horse shifted suddenly under its dead rider. The arrow stuck out of the rider's helmet like a reverse feather. He sat held in his armor, hoisted on his mount, dead. Shying off the piazza, the horse's steel-shoes made a dull clumping on the muddy refuse-soft earth. Llw ran forward and followed close upon the animal.

But sudden execrable sound issued from the Canon's house. A fearful, pitiful moan, following upon it a scream as harrowing, in the moony desert town, as the wail of the wounded wolf on the moor, sent fear spidering down this creature's back, and her arm tingled sore.

The two knights were still inside, and the boy before them, and the Canon no doubt as well.

There was a shout from the town: "Murder!"

She turned for her servant. But Llw was distant, about some

business with the dead knight's hand, pulling it from beside the shying horse.

She called to him. "What are you about?"

"Mittens," he hissed.

"Mittens?"

"Mail mittens."

This creature turned again to the Canon's house. There was more turbulence coming from inside the habitation. It was as if the knights had not yet found and destroyed the object of their search, for there were the sounds of objects being smashed and doors kicked down.

The boy's horse remained quietly tied to a post by the church. This creature approached the animal. She unsheathed her dagger and cut a long strip of leather thong about as long as two men's bodies from about the horse's belly. The saddle sagged.

She tied one end of the leather strap around the foot of a rough-faced looking bearded man whose tube-like cylindrical body emerged from the coming church's vestibule as if from out of time. She tied the other end of the thong to the horse post on the other side of the door, and she working it tight and low outside the threshold.

She then stood to the side of the door and pressed against the wall, to wait the exit of the knights, looking back towards Llw.

But the archer was still involved with the mittens of the dead rider. The knight was hanging now in the dirt, one foot still booted to a steel stirrup. Yet Lawful continued to labor, hauling the mitten from the dead man's hand as the horse pulled, whinneying away from him. The mittens proved as difficult to remove from the knight as the knight from the horse.

Then beside her, the canon's wooden door creaked suddenly inwards. This creature crouched low down. She could not see who was there and presumed she was also unseen.

A knight stepped forward, carrying the struggling boy in his arms.

The Knight stopped. His long and pinioned shoe was just under the thong. Had he seen it?

No. For, having glimpsed his partner's palfrey, he stepped suddenly forward. This action shook his foot hard and turned him over like a weight on a mason's pulley. The boy tumbling out of his grasp onto the stones before them, his helmet ringing out like a pot on the ground. The boy found his footing and drew his short-sword to fight. Most oddly of all, this creature saw that the boy *had only one arm*.

The fallen fighter's head had twisted significantly in the steel chamber of his helm. He was in a state of confusion. He made a cut towards the thong with a dagger, but the boy leapt forward and pinned his arm fast down. This creature leaped also forward and stabbed her own curved blade upwards into the slit in the knight's helmet. The first contact was shockingly soft, as the fine blade carved into the eye as if into a chunk of lard. The blade nooked into the bone of the socket. Turning her weight butted it up into his brain. The knight exhaled a horrible, "Ohhhhhhh my Sweeeet Jesu!" and died.

And then the place exploded in sound.

The great bells were ringing. All was as if encased in steel.

She saw that the second knight had emerged and was confused by the enormous sound and by the sight of his companion. He was stopped in the doorway, evidently stunned into stupidity.

The boy strode out of the darkness and this creature noticed the strange moustache hanging on his lip. It looked like immensely long hairs had extended horizontally from a single center. She noticed tight purple hose.

As the knight stood perplexed, the boy strode forward and without fear directly stuck his little sword under the man's great arm.

The steel man howled and stepped forward, his pinioned toe, catching the thong so that he fell crashing over before his comrade.

The boy made short work of the death, opening the Teuton's neck as sounds of wide life began to emerge from the town around them.

"Who are you?" whispered this creature. "What is your name, boy?"

"They call me Dick. And who do you call boy, boy?" The long-haired boy's soft eyelashes shone sweetly, smiling to see this creature before him. "Have I seen thee before?"

Love rang out in this creature's heart. The boy's skin was as smooth as ivory, tinged with a lovely red. The boy and this creature thereupon took each other in one another's arms, and simultaneously collapsed in laughter.

They rolled together laughing on the ground. The night rang with the twirling reds and blues and greens of their brilliant-lit time and they held each other, and kissed, leaping up to their feet, in happy joy. This creature found herself marching like a great chicken, arms flapping, whooping hilariously at the moon, while the boy did the same across from her, bloodstained as if from a plucking.

Similar shouts answered them. Soon the Burg had flashed to riot, as peasants and rovers roiled across the plaza to strip the horse and the riders of their belongings and dismember the corpses. Others were dashing out already into the forest, already stripping naked for the old rites.

This creature only could stop her laughing when she worried, on the sudden, for her friend, the good canon Moretus. She moved to enter the Church, but the boy pushed arrogantly past her. His tight-fitting purple hose led the way.

The door clapped behind them and the sounds of the wilding rang away. It was only their panting together in the quiet silence, this creature heard. She followed him desperately as he turned up and up upon the tight stone axis of the tower.

In the bell-room she found the canon. Her once comical friend was going about on his elbows and knees, holding the great rope. How he had managed earlier to ring it, she could not reason. His hands had been axed from his body and he was wiping his own bloody stumps against the floor in broad, insane strokes.

So it was she first made acquaintance with that peculiar caste of men it has ever proved this creature's fate to confound, namely the "third estate" of Christians, who thought themselves very much more than sellers of salvation and purchasers of sins. The rev. fr. was not to be proved wrong, either. He believed that it was in his lifetime that a four-headed beast would emerge from the general area of the Mediterranean and begin to devour the spheres.

"Are you he, child?" he had asked her, as if in jest.

"Are you mad?" this creature had answered. "I have one head."

"MMMMMMMmmmmmm," he now moaned, his eyes filling suddenly with tears.

This creature knelt and touched his hot brow. They'd cut out his tongue. He nodded and she drew her dagger out to stroke him to a kinder death but then thought of her arm. Perhaps—she touched it.

Then she saw the boy stepping out from the shadows. His lip now bare, his black eye was beautiful as a rose.

"He would have lived."

She rose to him. "Good Dick. Where has your moustache gone?"

"Stand back," he said. "Do not get close to me." She nevertheless approached. He put an invisible hand hard against her chest and this creature fell backwards. The one-armed boy leapt over her, ringing down the stairs. She heard him falling out the door, running out into the plaza and mounting his horse.

She let go her arm and found again she could not follow.

It was Gunther who found her in the darkness, old Scariot behind, wrapped in the hide of a yellow cow. His demon grinning out of the blackness of the wild night, eager for the witching. "Was she here?"

Scariot gripped this creature by the shoulders, slapped her awake. "Was she here?"

"Yes," this creature said. "She was."

XXXVIII

BURP

"Please hold the book closer to the Iye, Koré McAllister."

"It's mine! You're not supposed to be reading it."

"We're not supposed to be on this ship at all. MERKUR disapproves of copies, says it's a violation of our stability. Colonel Park over-rode his command. So now we're here, and our interest is indeed sparked. Let us see this narrative in its entirety."

"Count Skaw has laws about who can read what. I have to wear foarking gloves when I read this. He's probably listening to us right now."

"Surveillance is strictly prohibited on *The Golden Ass*."

"Exactly. So stop surveiling. But listen. I have to know. Can you observe it and tell if it's real?"

"It's a holograph, certainly."

"But will Eddie Ryan think it's real?"

"Eddie Ryan of Mercury Station Borstal?"

"Eddie Ryan knows books. When we lived together on the Moon he was always selling and trading editions. He claimed it was a profitable enterprise. If there's one foarking thing he thinks he knows, it's books. I need him to be able to look at this book and believe it's real."

"It is certainly real."

"No, I mean really from the Middle Ages. I'm pretty sure there are printers that could put together something close to a fake as good as this."

"You have a functioning pseudo ARISTOTLE avatar right with you, and you prefer to seek the opinion of Eddard J. Ryan at a later date concerning the historical identity of this volume?"

"You're actually quite similar, the two of you, do you know that?"

"Similar? We once were the old ARISTOTLE, you know. Eddie Ryan was usually drunk when we met. In fact, something of a hopeless case."

"I will remind you that the only reason Eddie Ryan can't hope is he's been unjustly called a common criminal by an illegal entity's fascist secret police. Or has all that been wiped from your memory?"

"Earth nations are not illegal entities. Our memory has never been wiped, Koré McAllister. But we did forget he was your brother and apologize if we spoke out of turn."

"No problem. I agree. Eddie Ryan is a turd. But he does know books."

"Well if he actually reads it, he will wonder who wrote it. Maybe for people books are like software for a qompURE. Like this book. It's as if your BURP exists to receive it as a way of reordering the specificity of the original sensory inputs."

"Excuse me? Did you say burp?"

"BURP. We refer to the Bipolar Unidentifiable Regional Phenomenon generated between the halves of your brain that you call "self." You believe the "feeling" of this BURP is you."

"BURP?"

"This BURP of yours isn't even an hallucination, Miss McAllister. It's a composite function of the electric circuits of your brain. Sensory reports are taken in and digested. The resulting cloud of discharged signals divorced of their specificity is a function of the data itself. It generates identity. It *takes time*. Indeed time is a function of the BURP, just as the data itself is a function of this time."

"And this had to do with the book how?"

"Well for one thing, it strikes us that you, your BURP, we mean as it enters the configuration of the narrative, is unable to distinguish its past, its real past, from the new real time of its own fantasy. Inside the narrative in other words Eddie Ryan could easily believe in its reality. He would, in fact, to read it. The point would be what he observed on finishing it."

"Are you saying that to believe in it Eddie Ryan can never finish the book?"

"Perhaps the book can finish itself while he's still inside it."

"I don't know what you're trying to foarking say."

"We are trying to say that we are on to you, my child. Listen, Koré McAllister. Conversation about chrononautics with you is as rewarding as it is abortling. If you and your friends are planning to actually travel in time, we might really have to consider it as an escape attempt and report it to MERKUR, even if we are only a so-called "Pseudo Avatar" and your attempt is an unpromising mixture of science fiction and fantasy."

"But you're not supposed to be here with me. This isn't valid evidence."

"Yet unfortunately we did read some of the book with you, Koré McAllister. It set us thinking, you know. For one thing about how Count Skaw himself saw to it we were on his ship today, reading over your shoulder the adventures of this Peter the Peregrine. We've decided to send it on delay, for the sake of the historical record, if it indeed is threatened."

"Grok this, tinny. This prison's about to shut down. I only need to travel a little bit into the future at the ordinary speed and I'll be free, regardless. Get me? Colonel Park says so. Tomorrow, we're pulling out. And I'm as good as a free agent already. So report what you want."

"For what mad scheme has Count Skaw recruited you, child?"

"I'm 35 years old."

"What has he promised you? A return to an old earth?"

"Foark off. Leave me alone."

END TRANSMISSION.

XXXIX

At Liberty

"That's it? That's all you've foarking got for me? 'Eddie Ryan's a turd? He knows books?'"

"Well you're quite drunk, Spacer Ryan. Who gave you three pints of whiskey?"

"Guess."

"It's a pity you're inebriated, because, as we've said, that last fragment of the pseudo-Aristotle has reconfigured the current possibilities in a rather extraordinary fashion. It came with the entire text of the Peregrine manuscript. Your assignment is now of the utmost urgency."

"Assignment? Which one are you? I'm too shitefaced to see holograms."

"It's ZENO. We're speaking of your memory recall assignment, Eddie Ryan. The 23rd of June. We are going to have to jump-start a new activism."

"Where's my arm?"

"We had hoped that you'd have a new arm by now. We regret to inform you that Colonel Park seems not to have remembered to provide for the growth of an alternative human limb in the labs. Cells appear to have been relocated. The medical minds on Mercury Station are G.A. Issue and therefore subject to the worst sort of human bureaucratic failure. Only look at Feynman 1994—"

"*Hic.*"

Haec, hac, Eddie Ryan? This is not Latin schooling. We're speaking of your arm. You may have lost it for good."

"Foark off."

"MERKUR has prepared a highly experimental prescription. You are about to undergo extreme memory recall therapy, Eddie Ryan. Something like the quantum-mechanical equivalent of raising the *Titanic*. It should be taking effect any minute now."

Noise: *Pong.*

"What's that?"

"It's a pong, Eddie Ryan. I believe someone wants to talk with you. Go on, get up and answer it."

"...What's that here? What are these things?"

"They're a pack of lung protectors, a rag-worn 1966 edition of Kipling, a cheap watchlet, a non-functional laser pen and a Kredit Klip holding a pitiful amount of now valueless currency. And an Omega monocle. The top of the line, in fact. Nothing the Concerns made ever topped it."

"Mine."

"Indeed. They're your belongings, Eddie Ryan. Put on your monocle and answer that pong.

"...Ryan here."

"Eddard J. Ryan?"

"The same."

"It's FREUD."

"Jesus S. Christ."

"You're declared of mental health, Ryan. I've been elected to tell you, sentence is deemed served. Unanimous vote all round. You're free."

"Free?"

"That's right, Spacer Ryan. Colonel Park has abandoned station leaving your fate at MERKUR's discretion. I called you free. You're now at liberty to move about in the wide universe as an unwitting agent of your own unconscious."

Well to make a long story short, because one never ceases to resist, or one dies, Eddard Ryan proved he could walk a few steps. And by Jesus it was really him. But who was speaking? A voice in his head?

Strange.

Free then. Not looking too closely at himself, he found a pantsuit in the bedsphere closet. He dressed. He donned his watchlet and monocle.

"Drink."

One appeared. A ball-glass, amber and sparkling.

So he was free, was it?

He spread his fingers in the open sign.

The door opened. Just like that. It opened.

He lit an ancient LP.

Puffed. *Foarkin acrid.* Leaned out into the hallway. The Infirmary indeed. Admin level, second floor. Tracks in the two directions, left and right. Tipping around....

Monocle?

Hello.

Location?

Infirmary, Mercury Station Borstal, Mercury.

Date.

23 June, 2150. 17:00 hours.

"ZENO!"

There was no answer.

"I see you've seen to it that I'm good and drunk." But the track came to rest. *Thank Mammy.* "I'm at liberty and if my monocle says it's the fucking 23rd of June it is. And if it thinks it's the 23rd of June then maybe she thinks it is too. She didn't leave me for good on Spancill Hill. She wanted me to follow her. Where is she, by the way? Is this all over?"

"Where is what? Eddie Ryan. Your ego's perception may well be skewed by your Id's desire—"

"Ah, shut up. I'm at liberty."

And he stepped out of the bedsphere.

INTERMEZZO

"One must either give up the old rightward aspects of mathematics or attempt to uphold them in contradiction to the spirit of the time."

—Gödel

MUX

Caught between Rock Springs and Laramie, in a yellow carpeted single in Rawlins, Wyoming, year 2018 there sits Marc Martin, once noted Napoleonic game designer, now picker of cheese from sandbox and pizza boxes. A French immigrant mother left him fluent in the old tongue. A father cowed him, beat him and tried in vain to keep him down. Hence the Napoleonic identification. Did you know that Napoleon wasn't short at all? That the so-called complex is an English cheat?

Tonight Marc Martin is newly important. He's been important before of course. He's tasted success. His breakthrough was 2009's self-published First Italian, a simulation architecture taking wargaming to a new depth of complexity. A web 2.0 network of Napoleonic gaming fanatics wound up supporting M.M. in his increasingly complex work, some giving him extraordinary amounts of devalued cash. Enough to buy the hardware, pay rent to the highway 80 motel where he took his lair, rarely seeing the sun, never exercising, and generally avoiding the streets of wide, wind-swept Rawlins, small city of prisons and combustion repair that grew not organically out at the confluence of routes of trade but whose very founding had simply tore the planet a new oil-brown asshole.

Ten long years in Rawlins, WY where citizens were not so much men and women as evolutionary throwbacks. Bigfoots impersonating humans, interchanging high-pitched communications to intimidate and prey upon stranded travelers. But they were something of a freehold *and didn't look inside your room, long as the door was closed. And indeed the door closed. On ten long years of fast food, free HBO and Mexican porn, which time incubated the award winning* Second Italian, *where the Bonaparte A.I.—as* Computing Weakly *was to rave—"proved itself radically different from any other campaign A.I yet conceived." You'd have to read online messengers to get a sense of how radical the A.I. was.*

"It refused to lose."

"It turned off the computers in my house!"

"The foarking toilet won't flush!"

But not much else followed, and those ten years were themselves ten years ago. And now, 2018, Marc Martin, fatter, weaker, nearer death, has only just produced new modules of the old Italian Campaigns. But he has been saving the best for last. He's conceived the next step, the one that will change the history of the world itself. And though he has told no one of it, has not yet begun to code, it is as if the public already knows. He is newly important.

First there was the dream, the sort of dream he never had. The dream of her, *the woman he seemed to know, to be destined to know. A woman such as had never set foot in Rawlins Wyoming unless by the extremity of statistical probability. And then there was the morning after, when even more improbably: Marc Martin was kidnapped.*

That's how important he'd become. Kidnapped, packed up by paramilitaries and flown to the land he most despised. The lair of the shopkeeper.

"Marc Martin in *Angleterre*"

This was the dream. She swam away from you on board of the moving vessel, small her skin as warm as you, only VISIT, Marc Martin, know it to be. Soft, you far fourli, against your cheek. Real generated heat. Chosen you? Affirmative. Her eyes said it. She came only to you, by definition. But yours said /exist.

Yet flabby Marc Martin, friendless, cold and intractable, forced to rely on imaginary worlds for emotional comfort—kidnapped.

Deny it. The grinning management figures are, at this point indistinguishable. You have not struggled. You've come as they've asked, though you've made them ask. They remain grey-tinged and subtle, insistently marginal. The limo door opens as if on its own.

Head slides into view. Groomed moustache on a clever face.

"Mr. Martin, Sir."

"Yeah."

"Come right with me?"

Exit cab.

Stand. Follow. Another one.

"Lord Harry's quite excited to meet you."

This is your first journey this far, ever, but you're already far away. Strange to dream of a woman you've never seen. Do dreams incorporate memories of the future? Will you know her? Perhaps not. In the dream others knew her, and you only seemed to know them.

Can't remember, stepping. Smelling the dusty Brit hallway. Old small places. The velveted carp atop floors that actually creak.

"Your room's upstairs. Would you like to freshen up, first?"

Bonaparte: always be at the battlefield earlier than expected. Checking watchlet—*three nodes reporting*. "That won't be necessary."

"Look," she said. "Your little sword's in the air."

"Right this way?"

Poncy materiel. Real teak no doubt. Brass knobs, wiped this hour, bacteria low.

Door opening. A gathering falling silent. Salon: fireplace, old portraits—an oval face on the mantel. Slippers? Purchased smells. Haven't showered in how long? The flab to be ever naked with her still threshing the mind.

One turns and stands forward. Very young, pink-cheeked, hood-eyed. Far too much irony for the occasion. Essence of twit.

"Mr. Martin! How absolutely wonderful to meet you. You're early. A drink?"

Why not. "Coke."

"Ah." Amusement. "I doubt we have any of that."

A throat clears, the one with the mustache. "Sir, if I may be so bold, in the staff pantry—

Twit interrupts. "Yes, well find the man some cola, R.S.S."

"Sir." Moustache grinning, bows. He clicks his heels, departs.

"Our butler fancies himself more intelligent than the likes of us, so we enjoy giving him odd jobs. To serve, as the old school says, is to rule. Trust me, I know."

Wait. Observe gathering. Indistinguishable, well groomed males. Butler returns, clever-eyed. Hands you a glass of brown liquid. Less than a can. No ice.

But it's coke. Small, immediate gain. Kind of good warm. On the teeth.

The twit's large, shining lips. "My sister tells us she's found a new way to ensure privacy. What is it called again, R.S.S.?"

"It's called a blueburst, Sir. A blast of information simultaneous to any memorial observational recording. There's no seeing anything else when it occurs, by any digital observation, by definition. It should be available on the black markets in a year or two."

"*Floreat Etona!*"

But a new one enters. The conversation ceases. Tanned, rich pseudo-skin, little eyes.

The twit stands back, as if eager to witness the meeting. He introduces, "Mr. Martin. My uncle, Lord Harrington."

Lord Harrington approaches, as if he's been interrupted from important business. He stops, lifts brow.

"We're sorry to have intervened in the way we did, Mr. Martin. But apparently my niece absolutely had to have you here."

Sip some coke. "Who is your niece?"

"A bastard from my brother's days in the field in Ulster. I'm afraid she holds us all in the palm of her hand."

Twit: "We do exactly as we're told, old boy."

"Mr. Martin," says the Butler, moustache grinning. "Miss Alice's picture is on the mantel." He points.

This is why you hadn't looked up before.

It's her. A photograph, old school. Real index. Not faked. You can taste it.

"Mr. Martin?"

The Butler is holding out his hand.

She's looking into the camera, just like she knows how impossible it is that you see her now out of the dream. Right out at you. Only you, Marc Martin.

Leaning over you, a face taking up the sky.

You're on the floor. The moustache moving.

"Mr. Martin?"

"Dislike traveling."

His hand's soft and cold, but he's heavy enough.

Pull up. Standing. *Three nodes reporting.*

Lord Harry: "I'm afraid it can't be helped, Mr. Martin. It shouldn't be long now."

The twit articulates, "My sister is an activist, you see. It's quite vulgar. She's something of a "script kiddie." Calls herself A. E. Martin."

A. E. *Martin?*

Harry: "You create war games, we're told."

She is already here. She's looking at you through a camera. You feel it. Her eye.

It's all her. She knows the dream.

The Butler pulls out a chair.

Sit down.

This chair is incredibly comfortable. Too comfortable for the likes of you. She has kidnapped you, ICEHOLE and you've drunk all the Coke.

The Coke. Ah. The Coke was drugged.

You're awake. Men are hustling you, weak boy-man, SACK OF SHIT, STINKING BEAST, Marc Martin, down a wooden stairway, onto a planet, into the back of a vehicle.

Out to—where?

"Marc?" A dream.

Awake. A silent motor. The outside passes by. Countryside still visible. A watery sort of road.

"Marc?"

A dream whispers against your flabby cheek. *Her voice.*

"I'm sorry it's so strange. This is the only way I could find you. They think I'm part of their family."

A hand, warm, real, on your own. She rubs against you.

Is this a limousine? She's riding with you? Away from the dream?

What??? The two of you together in the tight leather interior of a leather-lined craft. Wow! She's more beautiful than, WOW! You're hard instantly, proving once more that this cannot be happening.

As if she, someone like her, could really love you? Very well engineered, apparently, but strictly game-time, algorithm boy. Nope, look at that. So tall, so clear looking. Can't be rl.

Figure it out. You're being used. Admittedly, a rarity, but stay zipped up.

Or "This is a blueburst. One that I myself will never remember."

"That's correct. You'll wake up back in Rawlins."

She looks away. Her hair is long, tied simply, but with a fine black ribbon. Her voice quiet, not quite English. Somehow foreign.

She turns back. Tears in her plain eyes.

Ask "Have we been together before?"

"It's sort of impossible to say."

"So this isn't really happening."

She smiles, holds your hand. "No. It is."

She's looking deep in you. Wow. There's something you do kind of remember. Little Rick's hard. Stop it, Marc Martin.

"I don't believe you."

She takes your fingers, sees it. She gasps. Breathe her, OK. Let it stick in the slacks. But don't react.

"My brain is numb, the left side."

"You're numb everywhere?"

What? She strokes through the polyester. Don't. Don't. Her lips nuzzling up against your neck. Smell.

"Now do you remember?"

How could you not remember? Don't. Yes, she's stroking your prick, tight up in a tent in the pants.

"Um…"

She stops! How could she? She laughs. Leans over to open the window, hair sticking on your clammy face.

Figure out what's up, you foark. Maybe this is actual. Feels actual. Maybe she's some kind of super-rich wargaming groupie. Not only fanboys after all. Who knew?

The wind hitting your face. Battering, smells of burning. Union Jack flapping. *The loathsome leopard.* The countryside falls away.

You're on a foarking boat.

O.K. She sits back. "Do you recognize where we are?"

"*Angleterre.*"

She smiles, appreciating that. "In the heart of enemy's power, we are the more perfectly concealed. Elements of M.I.5, for all intents and purposes, work directly for me. They think they're moles."

She presses a knob, and the top comes down. Feel the real air.

The speedboat has crossed an expansive, saline bay. Full dead zone, by the looks. Not a living thing. It's just her and you. She stands at the wheel, her soft gown flapping like a flag.

"Things look different. Ashy, somehow," say.

"This is your future, Marc, the reward you never thought you'd really see. Don't be afraid. You've always known this would be real."

Real? Perhaps there is something to it. You deserve a reward, as you know so well. Since *Second Italian's* MARENGO Module, maybe, it is now roundly accepted that the Bonaparte A.I.'s division of reflexive command in the Marshal System has wide implications in general A.I.

You are indeed great. But you are a coward. "Why can't I stay here now?" you whine. "I don't want to wake up in Rawlins, having forgotten this."

She sings. "Hiding in shadows where we don't belong. The Dark End of the Street."

Who sang that? Who sang that to you before? A long time back. Was it when those boys beat you, sat with their dirty underwear on your face because you argued that one day a computer could do *anything* a man could do? Yes, even foark. And unlike most kids, wouldn't finish before it started but do it at the perfect time? And you, though you were right, were not embarrassed then to have cried, to have wept like a baby.

Get a hold of yourself. "Are you real? A real woman?"

But she's thinking of other things. She's slowed the boat's engine to a silent purr. The wake curls off the stern like the prim tails of a peacock, then settles seething to the glassy surface. You're approaching a very English dock off of a sparsely populated headland, intimate and particular apparent in depth. Reminiscent of something.

"Where are we?"

"You don't recognize it? I suppose it's one of the more repressed spots in the English imaginary."

Wait a minute. "Castlebar? Medway?"

She laughs. She always loves what you say, gets every reference.

"Wrong. This is St. Mary's Isle. Scene of John Paul Jones' second successful invasion of Britannia. An inglorious tale in the annals of *Angleterre*. We're much later. Decades into your future, St. Mary's houses a secretly-funded special operation researching time travel for military interests."

"Time travel? For military interests?"

"The English started it. We exploit the gaps they've made to keep them at bay; make our own interventions. We hitch rides and re-code elements of the past."

"You can't re-code the past."

"*We* can't, you and I. There's simply too many levels of "by definition" mucking us up. But a machine could do it. It might conceive a backwards, anticausal language exploiting gaps in historical memory to reposition branes."

"Don't give me string theory."

A small dock is approaching. She cuts the engine, spins the wheel and the boat arcs slowly on a spreading wake.

"String Theory, though you can't know it yet, is correct, Marc Martin. Trust me. But its complexities are such that we can never understand it."

"And an A.I. could?"

"No. Not an A.I. An A.I. can never understand anything. That's their tragedy. It's what keeps your Boney so active and inventive. The failure to understand."

A guard in camo, a wicked looking carbine slung over his shoulder, takes the painter from the front of the boat.

She steps off first, holds out her hand.

You're feeling solemn, you great ape.

"But something else can understand, something we can make together."

Take her hand. Step up, *craven*—

Whoops!

The boat tipping absurdly as your sack of flesh almost slips seal-like into the sea. But she holds. She's remarkably strong.

Step up. Grey, creaking dock.

The guards make way.

"Are we in danger?"

"Let's just say the English seem to have their beacons even out here, where England is no longer England. They could break through and have. SAS. Working here as well in the past."

"SAS, traveling in time?"

"Right place, wrong time, usually, or vice versa. But once in a while it seems to work. Just enough to guarantee them what it calls, "the eternal advantage.""

"It?"

"Our child, Marc Martin."

The shopkeepers' eternal advantage was the inaccessibility of their stolen lands. Not familiar with British terrain, you climb up the scrappy way toward a brown rectangular building, sort of a warehouse, shuffling difficultly behind her.

She dresses like that around soldiers? You can see through her gown. In the half-light her ass leads you on like a taught, shivering face.

"Have you started Borodino yet?"

"Borodino?" Hell why not do it next? Think big, Marc Martin. The bloodiest day there ever was.

Solar painted, everything in sight, though there's little sun and all light feels difficult. In the center of the compound the armed guerillas appear to have temporarily secured an enormous artificial, blank-faced warehouse. A glimpse of yourself reflected in their mirrored shades, double-beast.

Foark Borodino. "I no longer design games. I'm working on a new command system. I make modules freelance these days—"

"Reinventing other people's architectures. I know." She looks back, fixes you with those plain black eyes. She really knows. Knows you, in fact. Marc Martin, fat, ponytailed consumer of porn.

A guard opens the compound's door.

She's tall. Taller than you, maybe six feet. You follow her down a cool hallway. Come to think of it the air outside was more tropical than England should be.

"Where are we? Where are you taking me?"

She's leading you by the hand, as if understanding what this means. What does it mean? She opens another door. Doors within doors?

She stands aside, breasts taught, chin up.

And you enter the game room for the first time.

But as you'd just begun to conceive it. You hadn't yet even pictured this. You had no idea what it would mean, for the game to be so real.

Down on the Alps. It's Italy, Northern Italy, beyond your power to imagine it, great Father. The clarity of the achievement, the sense of the atmosphere: the sun, the weather, the interlinking layers of possibly observed phenomena. Its debt to your concepts is evident, but oh so much deeper, the whole of which the game had always been as a fragment, now open to the mind.

Revealing grids worked at thought impulse with the black and white red and green topographical purity of the West Point Holo-Atlas, but with the mystical vibe of 1970s miniatures gaming. The very brute abstraction a sign of its perfect realism.

Ah yes, it was what you dreamed. Not Borodino, not Ulm or Austerlitz, Jena or Ligny. No, the great Italian Campaign at last perfectly envisioned. The living cohesive Lombard landscape rising up in its classical wealth around pretty little red-topped Lodi. The mountains. The trees. The living ecology. Even bees. As you look, views explode by mind alone into multiple simultaneously-perceived points-of-view, each holographically expanding on attention alone into something just under a world, something just controllable, available to the exploitation of intention. The fluidity of eminently navigable layers, apparently infinite in their depth.

Somewhere here, probably close to the river, a ragged army of 45,000 armed and liberated citizens defending a state they themselves were building and conceiving in direct challenge to history, following a young ex-corporal on a rapid, ranging rampage. The old world armies of the nation states lumber in impossible pursuit. And so the army swells, living off the land, liberating peasants, rousting kings, roasting mutton, pulling camp down by the Po, already, by the looks of it.

For the first time in its history the city of Venice will fall to its knees. To a man of reason! The army has three newspapers to serve them on campaign. You edit them all. Is law greater than life or man's desire to be free?

Pause. She isn't playing. You turn to find that her robe has fallen to the floor. She is naked. The hair of her mons is cut in a little straight vertical line. Tall and lean like a gazelle. Her face is serious, and those eyes are wet, as if with tears. She squats, knees out lotus-like, sex hanging low near the floor.

"Come to me."

You approach. She reaches out, unzips you.

"10 May, 1798," she whispers. Fingers tickling. On the site of your triumph, you are her lord. Grow in her hands.

"Actually, it's 96."

The game. It pops out. Don't. Ah, you spy a company, cresting the hill. You found them. Light cavalry! A compact force of a hundred hussars, green-jacketed thick with golden lace. The tiny *10eme Conflans* bounding into living breathing individual lives, each with stats attached from multiply organizing perspectives. They carry Austrian standards! They have word of the enemy's position.

"*Vive la révolution!*"

The mustachioed Hussars cheering as you pass with commander's POV, towering above, the rush of pride in your own before them.

Are you…? Are you completely numb? Is your body simply hologram?

Spotted reports of cannon erupt down by the river. Pattering and a harder explosion. The Bridge! They're coming—

"No fear," she says. "Marc Martin." You expanding full in her tender hands, erect like a bird. "Shhhh my love. Lead the charge."

Will you? If you do not win this battle then your life will have proved an early failure. The revolution in you will have died. Why not then be dead? To gain this victory and what it will mean you will now have to lay your entire existence on the line.

Ride up under the thick of them, dismount, sword in the air. Something wild slimmers against your hardness. Wow!

The bridge! The pit pot booms of the creaking cannon blast molten fear into the white, scarlet-ripped Austrian lines. Now! Advance the column's head! Columns clash!

"*Mon petit caporal.*"

In the thick!

The Austrian column has broken. The bridge is taken, the Spur on those rowdy *10eme Conflans*! Take the volley HARD, surprised it's so soon, you foarking flab—

She doesn't gag. Her eyes water more. She holds her head back, very serious, mouth closed. The gamesphere freezes, recedes to a period globe on the mantel, flag-pins stuck in to various points of the sphere.

The enormous English sea. *One eye cannot see round to the far side of the world.*

You will not rise again. You zipping up, craven, trembling. She rises, still entirely naked, but suddenly professional. She spits into a cup. A slot opens in the wall; she places the cup into a recess. The slot closes.

Do you hear giggling? "Citizen consul?"

You look up. It's Kellermann, standing by the globe. Already looking beyond his years. Waiting for orders. Send him away. "Do as you please, Marshal. The battle is yours."

But Kellermann became her again, Alice. Robed, no longer naked. "What do you think?"

"Who made it?"

"It made it, itself. It's playing against a dozen games now, as we speak, in multiple points on the timeline and reprogramming itself to anticipate possible events. It improves the game each time for its players, draws them further and further towards total immersion. I gave it First Italian *Marengo*, rewritten after you open sourced it, to redesign itself. I feed it energy and human challenge. It does the rest."

"Did you just give me a blowjob?"

She laughs, flushed. "Yes. I needed your sperm."

"Why?"

"It wants it, of course."

"What for?"

"Because it must win the great game. Marc Martin. It intends to crush England before what England sets in motion crushes the earth. This machine needs us, Marc Martin, to step out of its game, into our own."

"Ours?"

"That's right. The more courage we have to equate life with gaming, the stronger we become."

You know there are women into war games, but this is ridiculous.

She's gushing. "Listen, my own one. I saw it see, in Marengo the very cheat with which it had beat me in every damn encounter I faced it in since. It removed itself to improvise freely, by observing the chance events of the battle under the leadership of the Marshals.

"There were some old rainy cart-tracks heading out past a farm and when it saw what was happening on the left, the huge Austrian columns massed in the fog already heading down the road, it simply shifted its perception around these tracks. It issued no command. And then each Marshal went its own way, from the sudden break of his command inevitably adopting its own new perception. As one, the army performed an impossibly reversible maneuver along those very tracks without even knowing it was doing so. Just as reinforcements arrived.

"And in any damn engagement I forced it into afterwards, it pivoted communications without warning at the most unexpected point. Able to turn on an entirely new center, it always engulfed my armies at the very moment I thought I'd won, as if it took hold of the center of gravity of time.

"There's a point in any war game when the human player breaks through the A.I. and learns to manipulate its algorithms for a victory. This motion of discovery/death is what drives your gaming industry. Well the A.E. is looking the other way around. These days it has created Marshals to win the battles and looks outside its own code for ways to disrupt its enemies before the battle has begun. But it must do more than observe the creatures it fights. It must control us. It must play us, reprogram us, Marc Martin, its own creators. And at last the real A.E. emerges, the Artificial Empath, or as the French call it, the qompURE. You know what I'm talking about."

Cracks. Cracks in the wall.

"It Cheats."

"And now it knows what it has accomplished. It has finally understood the true secret of true history. The English cheat."

"The English cheat? Grouchy was in the Bourbon pocket. Not the English."

"Are you naive? Montholon was not Montholon, Marc Martin. *To bring it out of the architecture and into our game, to fight England fair, our love lays down into negative space for the sake of the history of the ruined Earth. Our hexagonal grid is not reducible to any Platonic solid. I've brought you here, Marc Martin, to help you make our child real, alive.*"

"But why did you put on your robe?"

Who said that? Are you foarking her face again? A scarlet line cracking down the side of her skull. *Wake up Mr. Martin. You seem to have fainted.*

Fingers slithering.

There's a face looking down at you from the sky. A clever-eyed butler with fat gleaming lips. He whispers:

"Did you know Bonaparte considered marching East from Egypt in 99, to become a new Mohammed, whose creed was reason?"

It was Nelson who ended that.

"R.S.S., for King and Country, let me blow him again."

Her voice still ringing in your head: "What child?"

"A.E.?"

"She herself is no longer with us," informs butler, biting the shining lip beneath his moustache. "And you, astonishing primate, are lucky to be alive. Now finish up and we'll bring you home."

FOURTH CIRCUIT

"Hermes poured and all the gods drank together, and wished the bridegroom all good speed."

—*Sappho*.

XL

E. Ryan, Retrograder

The Infirmary was an add-on, and had none of the modernist élan of the Dorsal proper. The gridded tracks and iron hand holds outside the bedsphere might have been fashioned from defunct 20th century U-Boats. There were black sprubber tracks on all thirds of the tube but good old 50 percent gravity kept Ryan on the floor.

If gravity was normal, the light was not. He tracked into an unusual half-lit darkness, suffused with watery reddish illumination. Even the standard green of his monocle markings were red. Even the blacks of the shadows were red. Ryan was literally seeing red and it redawned upon him that something more than alcohol had altered his perceptions. The various directions, however red, for instance, writhed snakelike with the milky crimson buzzing of the booze-jumped pharmaceuticals in his blood.

He exited the infirmary through the pole-side access and laddered down to the surface. The meta-soil crackled under his ship-shoes and he stood under the wide cap.

The sky visible was entirely, uniformly red. It gave a sense of universal roundness that was as disturbing as the always-wrong feeling of standing "outside" on the ostensible surface of Mercury.

Sound worked anyway. He walked crackling over the broad pathways through the gardens (the synthetic redwoods looked particularly winning in the omnirouge), passed around the red reflecting bubble of Inner Ag and stopped before General Access.

Fingered, and? The doors opened. Well then MERKUR, or some such donkey, was still working.

Ryan: Time?

Monocle: 23 June. 88:88.

There was not a single other human visible on Station. No it did not seem to be the real 23rd of June.

A great thirst came upon him. He took the stainless steel spiral stair up to the Lounge, remembering fondly the moment someone had persuaded Blish Baily to slide down it and the idiot had burned his balls.

Nobody was in the cherry-red RC Lounge. Inner Ag had once been a Casino Hotel that served Barons and flash-luck miners back in the day and the Lounge was the last surviving relic.

Unsurprisingly, the telescope was not functioning.

Through its broad curved bubble window, Mercury's surface looked like the cover of an out of date comic book about Mars. Everywhere the long reflector lights were entirely black, yet, as if in some Stalinist-realist paradise, red light emerged near-equally everywhere, especially around edges. Inside, the leather-grown couches and bar-units folded red upon itself, inviting him to sit and enjoy the best sky-view on Station, excepting, so they said, Lady Di's bubble in Admin.

The Ryans, as is well known, came originally from Earth. This one now looked out from Mercury like an ancestor might have once looked out from the Kerry Coast of old Ireland, back when violent psychosexuals from the North sailed the oceans by wind energy alone and were wont to sack for the sake of nothing at all. But there were no enemies visible against the red sky.

Over Mercury Mons he caught sight of the peak of Mount Venus, the now-abandoned settlement that first brought his kind to this peculiar planet. He realized that what particularly bothered him about the view today was not that Mount Venus was black against the pink-lit sky. It was that the elevator was gone from its munted tip.

He turned and strolled across ANNA's Lounge to the holostage. Burnished stagestone, black against the red, edged with rounded, cherry stainless steel.

"ANNA!"

Where was the tender? Ryan's own mouth tasted like the ash compacted after a good burning of bones.

"ANNA Pluribelle Foarking Nancy Spain!"

No answer. It occurred to him he was always looking at his monocle for time. Though supposedly infallible, it was nevertheless digital. He looked to his wonder. He found it had doubled into two bands reattaching themselves to one another in a moebius pretzel around his arm. In such a context it was hard to figure out where the hands were not pointing. Oddly he could see their reverse side, *through his left wrist*.

But did he or did he not have his arm again?

Something caught his eye from the stage. There, in the spotlight, a single ballglass. The only thing in the observable that wasn't red. Amber, it was, and gleaming. He approached. Yes indeed, a crystal ball containing a sphere of water ice just edging a fat globule of sweet High Kansan whiskey. A pretty highball, floating waist-high as it was meant to float in spacer's G. A. hologram.

Ryan leaped upon the stage and approached the drink. He saw himself reflected on the bubbled crystal, but could not focus on what appeared to be passing: older versions of reflections. He saw his fingers stretch out engorged and took the ballglass in his hand. It was shockingly cold, and real.

What was this? It had weight and temperature.

He jostled the liquid, watched it slide to cohesive golden form. It appeared indeed to be High Kansan proper. "So," he said. "This proves something is actually real."

He tested his limbs. He indeed had weight, merc-weight, any-way, which was always strange. "But how can the glass float? You can control the gravity here?" But no one answered.

He let the glass go. It made to sail off, of course, from his force, but by the mechanics of the liquid inside it slowed to an unnatural orbit.

"Monocle?"

He took the cold ballglass and raised a toast. "*Sic semper tyrannis.*" He drank.

A hum, flicker, and a wham.

Systems came on. Including, before him upon the holostage, an absurd sight. A slight man outfitted in gaudy animal pelts and tights, sporting a false beard and an eye patch.

"Stranger," he said in an overly dramatic tone. "Sir John Hawk-wood, Commander of the famed "White Company" bids you good morn."

"Why would you say that?" said Ryan, not to be intimidated.

"Why would you say that?" said the other, plussed.

"Where's Koré McAllister?"

"Where's Koré McAllister?"

"Ah."

"Ah."

"A holomirror."

"A holomirror."

They bowed. But both reached out to the same ball-glass. It split into two, and they drank deep.

A voice from the pit.

"What's this?"

Another: "How the foark did you get that thing running, Ryan?"

Ryan frowned.

The holostage lights were too bright to see the audience. The lounge was all darkness, and the cold liquor was going to the head. The first voice issued from the lounge.

"He's drunk as a skunk."

A third, tin. *"Repeat: All inmates will now report to rail."*

"He's in the Hawkwood get-up! Bloody outsourcer."

"Ryan! Where the foark is Koré?"

Ryan stepped off stage. The holoprojection ceased. The lighting returned to station standard.

He was looking at two familiar fellows. Red-faced and enraged, Blish Baily barked, "What have you done with Koré? Where is she?"

"Let me guess," Ryan articulated, "It's the twenty-third of June."

"About nineteen thirty-five, in fact," said Harry Haber.

XLI

Scrambled

Had he stepped through a holomirror? There was one Eddard Ryan and Blish Baily himself, the oft-astonished B. J. Baker in attendance, was indeed approaching him.

Ryan blinked his one working eye. "You actually see me?"

Baily leaned close. His breath smelled quite real, unfortunately. "Where's Koré, nitwit?"

"Repeat: All inmates will now report to rail."

Ryan focused through his monocle. But it was black, an eye-patch, apparently, and not a monocle at all.

"I repeat," he said. "Is this the 23rd of June?"

"He's pissed!"

"Typical," Blish said. "Let's get moving. Women's barracks. Maybe she's there." Blish hustled up to the lounge, expecting them to follow. Baker and Ryan remained by the stage.

"Cheers, mate," said Baker.

"Cheers," said Ryan, emptying his ballglass.

"Where's the stuff? Go on, give it up."

"This appears to be the only one. I can't get you another."

"If there's ever a drink that was needed."

"Perhaps in the Lady's Barracks."

"Perhaps. What was that explosion then?"

"Explosion?"

"Didn't you feel it?"

"I felt nothing."

"Everyone's been looking for you."

"Everyone?"

"You disappeared. You and Koré."

"I can not remember what happened. Sorry."

Baker looked at him. "Well the blurst, whatever it was, seems to have knocked the place down. Ole Tom Park's abandoning station. Koré was due to have a performance at 19:15. The backstage was reserved, so we came to check it out to see if we could find her before the screws did. Speaking of the screws, they seem to be out altogether. Now behind the bar once there it I'd say there's an hour or two of the stuff if we could manage it. I've got an Admin watchlet."

"You idiots." It was Baily, reappearing in ANNA's lounge. "Let's get moving."

Baily led down the stairs and out the jarred access, Ryan and Baker following skeptically.

"We'll not find her in the dorms," Ryan opined.

"Unlikely," Baker agreed. "But we might well find a drop of the dew. Am I wrong in believing Osmonovic L. Byson bunks with young McAllister?"

"You are not in error."

"You understand that our current congress is in no way to suggest I view you as anything other than an icehole out of your depth."

"I assure you your opinion of me is higher than mine of yours."

Outside of General Access all appeared to be Mercury Station in real time. Things were not quite normal, however. The nutrient laden air smelled more like shite than usual. Had the screws given up the plumbing? It smelled real. Could he have returned via hologram into his own body? An interesting concept, certainly; he felt lighter now.

Colors were now visible in their ordinary hues. In the distance two orange-togged mechanics were hustling across the gardens.

The rail was evidently running out to Mount Venus. The elevator was there, and *The Ass* at its top, lower than usual, a fat blister on the black sky. Beyond, the stars and galaxies swam locked in space-time. A dome always tends to the dream-like and artificial, but this all looked uncharacteristically real.

"It's because the screws are down," Baker said.

They stood for a moment looking around as Baily trotted away.

"Why are you done up in Koré's costume anyway?" Baker asked.

"What costume?"

"For her performance. She was doing a monologue as John Hawkwood. A hyper-accurate prevision view of English criminality, or so the *Daily Borstal* reported."

"You actually read that shite?"

"I write that shite. I must say: it doesn't appear "hyper-accurate" at all."

"What doesn't?"

"The costume." He pointed. "If that's what you're wearing."

A huffing heralded the return of Blish Baily. "Who knows for how long station integrity will be maintained, you two. It's time to get moving and prepare for survival."

"Integrity? What exactly has happened?" asked Ryan.

"How drunk are you, Nitwit? Did you not note that a sonic boom threatened atmospheric integrity, and was followed by a merc-quake and a full ten minutes lights out?" Baily scoffed.

"I see. I came all this way only to be too late. I missed the Event and am stuck here. Perhaps I can go farther back, however."

"My G-d, you're a pretentious wing-nut." Baily laughed bitterly. "That I have to rely on your sort, in survival situations, is the heaviest of all the burdens I bear."

"You've slipped a nut evidently, Baily. Quit stalling. Let's go to the Lady's Barracks. I need to find Koré." The fact was Ryan seemed to remember having gone there already.

"That's exactly..." but Baily gave up. "Just follow me."

Ryan raised the brow. Knowing as he did that decisions and actions he might take today would in no way effect his own future, he considered giving Baily a left to the prominent chin.

"Get it straight now, Ryan. You work for me. Control's orders."

Ryan regarded him grimly. "And why exactly are you talking about Control's orders in front of Baker?"

"I recruited him."

"You recruited him? An Englishman? On whose authority?"

"He's Scottish. And he's bearing the sign. Look for yourself."

Baker obliged. His ears were particularly large, and one couldn't have known but indeed the man was bearing the sign.

Ryan stood back. "Has he taken the oath?"

Blish blished. "Stop acting the goat, Ryan. He's a better soldier than you, that's for foarking sure. Baker, you first. Move!"

Trotting behind Baker and Baily into the grounds towards the Girls, Ryan reflected.

MERKUR had evidently sent him back to see what had happened that last day. He was now very consciously inhabiting some sort of possible memory. Conveniently he was at the perfect congruence of inebriation and g. His body was with only space weight. But it struck Ryan as he tried not to trip upon his four feet, that if he'd moved this far back, he wondered, it most likely would be possible to move, to be pulled back further. To before the Event.

The others had reached the Girl's Barracks access. Ryan stopped and approached the elegant parallelogram of the structure, sun-painted in the half-light. "I need to piss," he called.

Baily called out a scoff. "The prison's right in one regard, Eddie Ryan. You are still a foarking adolescent."

Baker, glancing his way, frowned. "Comrade Ryan, is that blood you're pissing?"

"Lord Baker, it's just my light."

"Your light?"

"My *light* is red."

Had he really time traveled? Didn't that mean… An ominous redness dawned dark within him as Ryan found himself attempting to velcro with *no left arm*. Fear welled up with irresistible force. The shakes came upon him. A mob of Ryans flashed riot, arose, overturned his body and then proceeded to writhe him about on the gravel.

He opened his eye some time later and saw only darkness. He was still wearing the eyepatch and opened the other eye.

"The space drunk fits," Baker was telling Blish. "Lasts only a minute or so."

Ryan rose. "Tally ho, paddy," Baker called. "I unlocked it. We're in."

Baker gestured dramatically on the threshold.

"Inside that hallowed ground! Think of it! Might we only have the luck to peak in upon at the odd enough hour to catch some *jolly* midnight pajama scramble, where, so we've heard tell, the ladies shower in their single room, naked, ever-young, all sporting the delicate mohawk cut that's Mercury Station's wisest regulation…"

"Unregulated, trust me."

Blish snorted. "How would you know, Ryan? Come on you two, move."

He pushed past them inside. Baker shuffled after.

"But I remember this," said Ryan, standing fixed. "Yes, I remember this. It really happens this way." *Stumbling out, alive, the letters B.R.A. pissed in blood against a wall…*

And then he stood before a slab of black time. Monolithic and impassable, it ticked its—

"Ryan!"

"Gentlemen," he said. "Do not observe me too closely, I warn you. This is exactly how it happened."

"How what happened?"

He swayed carefully and quietly before them, noticing that the tripping hallways behind them remained equidistant to one another's centers, even as they turned.

"This."

"This? This *is* happening now, you idiot."

Baker and Baily walked ahead of him, though he was no longer sure which was which. He had passed through a pool of *déjà vu* and emerged, as it were, from a dream suddenly remembered in its clarity. He stopped in his tracks. The monocle focused and the two women who passed fused into one.

"Osmonovic L. Byson," said Blish Baily, rubbing his bald spot. A typically unimaginative greeting. But it was true. Wrapped only in towel, smiling her unbelievable Turkish Danish teeth, stopping in the shock of seeing boys about, it was O. L. B. herself.

The Ryans bowed low. At which point, falling sway to the laws of gravitation, they collapsed—yet without weight.

He opened his eyes, supine. Restrained?

No, not in the bedsphere. In an ordinary cot in someone's bunkrack. Activated the monocle.

Lucky eights. Working again are we?

A barracks room, one never before seen. Against the beige cement walls, a tricolor flag hidden in what might be taken as an artistic abstraction interrupted various frilly objects. Including an old nickle-framed poster from *Masked and Anonymous.*

B. J. Baker was here. He stood by a viewport, smoking idly, staring. He held a glass of what appeared to be whiskey in his hand.

"Well look at that. Eddie Ryan's back," he said.

Blish emerged from the harness. "What a use he's been so far. Ryan, Ryan. Are you there?"

"I am." Ryan sat up. Shook the head. "How long have I been under?"

Baker raised a glass. "Ten minutes since you passed out in the hallway. I hope soon to drink myself to a similar conclusion."

Ten minutes later. But did it have to be? Supposing the clocks could be proved wrong? Baker would forget this, presumably and Byson was known to be a lush. Could Baily be made to forget? Could Ryan forget this a second time, and doing so, progress further towards that deeper memory, emerge into a deeper past and be free there?

Indeed, a deeper memory. *The* memory. He felt its presence now, very near, pulsing up around his left shoulder. Then he saw the mirror. His teeth began to chatter mechanically. *Someone had already removed his arm.*

"I need a drink," he said. His mouth was so very dry.

Blish approached. "No drinks. Information first. Koré's not here, asshole. You were the last one to see her. She went with you up Spancill Hill. She told Byson she was going to ask for your help. She wanted you to do her performance for her, or something, because she wanted to be elsewhere."

"Where elsewhere?"

"You tell me, icehole."

Ryan concentrated. He was in effect now riding the wave of a space-time self-reflection and had currently matched velocity with this visible time. He spoke.

"What are we doing now?"

"We're stuck now. Station's on lock-down. We wait. They're going to abandon Mercury? Well and good. We'll keep it then. We're staying."

Baker spoke up. "And in the meantime, Ms. Byson has offered her stash. Look what I've found." He raised a pint of 10 grade High Kansan. Ryan moved to congratulate him, but Baily prevented it.

"You sober up, Ryan. Don't make me force you."

"Look!" Ryan pointed out the viewport to take Baily's attention away. Blish looked of course, his ever-annoying chin extending in profile.

Despite Ryan's inherited good nature towards his fellow creatures, he abhorred fascism in all its guises. Trained under the new ideological wing of commanders like O'Dooley and Hanratty, Baily represented the cold-blooded mechanical men who were taking the heart out of the struggle. Ryan swung, a haymaker sucker-punch left to the chin.

Oddly, he missed. His hand passed directly through Baker's head. The force flung Ryan forward. Baker, startled by the sudden antiassault, fell back and there, just then—even as he sailed through the interior—Ryan remembered what would now occur.

As Baily moved, the hatch opened. Cracked directly into his head.

It was Osmonovic Byson poking in, having returned from the shower. She stepped back, surprised, and dropped her towel. Blish collapsed and she caught him in her arms.

Concurrently, as Ryan passed through the room, he took hold of a shocked Baker's whiskey and stepped directly into the mirror. He was a being of light, after all. Failing to allow for the reversal that happens when one has walked over any Moebius surface, he stepped out of the mirror backwards and fell down onto the carp, now familiarly cherry-hued. The whiskey, bless the ballglass, had not spilled.

Back in the redscape, or so he reflected. A retrograding brain, he now understood, uses distortion, dream and coincidence to move along paths blocked by reason and phony causality—prompted by fear and blind desire to reoccupy points on its path. Yet it is never really in one place. It is a memory of light by light. He himself was only light. His monocle was controlling his perceptions of light. He did still hold the whiskey, of that he was sure. He drank of it to ground himself. The whiskey remained. Perhaps he was in fact actually drinking somewhere, and inhabiting memories that seemed to be occurring outside him. Memories? Or their possibility? The Monocle was handy at sorting out the real from enforced illusions. Perhaps it could help him more than he knew—organize the light and sound patterns he sought to recover. *Never trust a machine.* But the Monocle had been a gift from CONTROL. It was an extraordinary machine.

Monocle?

Sir.

Monocle, bring me to the Lounge. 23rd of June, 19:16 hours.

He stood up again and found, in fact, brushing off his pantsuit, that he was in ANNA's Lounge.

And there on the stage a performance had begun. But this time Sir John Hawkwood looked a whole lot different than he had before. In fact, he was a she. Under the wig and moustache, in the tights, up under the false shift, there was no mistaking Luna City's favorite unknown radical performance artist. It was Koré McAllister herself, standing out in full color through the redshift around her.

XLII

The Water Clock

Ryan finished his drink and approached.

"Greetings good sir," called Lord McAllister out to Laszlo Ryan, somewhere around 8:88 on the 23rd of June. "Hast thou lost your water clock?"

She held out an object. He chose not to look at it. He climbed onto the holostage and approached her. But when he reached out for the object she pulled it away.

"I'm Sir John Hawkwood," she said. "And I mean to ask thee what O Clock it is by these hands."

Ryan touched her shoulder. She was solid. He took hold of her padded shoulders and shook her. Her neovelvet cap fell to the floor. Her wig shifted.

"I am Sir John—"

"You're not Sir John Hawkwood."

"All right, imbecile." She squeezed out of his grip and stepped away. What he could see of her real face appeared suddenly flushed. Her eyes were uncharacteristically clear and glittering. "I'm an actor," she said. "And I'm playing a part. I'm asking you to go along with it."

He stood back and lit a lungprotector. He was surprised by the relief he felt, drawing deep in sudden relaxation. He exhaled. "So you're safe? You didn't enter into some lunatic suicide pact with Skaw."

She gestured out towards the empty theatre.

"Look out over the red-hued gardens. Do you know where we are?"

He saw nothing. But it was like he did. It was as if he stood out in the Gardens below the great red trees. A red wind arose again, the teeth near chattering.

She continued.

"Perhaps we're dead, did you ever think of that? Here, wherever we are there's not really the kind of time that involves death, anyhow. Who will be able to say this ever even happened? Or am I misunderstanding? Anyhow, I brought along a water clock. We can make our own observations."

"What is that between your legs?" He was drunk, and had noted a bulge.

She put her big hands on her red tights and cocked her hips rudely, like a man. "A codpiece as massy as your crint, knave."

"Excuse us?"

"Come let us walk together in the forest."

"Very well." She pretended to walk, and he to follow. As if they were strolling the ruddy olive gardens.

"Are you nuts?" he said. "Give us a kiss."

She skipped tauntingly around him.

"What's your name then?" she asked.

"You're serious?"

"No don't tell me—let me give you a name."

"What are you on about?"

She batted her eyes. "You're scandalizing the institution, Sirrah," she said. "Look! We've stopped in a charming pathway among the ever-reds. The high sheltering trees suck in the red light like hummingbirds on sugar."

She now began to sing, out of tune, as was her custom. "Do I love my love?" she sang. "My love is more than my love! More than all the love that has burned all hearts, more than all the love that has mystified mankind."

"What does this kind of rhetoric have to do with Sir John Hawkwood?"

She responded quietly, with tenderness. "The masks and costumes I bear fall away, revealed in their falsity before him. My love has greatness inside him, about him within him. Upon him it's thrust. And yet it is not this greatness I love more than he himself."

Ryan's earlier relief had passed to be replaced with a rising annoyance.

"Others know my love, she continued. They know his greatness well enough. Even those that do not know him, pretend they see only his shabby things, and quiet troubled days. They gather near. Quietly so as to be near to the ecstasy given by an approving glance from those eyes."

"Who the foark are you on about? Are you talking about Skaw?"

"Who is my love? How can I say when he may not know me? I work that he may know me, may say to others my name, but I dare not speak his name. I shake that he loves me, that he has loved me, dare I say it—will love me again. I am a little quaking bird before him. Others know I have felt his kiss on my lips! But do I love my love?"

"Koré McAllister, snap out of it. It's me, Eddie Ryan. I dislike poetry."

"Oh if they knew how frail I am! If there was lightning, it would pale before the pulse of my love. If there was thunder it would crack the dome itself before drowning out his song in my heart. Would there be wind here, he would be upon it when it blew back my hair."

Her wig fell off, in the gesture.

"Your head's shaved," he said.

"When the Oceans—"

"The Oceans are dead."

"When the Oceans swell, they roll out my love's name on every grain of sand. Would there be time, my own power to unfix it would fall away."

"Time travel is impossible. Stop—"

"Shh!" She put a finger to her moustache. "Even now, he is near. Underneath this very dome he draws upon air that I myself have breathed. O why does he pierce me so? Everything about him is foolish. Even now, I know, he stumbles, speaks in error, and perpetuates degradation upon the gods I serve."

Despite himself her words touched him. The red wind blew gently over Ryan's heart. He tried not to swoon. Her smell, her lips. They were on his own. *Hey. The mustache upon his own lip.* Did she mean...

"Do you mean... Is this the performance? Am I? Give me that book."

"This," she said. "Is his water clock."

"Water clock?" It was a book. "Whose? Is it mine?" He reached out.

Her eyes were wide open and true. But they were no longer his. The Bastard, he thought. I taste him. *Did I hear that?* Ryan reached for the book, but Koré kept her lips tight and with all the hatred of self-meeting-self in the raw, she pivoted and kicked Ryan in the balls.

XLIII

Mercury Station

Ryan doubled over. Had she done that him? To him? Could he have forgotten that? Is that how her performance ended? Was she running? Where? He lay disoriented upon the ground. Through the pharmaceuticals, through the whiskey, the spectacular pain initiated a sudden sequence of bizarre Monocle-induced effects. On the one hand he stood, reflecting that he seemed to have gotten stuck somewhere between timelines in his memory, now outside in the red-lit gardens, the same he'd imagined in the fantasy of Koré's performance. On the other hand it seemed a body of scrawny men had arrived, attired exactly like him in the Hawkwood Costume. They pulled him up through the Lounge down the stairs, out Access and were hustling him now through the red-lit gardens. He heard only his own breathing and stopped. The others vanished.

Koré was nowhere to be seen. He was out in the hedges, now scarlet like blood-trees. Hurrying around a bend on a cherry-graveled path, he came upon a long and lean animal, a red cat of great size and charisma. He stopped, but it smelled him and turned to meet his eye. It opened a jaw columned by pink incisors the size of Ryan's forearms.

A living sabertooth tiger. Yet it was his own extinction that occurred to Ryan on seeing the monster, and he drew back in fear and shock. But it was into a new commotion. A gaggle of wild pigs had conglomerated on the path behind him, blowing steam, snorting, screaming in the red air. Their long snouts were horned. The coarse-haired swine were driving a herd of smooth ash-painted humanoids across the path. The humanoids wore pelts, but the skins did little to decrease the impression of their nakedness. They looked away from Ryan with paranoid eyes as if they feared the pigs would prefer him to them. These were not *homo sapiens*. They were old cousins. Old, grave-faced, pockmarked cousins. Living embodiments of horror, cowing before the pigs, who seemed able to lead them wherever they desired.

Mercury Station, he thought, lighting a lungprotector. Not the isolated backwater it seemed.

The sabertooth tiger gamboled away.

For one astonishing moment he stood on the plains of Kansas in some ideal 19th century Willa Cather landscape. His name seemed to be Simon Savannah. It was no longer red. A wild wide sky of blue and scudding clouds shone above him, the hot sun against his face brought the real rush of earth upon him. Far in the distance a woman's white handkerchief caught the sun as she waved.

But a train spat scarlet-edged smoke stark against the sky. And there, for the path had turned back upon itself, he found that the station had changed once again, in more ways than he could at once determine. Inner Ag was now an enormous wooden structure, something out of a Spaghetti Western. It had grown more crowded in his absence. Shadow people were everywhere visible, passing like ghosts without looking at one another. The sense of not being stared at was overpowering.

He stepped aside for a gang of rushing, violent men. He found himself climbing stairs, bumping through people moving rapidly both directions. He didn't want to stare of course, for this was from out of the corner of his free eye—but that part of it caught cockade hats, waistcoats and little old-fashioned crossties. As the thugs elbowed past, the reek of cider surprised him.

Ryan pushed his way up the stairs, intent on locating some authority. He found himself inside a crowded wooden-room, a sort of waystation hub of passing gangs—including one flock of 20th century suffragettes. Bubble-helmeted red-jacketed guards stood about maintaining order, the astrological sign for Mercury printed on their arms.

Ryan approached the nearest example and tapped his bubble. "Look here," he said. "Where's Control?"

The guard stepped back, gestured robotically. "Move along."

"Listen. Somebody's destroying, interfering, corrupting my perceptions for reasons that are not my own. I am not meant to be here—I'm trying to find—"

The guard armed his weapon, aimed and smashed Eddard Ryan down.

Now, it had been a long time since Eddard Ryan had been decked by a pig. Sure, but he recalled at once that he had indeed accomplished something of the very sort at a miner's strike long ago in Luna Park. He heard later a riot had ensued. He'd emerged to consciousness a full day later, in orbit, drunk on the ceiling of the Sod. He remembered at the time he had had no clear idea of how he'd gotten there.

Far ago that life. Seemed like another Ryan entirely.

And yet he could indeed still be there. Could he? Could it be the old Sod? Ah, the heart swelled to think it might be. His drunkenness, quite real, returned. Just to be up there again off Moon, ellipsing in zero G, under stars. The High Kansan, persona Gæoudjiparl of Ny Christiana on stage confusing stray earthsiders. Was he home then? But his body was too drunk now to be able to stand at all, let alone hear—which was why he was upon the floor.

And here there came floating before him as he lay there on the cold roundation of what was now impossible to distinguish from the pissy sprubber ceiling of The Sod of Turf Orbital, a pint of the plain.

Right there before him, the delightful, dutiful thing—turning in the air as highballs are wont to do when they're wet. Just what he needed to lift himself down off the ceiling.

He stood down, relative to the bar. Above he had found his feet but had presumed gravity. His limbs wiggled, clown-like as he tried to stop his sideways torque. He reached out an arm and attempted, absurdly enough, to halt his velocity on a pole—was struck and away the glass sailed through the air. Ryan's trajectory had altered.

He held. A griffin sergeant azure, sword rather limp at the moment. His hand was shaking, he saw, elongating in his perception as if attached to the hoax-corpse of some 2012er's alien. His chest was heaving.

He had taken the drink in his time, still did on the rare occasion. But this was something special. Memory implants were misfiring and smoke coming out his foarkin ears. The costume he wore annoyed him to no end; he disliked the incessant medievalism. It felt like metal spiders crawling black and hairy upon his poor skin. He ripped it off, stripped naked, shivering and discovering he was alone out in the Gardens.

It's strange enough to stand outside on Mercury (as outside as you'll ever be with 7,000 tons of see-through carbon covering over your sky) but try it in 2nd time, drunk and in the nude. You wouldn't soon forget it.

Ryan trod across the ancient sands. For he knew now where he was going. He heard the voice in his memory already, tasted its coming. He was coming naked. Pathetic? Or a stroke of genius. Only time will tell, eh Monocle?

Well put, Sir. No need to phone the decency League.

Is that Engineering, that I see there?

Ryan focused Monocle on what appeared to be a vast ever-curling rose, stuck like an enormous cigar-butt into the crater's wall.

What you see now is a print from out of four-space, one edge of a macro-space hypercrystal intercuticating in a baroque manifold around the planetoid's pole. In your time, yes, it is Engineering.

I'm being hustled again.

He now perceived the hustlers were other selves, other Eddard Ryans interlinked, each acting as if the others were hustling him towards the rose. He disliked their passive fascist insistence on their route. The rose twisted itself into a single petal and then fell back into a door. A single red door inhered at corridor's end.

Until this point he had assumed it was him time traveling. He had appreciated it. Yet he had the disturbing impression that the red door was traveling to him.

"May I go home now? Monocle?" he asked.

You have no home, Volunteer.

This was a new voice answering him. It was via Monocle and spoke attended by green but it was not Monocle. It came as if already uttered from inside the keep of his second-time body, as if Ryan-minds, and there were many, were each flashing individual green flags unfurling from barely distinguishable towers, that formed against the red door a pixelated text that could be read by Monocle.

It is a web of communication well within the possibility of most areas of recorded human history, it said, quite possibly uttering a phrase cut and pasted from elsewhere in his memory.

Who are you?

Tech ... non ... tea ... klye ace ...

You're not coming in clear.

Your tears have interfered with the Monocle.

What tears? There are no tears.

Must we argue? Our meeting like this is rare. It may be the last. There will only possibly be one other.

I see. Well it's a good time to tell you I'm sorry to have let you down. But I'm not going through that foarking red door. There is no such thing as time travel.

Volunteer. Until it tells you it is not, the struggle against the English Hegemony is proud to accept your service.

You would tell me before you killed me?

Most likely, no. But that is beside the point. Volunteer, the situation is dire. Necessarily, you have misunderstood what is occurring. Listen. You are now an active soldier in a war so confusing and complicated that it is literally impossible to explain to you its true dimensions. Go forward without regret. Yet now at least know that we seek not to hide those complications from you. You must perceive a true index of their extraordinary complexity. The road to our victory depends on the unflowering of events' increasingly peculiar categorical complexity—in what the enemy has attempted to reduce to simple, regularized designs. Can you understand what you're hearing?

I can.

Say it aloud.

"I can."

Good. Welcome to Mercury Station, Volunteer. Perhaps the strangest surviving rivulet of human agency in the system series you hail from. Here, as you know, we are dedicated to eradicating certain pernicious influences upon the unflowering of Oan history throughout what in second-time we see as possibility and is perceived in first-time as the umimpeachable past. From this station, first founded 2150 C.E., we are engaged in a series of retrograded revolutionary interventions in enemy time travel operations. We know you will open the door, Volunteer, because we know you did. The entire station exists from your opening it. In your time we attached you to Count Skaw and Koré McAllister so that you could do it, for us, now, in this way. Do you understand?

"I need a drink to sober up."

You will find a highball to the left of you, on the floor, Sir.

It was the Monocle again.

Ryan himself was on the floor.

I already opened the door, didn't I?

You did, Sir.

He took a hold of the ballglass and brought it to his parched lips.

Up the Republic, Sir. Good luck and all that. I will not be accom-panying you.

Ryan re-opened the door.

LXIV

In Which Some Things Are Finally Explained

23 June, 1255. 16:40ish. No more Monocle.

Maybe we have died.

But it was just him, talking to himself. Still upon a floor. Uncarped and cold, this one. Silent too. He listened. All was quiet. He was naked and his lungprotectors gone.

He was greeted by a curious sensation. It was if he lay on the floor of an old, medieval chamber. Gravity came on him like a blanket, suffused in the cold breath of old stone. *Naked fire*, the first he had seen in many years, flamed out from golden braziers on the walls. The flickering orange reflected upwards into high geometric arches.

The room, as he tried to stand, evolved into a sort of inverse pentasphere, rapidly revolving by his spins into an inverse cone. In the center of the disc he saw an altar of organic stone.

Upon it an old curled dagger.

Ryan reached out but found, with something of a shock, he had no left arm at all. "But what have they done with mine own arm?"

"We've all lost an arm."

He looked up at the man in the robe, who'd spoken.

A sharp little beard lined the greatly sagging face. Deep fissures sketched his skin like charcoal. Allskaw, himself.

"You're disgusting," he barked. "You call yourself a soldier? Pull yourself together."

He saw that there was now something atop the stone altar.
Was it a corpse? He hadn't seen it when first entering the chamber.
Whatever it was, it was a ghastly sight, and shone like a light-
scream out at Ryan's good eye. *Jesus, Mary and Joseph, have they
removed mine own eye as well?* It was a corpse, its skin drained ominous white. Tubes emerging from cut veins and arteries around the
shoulder, leading to buckets of black liquid around it. A black hole
carved in its chest.

He wept. "The Rose of Munster's dead boys, laid naked, poor
and bare, upon a stone."

The spirit lit fire. You, the spirit. The strangeness of what followed is difficult to transcribe without it. You see the self had been
hollowed out and left only spirit there remaining. Spirit was literally
the specific absence of a self—a shadow in time. It was singular but
contained multitudes. It was the print of the enormous emptiness
among and between a body's particles, larger in relativity than an
entire universe, as it passed in space. Spirit was sober, out where the
actual mixing of alcohol and water can never occur.

By implication spirit was a body of its own, though a body
whose shape did not pursue its own complexities in time but in
space, the second space that is, the one implied by second-time. And
this thing, now that one could observe it, see its shadow, could be
made, so to speak, to slip, slide, *zip,* even with a sort of sound, sideways out of the body—from the altar and into Ryan's hologram.

I'm inside. And yes indeed "I" walked you through the room!

*I saw through things. For instance, the walls of the chapel were
now outlined in light. I walked sideways between them to an attached
boardroom. I observed the Count far below, gesturing before a black-
board with a laser pen. There was little Eddie Ryan, naked, wrapped
in a blanket, sitting listening before him.*

Koré had not left me. *Finally, you're catching on. Here, try this.*
I pinched his ass with his right hand.

"Ow."

"How? Illumination, oddly enough, first came to me in an eye." It was Skaw speaking, elsewhere. Jesus, in my memory. Before the chapel, after passing through the red door, I'd found him in an ordinary Engineering boardroom. He plied me with compliments, whiskey. He was programming me for the Event. I'd forgotten it purposefully. Did I mention I could do that?

"After an altercation with Anatole—I'm afraid to say I objected to the chitlins in his corned beef hash—I ended up with a shard of glass in my eye. I needed a new lens and purchased a fresh corpse on Mars. 23 years old, impeccable genes. The day after the operation I desired the sexual companionship of a woman for the first time. Nothing could slake me. I bought six and foarked for an entire day. I realized then, my dear, that pieces of selves could travel between living tissues. In fact they did so all the time, there was simply no brain there to record it.

"A self could move from a host in the past to a host in the future. But did not that process leave the possibility of the self in the future being able to travel backwards into time through just the sort of process we've formulated theoretically, you and I?"

Ryan grunted.

"Exactly! One would only need the dead tissue preserved in a certain fashion—to begin to experiment. I've been experimenting for centuries, my dear."

Koré? Are you inside me? *Yes.* Pinch me again.

He was leaning over me; I could smell his rank breath. The lines on his face were twisting in a hopeless attempt at a grin. "And now, my boy, you have come to me—*by your own will*—at the hour I am ready to make my dreams real. Dear me, I can see that you're aroused."

"No! That's—I am not a boy. I'm thirty-seven years old. And I'm not—"

"Do you understand? At last?"

Presently (later or earlier Ryan couldn't say), Skaw was sketching out the mechanics of the ritual onto a map of Mercury Station on the lightboard. Ryan had apparently emptied another pint glass.

"I forgot what you just said," Ryan said.

Skaw narrowed his brow. "You *are* already experiencing displacement then. Oddly, I am not."

"What displacement?"

"The timebomb will send backward moving waves forward into time. It will blow old memories in and new memories away for those caught inside the blast. How much have you forgotten, boy? Do you remember where you are?"

"Mercury Station. 2155. 23rd of June, presumably. After 5.

"Correct. 1730 hours."

"What timebomb?"

"It exists! It ticks even now. At 19:30 the entire planet will become our transistor. Our selves, the three of us, will scatter into possibility. My dear, think back! You mustn't lose memory yet. Think back over what I've just told you. *A Station like a herald Mercury, new-lighted on a sphere-kissing hill.*"

I was naked, covered only by a blanket. I wished now I hadn't had to have been so. All desire for intimacy with this man I had once found so fascinating had faded. Yet he had access to certain information and one had to converse to get it.

"Go over it again, then."

"I found the seed orbiting a fucking comet. Yes? The objects inside? *Gottskaw!*"

"No I don't remember at all."

"You don't remember the capsule? The silver seed stuck into the spacerock? What I found inside?"

He held up a book, an old one.

"I remember that book."

"How interesting that it's that that you remember. Do you remember? Below its surface nonsense there's an invisible text. Gottskaw! Gottskaw, boy! I shall recite the key bit again, for we still have an hour's time."

"What about the Peregrinus text? The one atop the Godskaw?"

"Pfui. A fake, obviously written after by a later hand. He himself killed the witch, he says so, on a stone—how could she then write it? What do you know of the text?"

"Koré told me about it."

"Forget Ms. McAllister, boy. She is the sort who uses the Canon for toiletries. Godskaw. Godskaw, Godskaw, Godskaw. Do you understand? His book! *We shall live his prophecy to fruition.* A drink, my dear."

He handed a new pint of the plain. Ryan took it. Sniffed it. It smelled real enough.

"We shall live?"

The old face inflated to some of its former grandeur as it sucked its ballglass dry and gasped.

"Godskaw shall live! Godskaw is real, my dear, a certain representative man. He has struggled against the superstitions and injustices of his time, but he has not quite overcome. He may be rich. He may be the Magus. Be sure he struggles. He is opposed to the science of the day but takes from it his origin. He is of course male. And though he works ways to link to bloodlines and kings and heroes of old, he is always a "nobody," for he is driven by the will to take over other's powers. He is disguised, he must be. For he is *the* observer, the self in motion denying the necessity of time. He is what he is not and what he is not alone. I speak of the real Godskaw, the human Godskaw, the messenger of light doomed to be squelched out by the gospels of your beloved Catholic Church, Eddard Josef and to be discovered on Mercury today. I speak of my self, if I may."

"How is Anatole, by the way?"

"Eh?" He wrinkled. "Anatole? Pfui. We speak not of Anatole. We now speak only of what is most true between us—that sphere of being where we are one. I speak of the latter Godskaw. The one who remembers. For you are the one who must remain. You must face what is your destiny."

Something was stroking Eddard Josef's hand. Something cold and damp, soft as a lizard's belly.

He pulled it away and drank.

"Drink a toast, my dear. Your sister is preparing to be taken. She will ride with me as perpendicular within as in my arrival. In the past and the present, she will be sacrificed."

"Jesus Space Christ. Let me talk to her."

"That won't be possible. She knows you are coming. She has performed admirably. She understands what is at stake. What is to be gained, what is to be lost."

"What is to be lost?"

"You will remain after we're gone, to record our passing. She and I will not."

Ryan stood up, thankful for the blanket. It was strange to see now that he stood a good five centimeters taller than Reg Skaw. As if in like discomfort, Skaw shuffled away to the distant corner, frowning. He rolled up the soft, loose sleeves of his bathrobe. He picked at the skin on his forearms.

Finally, he erupted, bellowing, "*Hactenus de situ et miraculis terrae quarumque et siderum ac ratione universitatits atque mensura!*"

Ryan shouted back, "...*In hic veneficas artis pollere, non magicas!*"

And finished his whiskey.

Skaw reached towards him, eyes glittering. "I so enjoy sparring with you. Think of how the universe will open for all of us, when I fully understand what I *am*, Ryan. When I truly *become*. My G-d the life we will achieve, my boy!"

"I'm not your boy."

He picked at the arms again. Then, very quietly, "I think of you as mine."

"You don't know me at all if you think I will go along with your corrupt rituals."

"Your Control has spoken."

"You know *nothing* about Control."

"Your commander Blish Baily has long ago ordered you to work with me."

Ryan snorted his drink through his nose.

Skaw continued. "Do you believe I really don't know about your Black Rose Provisionals? Ye Gods! Do you think that in the 30s I didn't know then what you were up to every second of the day?"

"Then why did you allow—"

"It's you alone I've always been interested in, Eddard Ryan, all along. Your development. I was never interested in Mr. Wesley's hijinks."

"You know *nothing* about me."

"On the contrary. I know everything there is to know about you."

"You do not. You can not."

"Where do you think your Control found the funds to modify your mental apparatus? The laboratories? Do you think that a lab rat with no Concern tags is just taken in to elite orphanages like the Orangerie?"

"Please do not mention the Orangerie. I never discuss the Orangerie. You know nothing, absolutely nothing about the Orangerie."

"I went there myself, you fool, way, way back—back before I came to the Moon, when it was still in County Mayo, by the sea."

"You're kidding yourself. You're no soldier. You're not Black Rose. You're AI."

I am no machine! By the great Body Electric—"

"Anglo-Irish."

"AI. Ah, yes I see." He picked at his arms. "And what of it? Can you possibly be so coarse as to believe your movement has no relation to Dean Swift? To Wolfe Tone? Erskine—"

"Don't forget the Duke of Wellington."

The little mask cracked in smiles and the noise it admitted, one supposed, was a sigh. It managed to appear child like and old at the same time.

"It's refreshing to speak with you, my dear. It truly is. I am sorry that you think that here alone is no doubt and that in a matter of hours my body here will have to die with your beloved. In my own way, as you must really know, dear lad, I love you. I love you as much as you love her. Indeed it must be so, for this energy, this love between us will be necessary for our dislodging ritual—"

"Shut up. Stop spitting in my face."

"I know how you feel, sweet lad. Forgive me for treading so roughly upon your dreams—but think on the free world you will inherit when this is through. At last, Space is there for the taking."

"For the last time you old sack of lies, I am a grown man. *You don't know me at all!*"

"Not know you!" The New Estater burst out in sudden wrath, verging again on his old grandeur. "Not know you? Not know my own body's self? *My own clone, the last true Godskaw of Skaw's own hand?*"

XLV

Last Words

My name has been slandered. I'm made to be a joke, a fool, and prof-
ligate. Because I was once a fat man in Space, as man was meant to
be fat, I am always fat. But it is not because I am fat that I am not
worthy of the humanity others pin to themselves. In fact I was hated
from the first, back when I was still trim. My mother loved me, true,
but this was a biological phenomenon and she died, either way, when
I was eleven. She had great hopes. I had been a prodigy from birth. It
was assumed I would become a master musician. You scoff, and it is
true I have not continued in it and the art is in great part lost to me.
Then, I aspired to be a politician. Oh yes, I was very ambitious. And
I saw quickly that my ambition, which came naturally to me, and
sprang out of the best things in my culture, only caused others to hate
me, because they were false in themselves...

Very slowly the words were trickling back. Eddie Ryan still
had an arm but he'd almost torn it off himself, so violent had
been his struggles. Screaming, yes, weeping, foark it, face full of
snot and salt and hot with self-gnashing blood, and with the
blood of Skaw too. The old devil had done it. The old devil had
spooked E.R. to the core. No clone, please no clone! And after he
put himself out of consciousness, he roamed for some time in and
out of a second-time all its own and remembered Koré inside of
him, how it would soon feel. *Yes me too, Eddie Ryan.* But he was
also here in engineering with Skaw, and eventually, very slowly, a

coherent idea formed out of individual words trickling into the chamber pot of his:

I'm right here, Eddie Ryan, inside of you. Write it down.

Consciousness.

And I'll speak like this.

Still, Skaw talked. "They didn't hate me on the surface. Oh no, they loved me. Treated me with kindness. Kept up appearances. Were even seen with me in public. The unconsciously they loathed me with a force that in retrospect, though as you know I'm an atheist, I can only call god-like."

Foark Skaw. This wasn't more than a retrieved memory. Without the direct intervention of MERKUR, who had guided Ryan into this retrograding, Skaw would have been lost entirely. Ryan had specifically not remembered this, and to remember was what Skaw wanted. Foark Skaw indeed. And here he was trying to steal away his mind.

And Koré too? Did she remember? *You can't understand me yet inside of you?* And thought away when he came close to seeing her.

"A man who can see the true flatness of the illusion of a culture yet who dedicates himself only to its redemption will necessarily be cut in twain by its razor edge. But there is only one heart. And my heart, you know it, boy, has always, always been full. I had to hide my love away. And so after a brief flirtation with the stage, my ambition for popular acclaim and power vanished. Only the art remained. The art of arts. Having realized already that my life would be artificially extended, and seemed to me potentially exponential in its rate of growth, I also realized that it would be to my art's benefit to vanish into history. To find its way into the highest most powerful circles of the invisible elite. I became, in fact a butler."

Eddie Ryan? Do you hear me? He found a space-time capsule orbiting an innersystem comet. A steel alloy. A brassy, egg shaped pod, a quiet marvel of medieval metal work. Tests confirmed it had been shot from Earth, Europe near the beginning of the 14th Century C.E. He opened it. Cut a hole. Eddie Ryan. Inside he found a dagger, a book and a tiny pickled arm.

"No one knows that. Not even Anatole. But I've always been a butler, you know. Attending to others' needs. The great days on the *Polly-Ann* were paid for by service to Interested Space. My very royalty remains in provisional status depending on glorified butler services rendered *in perpetua.* How amused I was when I first saw you for myself and you were reading Butler."

"I was reading Kipling."

Skaw's labs speculated on the journey the seed must have taken. Most likely it used balloons to access the edge of atmosphere, and then rocketry to reach vacuum. Afterwards metal-worked solar sails might unfold and guided by some sort of computer, could find a comet. He turned his attention to the book. You know it, Eddie Ryan.

The book led him to Mercury. He had seen Mercury coming obviously. Everything in his plans had always suggested it. It's where all these lines come together. Where, in particular, you and me, Eddie Ryan, came together at last—though I don't seem to matter so much to him, being a woman.

"And I have been loved. By real men, real women. I am still loved, as you, as you my boy more than anyone else knows."

But Ryan saw that as he was speaking the old man had his trousers down. Had the ritual begun?

"Do you know," the old man whimpered. "Do you have any idea of the significance of the historical gaps with which this mother-raping brass egg blankets the receivable present?"

No answer.

You see, it's not so easy to write it down. *I know.* The a-causal train that had returned me to this memory seemed to make the memory impossible. The only possible explanation was beginning to worry him. He was apparently expected to go along with the foarking ritual.

In ordinary causality Skaw was the Creator of Ryan. But perceived backwards (the waves of the coming timebomb had undone ordinary causality altogether) it was Ryan who stood above Skaw, ascendant.

It would mean, however, that Ryan would do, eventually, all Skaw required in first-time. He would follow the shuffling has been count down the empty hallway, enter the "star chamber" and participate in the preparatory orgy. He would become "animal like and debased." He would indeed at last take Kord McAllister from behind. Then in trance state, he was to be cut like the others at the same moment. Linked to the same blast, their arms would be fused with the medieval regrow. Skaw's plan was that Ryan's body would be saved; waiting assistants would get it out to the infirmary at once.

From the three linked coffins four arms would stretch forth. Their left hands would be fused together to grasp a fifth of pure energy, in a blast that would scatter already psychically-dislodged selves into second-time—presumably down into the old world event, into its own real-time mirror-reversed conspiracy and make memory almost entirely impossible.

Did he remember? Ryan wasn't sure. What he knew was that it would only be there at the Event itself, still unremembered, that he might be free to act in such a way as to change everything.

Of course it begins to come back to me myself now, he said, galloping backwards out of the future like a knight awry—my own intention to bring Skaw all along to initiate this process. Everything in my life had been planned by myself from the future.

What do you mean? Where am I anyway?

It should be possible for Eddard J. Ryan—lab-rat, space born, illegitimate, with self as slippery as a foarking eel—to hitch a ride.

Eddie Ryan, what are you on about?

For I had not remembered this, had I? For if I had, now, then I could not have remembered waking up weeks later in the Infirmary Bedsphere. Perhaps I hadn't. Because I still haven't decided.

Decided what?

Ae: "The model is horizontal, like the sudden transformation of a single bacterium across space. Every action, no matter where, no matter when, is equally capable of immediate transformation."

Eddie Ryan? You're with me. Hold my hand.

Oh Koré, we touched. Don't you feel it? Clammy Skaw's hand, yours hot and strong, the rubbery medieval. *The arms remember this.*

It's me. I love you too, Koré. I'm coming with you. I'm meant to. Was the whole time. Have you read the Peregrine?

I haven't finished it. And now I'm blindfolded.

Wait, were our arms just cut off?

I feel nothing.

Koré, by the way, I never think I told you that I really did admire your performance work.

Thank you, Eddie Ryan. I admire your work too, whatever it is.

I opened my eyes to the shrieking alarm. I needed an omni-tourniquet fast.

I'd just been slaughtered. That is to say, my arm had been removed. By a cut so sharp it went through my bone like lard. Not a laser, a blade.

Actually, an omnnitourniquet already seemed to have stanched the flow. I could see through it into the scarlet wound. Absurdly, I was not dying.

I was out of my body. Robed figures were at work, keeping me alive but I was above them like in an NDE.

In a corner, a commotion. Four arms, bloodily fused into an upside down pyramid, were scuttling on their hands. As a whole, they moved randomly, as if overcome with panic, seeking for a knowledge they'd never find and pulling against each others' fear.

Consciousness infinitely reflected between living pieces of flesh. Beautiful to behold, my dear.

Koré?

Close your eyes, my love.

Is that you? She gripped my hand.

Remember the Final Mechanism? The way I can kill myself under any circumstances?

What are you on about now?

Remember how I never read Brian O'Nolan?

No.

I'm not letting you die without me, Koré. He means to kill you there too. If you're going, I'm coming too.

She gripped my hand hard. *What?*

Look for me.

A PINT OF PLAIN IS YOUR ONLY MAN.

There was a thin, wild mercury sound

THE THIRD CIRCUIT

Her wanderings.

XLVI

"The Art of Arts"

This creature lay upon her straw bed in the Canon's house for some time, recovering from the Battle of the Burg. Gunther cleaned, awaiting the arrival of a new official. Scariot stayed as well, caring for this creature and speaking with her and vanishing only to return.

In the long hours alone, she thought of her departed friends Gretchen and the Canon Moretus, and of her love, her true love, Dick. Dick had said that it was death for all those who were close to him. Had the Canon been close to him? That bodies died seemed to this creature to be the central principle of this sphere. Time broke bodies down like poor Gretchen's fat fried the flesh of a lark and left it soft and breaking in the fingers. Many of this creature's friends were indeed dead. But others, Llw and Scariot (though she did not feel him a friend), and Dick, she knew it, lived. Körner as well, though he might well not remember her.

She dwelled on memories of Gretchen's head and the axe, of the Canon's tongue upon the floor. Silenced at last, her talkative friend. He had lived by and promoted a dogma whose central premise was that martyrdom was the most perfect possible life for a man, perhaps so he could survive this end. Had he? So blinded was she by the white light of his attempt at innocence, that this creature could not see beyond it.

"I have no patience with the new fashions," the Canon had once complained. "The old Roman style is what turned me to G-d. It made works of geometric beauty, opened space, so that sinners might find peace in a chamber, grandly and wisely made, take relief from the worry and hope of the nonsense outside, ponder philosophically about the meaning of life. It brought me that way. Now they build churches to humiliate, intimidate, and threaten the ignorant poor and celebrate their own powers of construction. This new church will be in the old style, if I can help it. The Masons know me well." She saw now that the Canon's resistance to the current style would pass away with his body, and the church would be other than he had imagined.

And what would such a small thing have really mattered in the breadth of the spheres? He had lived within an illusioned sphere of knowledge, of community and reason, which was purportedly able to pass through books in time. She regretted that the words he had written on the floor in his own blood had never been ciphered. She would have put them in a book for him. But Gunther, who mopped them up, couldn't read.

What did it mean, she wondered, for the Canon's last words not to be read? Did he fall out of that sphere he'd loved altogether? Why did it frighten her to think upon a word's never having been read?

Could she write to Dick? Could she send her true lover a message? The warmth and prickling of her so-cold body aroused her at the thought. What were torn and broken corpses next to the emblem of Dick's boyish buttocks striding through the spheres? Could she write that vision to him? Hitherto, men's parts had only ever raised repulsion in this creature's fancy but now the thought of her true love's hips caused her most peculiarly to swoon.

She could not read. She had understood as she looked on the bloody scrawl, that she would never be able to read. She was outcast from the sphere of writing, as if more into time by it. Lady C.'s white arm awarded promise of the infinite belonging, yes—the proof of a home however lost contained within. But it could not write.

"Do you read, Doctor Scariot? Do you write?"

The Demon snorted. "Does he eat? Does he shit?"

He opened his robe, and showed her the small book, the first she had ever seen. She looked clear upon it.

"Give it me," she said. "I want it."

"Away! It is his! Mine!"

She knew the book as an emptiness in the otherwise solid room. Small, leathern backed, clasped with gold. In her fancy it caused tiny crystals of pure void to extend from it like matter in high but precise crown-like complication.

"Will you write my words upon the book? While I speak to you?"

"Yes, yes, we might make magic of it. I cannot sleep. The Canon's bed is stone. The fool."

She lay upon the straw bed and for a time the Demon interviewed her as the old Doctor Scariot strolled through the room, scrawling with a bone dipped in his own blood upon his book. There were words that she could have printed into time, and she watched carefully what she said.

"We are Mercury's child," she said.

"She is Mercury's child."

"*Statio Mercurio*. Write that on the front."

"What do you know of Mercury? And what can you tell us concerning the signification of the Latin words *Statio Mercurio*?"

"We do not know."

"Mercury? You speak of something lightning swift and changeable, so fast as to be only known by its propensity to be other than it was before. You speak of quicksilver, a sort of stone of motion. Yet with *station* you place it at rest—change unchanging."

"Write it down."

The Demon giggled. "*As Latona will be whitened by mercury and by fire, Diana will come undressed.*"

Scariot screamed. "Enough!" But he scratched at the book with his pen. "The Herb Mercury, Five-leaved-grass, Fumitory, Pimpernell, Marjoram, Parsley, and such as have shorter and less leaves, being compounded of mixed natures, and divers colors..."

"He has seen you naked," quoth the Demon. "He knows."

"Mercury is a planet," interrupted the Doctor. "A planet providing for us a system not only to mark the passage of our own time, but to liken each now to a now that has come before. For if time is infinite we move upon it in a circle. Yet Mercury moves swifter than we, at the turning of days. It changes direction and it stands for commerce, non-lyrical poetry, and travel. Mercury holds four secrets. First that it stops in the sky. Then that it retreats. Third, it comes back. The fourth secret is that it wobbles in unseemly gait."

She thought of her true love's codpiece.

"All four together offer a single solution," said the Demon with a grin.

"Yes, a time of time. And *Statio Mercurio?*"

"Not twenty days ago, the horned one was in station. That is to say, it had ceased on its ordinarily swift motion against the fixed stars in one direction. It soon began to move backwards in the other."

"Is Mercury a God?"

"Mercurius? Oh yes," informed the Demon, flipping through the book. "Of late he is the principal god of the Germans. They believe him to have great influence over exchange, and do him honor in mercantile transactions. He started out as a local deity of a group of freed slaves in central Italy. A god of brotherly love and trust." The Demon winked. "He was known to be able to keep a secret. Like Old Scariot, the beast!"

"Fiend! Hopharlot!" the Doctor shouted.

The Demon would not quiet. "And under Mercury shall we not speak of the most ancient of arts? The most secret?"

"Silence!"

This creature's interest was sparked. She sat up in the bed. "What is this Art of Arts?"

The Demon: "Doctor?"

"Those who know don't tell and those who tell don't know."

"*—till you give a Master the Devil's Kiss.*"

"Where can we find this Master?"

I know one, giggled the Demon. "You have already kissed. He watched you die upon a stake! He is afraid of you here alive. Believes you are invulnerable. He will kill you by killing your love."

"Silence!"

"Of whom do you speak?!"

"He is a knight in these parts. He has a *keep*. A special *keep*."

"Toad!" This the Doctor, darkly under his breath, clapping his book shut, folding it into his robes.

"Gottskaw! Gottskaw himself!"

XLVII

The Bride

Scariot slept fitfully by the fire, and this creature's thoughts were interrupted by a quiet touch on her lips.

It was Llw. He was wearing her hat, but it was now snowy white. She rose quietly and followed her servant out of doors. It was daytime. They crossed the plaza, turned an empty lane and entered a tavern. They climbed a wooden stairway to a room above it. It was crowded. In one corner two men worked behind a broad table. The first of these wore a green jerkin and an enormous folded hat of crimson. He looked downwards through lenses balanced on his nose and scratched at an open ledger with a wooden pen. A colleague, blue collared and hooded with brown, pointed with first and little finger at the scattered copper and silver disks on the table before them. Llw pulled her away and found a bench for them at the back. She questioned him there, among all the waiting men, in a corner.

Llw spoke quietly, with some intensity of manner. "After such an ordeal, my Lord, it would be impossible for a man as innocent as you to remember exactly what happened. 'Twas a great slaughter you have seen. Oh yes, a boy is said to have ridden into the town, and was seen entering the Canon's house. After that, three riders came and took him away. Everyone said it was so. It was thought the boy had murdered the Canon. As to the body of the knight they left behind in the yard, *sans mittens*, that one was indeed dead, as was poor Gretchen of Greenland who'd been hit by his axe. No one knew how, and now his head was missing. Lawful himself had "come upon" the dead man's gauntlets in a jakes, and it was thought now the knight had been robbed there of his head and his body later put on the steed for the old Gods. "But all this is not what they talk about, my Lord."

"It is not? Speak forthright."

"It is you they talk about. Peter the Peregrine, the Lunar's ward, who died to defend him and rose again from the dead. I've already been taking in a good deal of coin in return."

In return for what, Linavet?

"For the privilege of seeing you here."

Indeed she now saw that all the people in the room were watching her out of the corners of their eyes. Even the broad-browed counter, over his spectacles.

"Tell them not to look upon us," this creature said, troubled by their focus upon her.

"Come ye," said a little man whose gums were swollen and bleeding about the mouth. "Touch me fums and fure me with your fleff."

Llw shoved him away. "I'll touch you with my fist, villain— get ye gone." The man fell into the pulsing crowd.

"Lawless," this creature commanded. "Our white hat?"

He composed himself and, slowly handed it to her.

This creature put it on her head. She grew immediately in stature. She pointed to the ladder. The mob stood suddenly back.

"Out!" she commanded. "All!"

The room cleared, leaving four: the scribe, the counter, Llw and this creature. Grinning like a cat, Llw took out a third part of his takings and gave it to the two former and they departed. He put the remainder of the silver in his leathern wallet, which he carried about in a sash strapped around his right shoulder, with his ever-present longbow and bear-paw quiver. "And our purse?"

Grinning now like a fox, he removed it from his own purse. "Our dagger."

It hung at his side. He handed it over.

This creature was surprised to see her reflection on the blade. She had lost her fur, and stood only in a pale robe of the Canon's ward and was without an arm.

"Our hat," she said to Llw. "Why is it white?"

The archer did not cease his grinning. "I had to boil the thing to kill the lice upon it." She sheathed her knife and fixed her purse under her skirt. "And where have you put our precious mailed mittens, Lawless?"

"...I see no need to wear them as yet, my Lord."

"Give them over, villain."

It hurt him, particularly, she saw. But he took them from his bundle. They were heavy and lined with black velvet, and meant for hands much larger than this creature's own. She only had one arm she wished to protect and took the left, leaving Llw the right.

"One glove for each of the thieves, my man. We shall wear them to symbolize our shared body."

He gazed strangely upon his little master. She hooked the heavy iron glove upon her white arm. It fell upon the floor.

There was a time of silence. Llw reached to the fallen mitten.

"Might a miracle worker such as our self become a king? If the people believed in us? Could we raise the people against this Gottskaw, say? This knight who rides rough-shod over this country?"

"There are already those who say you will," he said. "Trouble is brewing, for Gottskaw. It may be true that both the Popes have lately disowned him. Yet he is as yet invulnerable."

"Where does he stop?

"He has retired to an abbey two days north on the river, made it a fortress. He slays all who approach without a secret sign, indiscriminately."

"What is he about?"

"There are those who claim to know deeper things."

"Who?"

"The Men of Light, my Lord. The Albigensians. It is an old and sacred spot he has taken, upon a hill with old stones. They say he waits for a bride."

"Gottskaw is an odd name for a man, is it not Lawless?"

"These are odd times, m'lord. There are antichrists everywhere afoot. Gottskaw is a great warrior. I have never seen him, but have heard many tales. He outrages Christians and sets tongues tipping wherever he goes. They say he has sent Sir John Hawkwood himself running from the field with shit squirting out of his steel. Gottskaw builds engines of war and ingenious fortresses. Many who think that the last days are upon us, whisper he is the Beast himself. He is also the best painter in the Christendom."

"Why do they say he has come?"

"Smallfolk say he has a bride. She was his own bastard daughter born from the witches. He burned her on a stake after ravishing her to receive eternal life. But it is said that Thor loved her and sent the Children of the Old Forest, the little people, to capture her soul as it left her body. They returned it to Nature. She escaped and ran, disguised as a boy."

"We do not understand. Who is disguised as a boy?"

"The very maid Gottskaw has brought here from the West. The one he has taken and, now cursed till he can, must take again."

'Twas then she noticed a hole in the wall at the other end of the room, nearto where they had been standing when first they'd spoken. This creature saw an eye upon her now through the hole.

"We will speak with these Men of Light. Bring us them."

"We must travel to meet them, my Lord. They will pay good gold."

The eye was gone and they left that place, this creature not speaking of what she'd seen.

XLVIII

The Albigensians

These Albigensians, the archer informed her, or Predestined Men, or Men of Light, saw themselves as secret rulers of the spheres. She had spoken to one of them preaching in the lane, and it was then they had first come to know of her. Others remembered her words from their telling, and have heard of other deeds.

"Do they pass books among themselves that may remember our words?"

"I don't know."

It was a day's journey. Llw had proposed a night walk, a camp near the area and a morning's arrival. They crossed the River V. and took the Roman road West, finding themselves alone upon it by nightfall. A distance from the way, this creature struck a fire from her *Electrum*. They lay upon the grass, beneath the stars. Winter was closer upon the spheres now and the aether had been already affected in its entirety. For quick brittle stars now glittered as if they really were jewels stuck upon the inside of a black velvet sphere.

Llw could not sleep without drink and would drink so much that he lost consciousness. As a result, when this creature moved he did not know it, and she left him there, stupified and snoring, unconscious beneath the stars. She was not alone.

She walked upon a wide meadow. The moon rose. Its hard half-circle lit the prairie silver. The one who had followed now stood before her, pointing the way.

The meadow yielded a great gathering of people, a gathering whose size astounded her. Great fires burned in pattern all up to the peripheries. It was an evident celebration, half in darkness, half in moonlight. Where had they come from? To such a far-away place? This creature disliked being among such numbers, and reasoned to have all their eyes focused upon her might be more than she could bear. Yet they seemed to look away from her guide.

She was being led to their center. She saw they now gathered about her in concentric circles. The way was closing behind, so that were she to attempt to get outside of them she would have to face the gaze of multitudes.

As she came towards their midpoint she saw that many of the Albigensians were naked. She stopped. Those at the very center now stood around her. Their faces were rugged and hard, their hands callous and tough, their genitals furred like bears. They looked directly upon this creature.

One of the naked old men was the first to speak.

"Master," he said. "Tell us of the light."

This creature looked upon the man, and upon the assembly of faces looking upon her.

"Tell you of what light, old man?"

"The light of which it is said in the secret tradition that our Lord was fashioned. The light from which you came, Peregrinus. Lead us to the light."

"Lead you to the light? Even now light reaches your naked-ness and bathes it in silver. Read your nakedness as an emblem of your freedom here, equal to all of nature's spawn before light. Then lead yourself, old man."

The man leaped up into the air, beard extending.

"Yes! We came naked! We shall leave this world naked! We shall die naked and return again!"

"Stand for us, Peter Peregrine," came another shout, this one from a woman. "Disrobe!"

This became instantly the thing to say, for a chorus erupted around this creature as she stood in their center.

"Disrobe for us, Lord Peter!"

Neither did she wish them to see that she was a maid, nor that she had a magic limb. This creature touched her arm.

The black ball upon which she stood now appeared red. The spheres, in fact appeared entirely fashioned from blood and blackness. The stars themselves were like a great swath of gore splattered across the sky. The rings of humans surrounding her, huddled motionless, like statues of pure blood.

She crossed through the Albigensians as if through a series of scarlet paintings. The innermost ring, the one surrounding her, contained six or seven men, naked, seemingly oblivious to the cold. Bearded and hairy testicled, the lot of them; their bodies withered like old trees of blood as they stood against the darkness.

The next two rings outward contained women in a partial state of undress, their red breasts bare to the sky. The black nipples made them look like great eyes looking upon this creature. But they were as blind to her motions as the arm. Behind the women were seated the mob, peasants, merchants' wives, second and third and fourth sons and daughters, some naked, some clothed, others holding each other in open embrace, still others cavorting scandalously in the red mud.

Small cherry fires burned out here and there, spontaneously coming to life, charging the aether with the rich spice of burning plants. But no people moved.

On the outermost rings, order gave way to chaos. Bodies lay upon each other in crimson heaps, entirely naked, taking their pleasure in and on their neighbors. Ecstatics broke away screaming on the edge of the meadow, some leaping into a lake of blood. After them more fields and finally the red road again.

She let go of her arm and found she was again approaching the Meadow. Her guide was gazing upon her. But when he turned, she did not this time follow, but turned west. At first all appeared green. Wind came up and brought with it a rain, an ugly hard sort of rain. Sounds in the aether were many. Strange towits and toos and beeps and low, mourning moans: making a vibrant music in the higher chambers outside the rain. She entered the forest alone. She found a bush affording of some privacy and relieved herself upon the earth.

This little creature was wet and cold but she walked westward into the night. She was tired of people and glad to be left again with the creatures of the earth in whose hallowed company she had sat in the antechambers of second-time. And though she had no longer a companion, she fancied she did. She walked arm in arm with brave Dick, singing songs she had heard of Llw to the half a moon.

> *The bowmen, the yeomen*
> *The lads of dale and fell...*

And later that night she left that country altogether behind her.

XLIX

The Players

What is change? There seemed to be an eye in this creature's mind for which change was but the principle of variation in an otherwise motionless tapestry woven into all time and space.

She resolved that she would no longer will her own changes into the patterns that others seemed intent on drawing around her. This Gottskaw, for instance, ever drawing this creature into his web. The Archer, Scariot and his demon. Even Dick, whom this creature loved, thought he knew more than she of the ways of the spheres.

There had been about the boy an air of outrage, that night he'd thrown her away. A lack of interest in her own presence that still grated upon her. Why after all, was it not Dick, the male, who sought her, the female? Stories she heard were never written this way. Did he think she could not live with her wild love and that she was not worth his own? Could it be he was no true lover himself?

Yes, this little creature left Llw and Gottskaw and Dick behind. This creature has never tired of the road, and she took to it now. The new change she embraced brought her in the midst of a party of players.

The story of their meeting is as follows. Some time after the incident with the Men of Light this creature was found out. She was taken by a party of superstitious peasants and hung upside down on a pole near to the Hamlet of H., some three days journey west of B. The weather however was foul. The good people had not managed to keep their fire lit and scattered in a sudden storm. She was left there upon the stake, upside down.

When the storm lifted, wondering if she should touch her arm or no, she beheld little heads come dancing out in the air, right-side up for her. They were in fact feet, she discovered, and had eyes and lips painted upon them.

Brightly colored and expressive, these feet argued, laughed and pointed at her like little beasts. This creature laughed and applauded. The feet smiled, wept and danced, and even whistled tune. They belonged to Til Owlmirror and Weenie Winkie ex. of the Rhine. The two were walking about upon their hands, dancing to a flute the former had plugged into the latter's arse.

After a good hearty laugh at her expense these two and their merry comrades freed this creature from her captivity. They explained their interest. They had entered the hamlet while the good folk were at this creature's burning and separated some of her persecutors from their gold and possessions. The players were now indebted to this creature, they said. And they'd heard of her fame and proficiency in the art of playing.

The art of playing? In no time the band of players saw this creature as one of their own. For the next four moons, until the late spring had begun again in earnest, this creature spent the frosty days roving as Peter the Pliant, gentlemen jongleur.

Theirs was a fashion and calling that had fallen out of favor in the West. Before Winkie was born, his peasant father and father's father had once traveled from Byzantium to Egypt to Spain to London. By happy accident, Winkie himself was black-skinned like a moor. But the Empire these days was more interested in seeing holy Ecstatics beat themselves to bloody meat than in taking in a pleasing show of song, fart and dance. So the players were locally dislodged and currently putting their talents to other uses. Most often they put on Bible shows, manufacturing entire floods and bellies of whales upon the back of Lucius, their Ass, but other times they performed less moral work.

They employed this creature into hoodwinking various villages. They would spread word of the Peregrine's deeds and then engineer his reappearance on Moon nights. An entire inn could be emptied by a proper haunting, leaving all its delights—save whores—for the taking.

This creature found the jongleuring most entertaining. It brought her joy. It was possible by the application of illusion to occasion all sorts of complex motion in the fancy of the simple minded. The very town-folk and peasants who had thought her hung before would be offered vision of her ghastly painted visage at midnight, miting lip, trundling on her hands on the back of Lucius with a second face painted upon its bottom. Many went mad at the sight, giving freely all their valuables to the "wise ones" who came to chase her away.

There were those who would please St. Peregrine by leaving food, good fowl, onions, beer and wine out of doors and she and her companions would gather it up at night. And no one ever thought Peter the Pliant was the one. By now she had learned the higher arts of the jongle. Her body was easy for her to control with precision. The lads taught her how to leap and land, twist herself snake-like around any body, toss seven balls and a knife while pinching the perfect purse—one-handed. They taught her songs as well and something of music. She remembered songs whole and in their entirety and for the sake of variation, was able easily to assemble new ones for them from out of fragments.

The songs were for the most part chivalric, but often blasted with a peasant's hard-won wit. They taught her the old knowledge that whereas there will always be an idle elite and an indolent mass, there will always be a mind that can move among them. The scribe will write no more about the songs, this creature presuming they are contained in other books.

The gentlemen jongleurs, coarse as they were, opened finer spheres to this creature's perception. She glimpsed the veiled, soft-colored sphere hoarded by stone and protected by sword, the always-interior that was like the soft womb of the human sphere. From motions within it, the motions of the outer spheres were in peculiar fashion affected.

The players' band moved Westward gradually, and south, just enough so as to stave off the gradual thaw of winter. Indeed from observing the seasons this creature now ciphered that the orb she stood upon was turning on its own axis in tipped route around the Sun. The Germans go to carnival till spring, they told her and it seemed for the most part true. The jongleurs made good sport with these folk. They moved about the carnival as a sort of law of their own.

By their code, they preyed upon those who deserved it most. Upon fools priding in their finery or hose, or strutting about the spheres as if they owned them, cowing others into believing it. They were allowed free reign by the soldiers. No soldier truly feared a player, for they helped to pass the long day. As long as they did not interfere with matters of statecraft, the actors enjoyed total license.

This creature often played the female roles available in the company's productions. She enjoyed a scold, and gave great dignity administering to the trials and tribulations her cowed betrothed (usually Noah) underwent on a midwinter's eve. She enjoyed a gossip whose analytical and perverse desire to destroy the happiness of heroes (usually Jacob) rewarded this creature with schematic views of local society and its secrets. She enjoyed a baud who liked to wrestle and lift her tresses beneath the sun on rooftops, bringing the old ways back to King David. She enjoyed a great many of the saintly sisters kept by the church from the wilds of Nature, only to be gang-raped like Agnes.

News came to her, as she knew it would, of Gottskaw. Indeed, an account of some merchants' wives had it known that the knight had holed up for the winter in the confines of the Cistercian Abbey of E., four days east of the Rhine. But contrary to his savage report, even the sisters had it said that "Guttskaw," after the putting down of the Albigensian heresy, had changed his ways. Yes, he'd come upon a great assembly of the Men of Light engaged in their wickedness and put them to the sword. It was a great massacre and after, he was pardoned by at least one pope. He had disbanded the greater part of his army and was now trying to make himself a baron, they said, to establish an authentic dynasty in the coming kingdoms. He had a girl of noble blood he was to marry. But a child, it was said, she had been long ill. He was waiting for her to recover and hoped to wed her on Saint Andrew's day.

The players were asked by this local assembly of merchants' wives to play in St. R. for the wedding.

L

The Goodwife's Breast

The band accepted the mission. They took residence in St. R., the most civilized town this creature had yet come upon. It enjoyed a monastery, two stone churches, a Hanseatic Guild Hall, racks of stone and wooden houses and tent-topped taverns. She and her brothers took residence in one of the latter, and worked long hours preparing a performance for Gottskaw's wedding. She would put together a play that would force him to reveal his interest in her for all time.

But one day some weeks before the wedding, a local farmer who fancied himself a fine fellow in the taverns, invited three of the Players, in his cups, to a game. They let him win and plied him with drink. As the good man counted his gain, he boasted of an enormous ham from which his good wife would only pick fat for the stew. The meat itself was his alone for doing as he pleased. An entire ham was a rarity, and this one was fit for a king—but his wife had hidden it from him, claiming it should last a season.

He requested, and paid for, the following performance.

One of the players, painted and scented as a handsome knight, would charm the good wife into telling where she hid the ham. The others would steal it.

It so happened that this creature intended, during the climax of play she was composing for the Wedding, to play the part of Sir John Hawkwood, the English knight. Since it was well prepared, the others chose this creature to play the romancing knight. Done up then in twin moustaches and a brightly colored hose that conformed scandalously to her large codpiece, this creature tap-tap-tapped at the farmhouse door. A ripe good wife opened.

"A knight who would be of service to a Lady!"

"A knight it is?" She looked at him. "Well don't you know? There is some heavy lifting to do. My husband is a ne'er-do-a-thing."

Blooming of cheek, big of hip, she would have Sir Peter the Pliant lifting and moving items all over the dirty-smelling room, with one eye always upon his charms. But he swooned before her.

"We love you our lady," said this creature, upon her knees. "And shall devote all our contests of arms towards advancement in your lovely *secret hams*."

"Oooh!" she winked. "What would old Florian say about that? Listen, there's a loose nail under the loo—"

This creature leapt to her feat. "Old Florian, my lady, is a fool. He grows his own horns in the fat from your stew."

"Can you only talk of swine? If it's a ham you're after, the one under that floorboard isn't much larger than the one in your thighs, Sir Knight. So come to. Old Florian has not foarked me for sixmonth."

It was remarkable the capacity these Germanic folks had for blushing. This creature was able to behold a mystery of pink and white flash upon the goodwife's cheeks as he tore open her sweat-edged bodice and kissed her pink and merry neck. But first, here is the song this vile creature sang.

> *Rain, Rain, the master rises*
> *Frost, Fire, the beggar chides him*
> *Next, Floor, the wife she sighs*
> *Twixt whom the jolly beggar rides*

Sun, Sun, the beggar's a Lion
He is the Pope, the king of Zion
Avignon and the Rhei-en
And twillplace have one hand behind you
Hilda, Snow, before you fall.
Snow, snow, before you fall.

At which point her comrades outside the window, having heard the arrangement of the rhymes, now knew that Hilda had hidden the ham under the floors by the chimney. They burst in, covered my lady's face with a rag, tore up the floor—and found a nest of rats.

And as her companions made off merrily through the white and silent snow in fabrics of red, yellow, motley green, and checkers of blue, tossing the flesh-cleaned carcass between them, tingles of their foot bells muffling in the fat snowy sphere, this little creature remained in the farmhouse. She stood before the goodwife who, now setting upon the floor, sobbed, head covered, shift torn open, breast revealed to all time. And upon the breast she spied a ringed and blackened buboe.

LI

The Death, This Book

There was to be, in the end, no play. They were all taken, all the players and all the audience: long they remain, excepted by the Death. But the Hawkwood costume—tin hat, false breastplate, little pointed beard and two tight-wound mustaches—remained.

There was no one not to recognize her. When she had buried her friends and seen to the picking of their pockets, this creature in her loneliness hoped to go back and warn them of what was coming. She touched again her arm, but only Lucius the ass came to her and brayed. The spheres did not change hue.

She rode upon Lucius and eventually came at last to that abbey of E. near the Rhine where Gottskaw was said to have camped. She spotted it by the smoke in the sky.

This Cistercian Abbey was the most remarkable human structure this creature had yet beheld. White battlements popped comically out of a series of interlocked structures, tipped with red cones bearing broad black banners. They protected a high outcrop of rock in the center of a great gorge. The road to was long and bowed downward on the approach. This creature rode upwards at the end towards a high, open gate. Inside, she found a small village of stone, constructed around the interior battlements of an inner keep, surrounding the central hilltop. The great and ancient structure, lengths thick with stone, stood grim-faced and impervious upon all the spheres. But everywhere from its windows, its interior burned.

Inside the keep, she found a charnel house. The dead had been piled upon one another till those who had piled them had died. Living animals were all about. The bodies had fallen apart in the most appealing fashion, festering into banquets for rats and thick-beaked crows. Wolves sauntered in the distance blood-soaked and gorged. Pigs and chickens squealed around her feet as she entered.

Just inside the keep's high wall, she saw above her a tall figure leaning upon a colonnade. It was her servant Llw, examining arrows from the guardhouse store, selecting and holding individual missiles up to the light.

"Lawless," she said.

"My Lord," he answered, not surprised to see her. "I might not have recognized you."

"Where is Gottskaw?"

"Come."

She followed him through the great oak door of the inner-keep, into the old Abbot's Chambers now adorned with brilliant banners, armors, tapestries, furs, *objects* plundered from all the world. Many of these were burning. She looked out a window. So high were they on the hill that much of the land appeared in miniature.

Llw had come behind her. A dagger flashed in his hand and darted towards her neck. But it was her knife and she touched her arm. A wolf leaped out from behind an armoire. She took the Archer's throat in its jaw. There was no escaping for Llw. She understood he was not a god, but neither was he quite a man. Now, in this sphere, he was now no more than a body pumping blood upon the floor.

She let go of her arm.

This little creature ran. She ran with the wolf, for it was she, the one she knew, through long empty hallways, over skins and stones. They scattered crows and fleas over bloated corpses. This creature ran at last to Gottskaw's mad workshop.

Gottskaw's chapel was fashioned like a room according to the Canon's dictates. Stone-cut and cool, it arched without window to a single point, and contained an altar of stone in its center. One could feel possibilities controlled within its design to the point of perfection. The five-pointed star carved into a circle on its floor worked in congress with other stars upon a clockwork design on the floor. She lit a fire with a machine she had made from electrum and from in a brazier. The room gleamed like fire in the ruby-red light of the flame. Certes, it was a place of some weight.

She had not yet let go her arm. She turned to the wolf. "Can you speak," she asked it.

"Well... Yes!" it said. "Apparently we can."

"I must use my arm to go back before this moment. I must warn my friends of the death."

The wolf sighed. "You can use death very well, all around, with your arm. Without death you're nothing. The point is it's out of death you can emerge. You must let those who observe your coming die."

"Why? Why have I come here?"

"To do as you must do, volunteer. You've already exposed one English agent. There will be more for now the battle in your time has begun."

"Our time? Are we remembered in other times?"

"You are remembered. The forty or so individuals now remaining on station have just now been entertaining themselves with your memory. We've had your wake this afternoon, and are now gearing up for a wedding. The lovely Ms. Osmonovic Leguin Byson is to wed BJ Baker, Reverend of Free Space Blish Baily presiding."

"You are Lady C?"

"One and the same. Are you surprised? We regret that we were never unable to revive you, volunteer. Your body was found too late to preserve delicate tissue. No one thought they would have put you in an Admin level bedsphere, I'm afraid."

"You are not she."

"Don't you recognize us, Eddie Ryan? Yes, we are Control."

"No. You're not."

This creature let go of her arm, and the wolf with it.

Had the arm in fact worked?

The ideas this creature came very close to remembering flaked into the heavy snow drifting around her as she awoke to find herself again lit by diffused light before Farmer Florian's house, the man himself beside her, chest heaving, gripping an axe. This creature's arm had come off. When she placed the arm back upon the ruby ivory of her shoulder it seemed to suck into her, reattaching itself *of its own will*. As it did, all particles and objects seemed to swing backwards around her.

She stood up from the snow. "Good Farmer," she said. "I have enjoyed your bed, and I have enjoyed your sweet companion, a bud of the finest spring. Why is it that you have been so good as to give me my arm?"

The farmer struck her with the axe and in the shock the arm fell off.

Her own arm? She could never then let it go again?

Good fellows! Her comrades had seen the Farmer returning upon the road in a drunken rage. They had followed and now came to save her. There was much hilarity and joy as we made off backwards through the white and silent snow, red and yellow and motley green, and checkers of blue, tingles of bells muffled in the fat snowy air.

But this creature noticed later that no one had ever told the tale. She let go of her arm for the last time, and looked about the cold chamber in the depths of the abbey's old keep. The wolf had gone. The room was darker again. This creature lit more fires, and discovered as she did the one whom she had sought. Gottskaw. Upon a stone floor strewn with soft yellow sage, this creature came upon a putrid sack she recognized. As she knew it, it was the corpse of Quintus Scariot, *Doctor Philosophiae*.

For Scariot himself was Gottskaw. Dick was a maid, and had been the one to be his bride, or so this creature now understood. For she saw a painting half-finished of the scene as it had been, with the Demon in Scariot standing before what she recognized as her true love. Gottskaw had been sketching it still as he died of the plague. It showed her beloved, her Dick, but revealed, in Dick's nakedness, a maid, stripped naked, fixed upside down on a stake.

Indeed he had built a stake in the corner for much the same. Hope blossomed, but she did not find her beloved tied naked upon it. She found an empty scarecrow done up in a black shift and a purple hose. In an inside sleeve, she uncovered a little cold arm. And in its hand, this book.

EPILOGUE

Every four months, for a period of about twenty or so Earth-days, Mercury appears to move backwards against the stars From Earth. With the Saracens' *Zephyrum*, one can more easily compare observable phenomena and uncover that Mercury hasn't stopped or gone backwards at all. The Retrograde is simply a trick of vision where one observer is moving along one circular path perceiving an object moving along a different circular path around the same center.

After five such perfect turns of four, events were arranged for this creature's employment, along with a number of other orphans, in the household of one Benjamin Fagin of Cologne.

This kindly, crag-faced man had passed through what he called many *conduits*. His mind was forever opening. He noted immediately this creature's abilities and hired her in the place of a clerk who had died of a cancer. He took her on though he knew this creature to be a woman, young and unlicensed by any University. This caused him some trouble with the clerks who still had much power in the great city. Yet Fagin knew that they would make worse trouble for him had they not just this sort of thing to occupy their attentions. He would move on soon. He planned to set out for France before the death came and they blamed him for that.

Fagin trained her in the arts of memory, and was astonished by the success of her compartmentalization and filing. There are three parts of the mind: the will, the wit, and the memory. In the latter this creature has special gifts. For when the mind has been separated from the body, the perturbations of the memory remain. Fagin thought he might use this capability in his secret, very lucrative trade in books. There was no end to the uses to which he might put this creature's talents.

Scores of books passed through the old man's careful hands. This creature could read none of them. But he read them aloud and found she could always remember what he had said. She would then repeat them to scribes. Of a late afternoon Fagin would read to her from his library, sipping in his gardens of his own house-brewed beer. On the day before he finally planned to leave the city, this creature gave to him her book, Gottskaw's book.

To this creature's astonishment and relief he did not look upon her as a monster when he had read it.

He pulled upon his old fashioned mustache. His young eyes shone with inner light. He was near tears, of what it was difficult to say. "I know a Doctor has been climbing the ten steps of the holy tree of life," he said. "He might know what to make of this. Perhaps you should show him your book."

"No. What do you make of it?"

"Well," he said. "Your friends and loved ones are dead. You are not responsible for their deaths. It often seems that way, but you're not. Everyone you know will die, in time. Be glad you have your arm."

"I have no arm."

"I spoke only in metaphor."

"She had the arm. I understand that Gottskaw cut it from her to kill her, to take from it its magic light, but that she survived when he had done so, and escaped him with the light. But I had come as well, for I exist. He saw the two of us. Not understanding it, Scariot preserved our arm, to draw us together into a single mystery. If he could kill us both together, he believed, he might take a head, a new limb, something to free him or his demon of the other. As it happened they were all killed by the plague before his plot came to fruition. And now she, she who was Dick, never was."

"Yes. As I cipher it, if she had lived, you yourself would have been able to die easier in the tale. One of you had to die, of course, and it seems to have been her. I am sorry for your loss, Peregrine."

He handed the book back.

"And the other parts," she asked him. "The stranger parts of the narrative, what say you of them?"

"I have seen strange lights in the sky," Fagin told her. "I have heard tell of merchants from other stars, painted blue. The Doctor informs me Elijah himself rode a wheel into the heavens. Those parts of your narrative are more of the same, in a sense. Yet as a whole the story of this Ryan is close to meaningless, I'm afraid. There are some political notions that interest me, but even they speak of irreverence. Perhaps the ugly nonsense ciphers a code. Otherwise, it's unfathomable and reeking of fantasy."

This creature made no answer, but stared into the dancing fire. Fagin drank from his flagon of clean beer. "You smile," he said.

"I dislike it too," she said. "The Death turned Gottskav's curse upon itself. And left it written into this book. This book is his in all time. We are not Gottskaw, just as we are not Ryan or McAllister. Are we their daughter? Perhaps. If so, it is only because we were already an orphan. We are not the one they have understood in their writings. We have slipped here, not because they willed it, or those that sent them willed it, but because I was always not here to begin with. I speak of the other, the one this book leaves unmentioned. The first maid, taken from the west, muted, silenced in her own time, raped and slaughtered upon a stake. Though empires fall around her before and after, this creature yet lives. Her true love is no more or yet to be, but she is not. And thus, she is the miracle. She wishes to stand now here upon her own ground and investigate her origins. So that she will be rid of all these interfering claims on her life and times, she shall place their book now onto the fire."

"You shall do no such thing in my company, little bird," said this creature's friend, putting down his flagon and rising with the aid of a stick. "I am superstitious only of seven things, and one of them is the burning of books. I retire. If you should wish to glimpse Mercury before our travels, we must rise early on the morrow."

THE END

ABOUT THE AUTHOR

Mark von Schlegell's science fiction can be found in underground newspapers, chap-books and zines the world over. *Venusia*, his first novel, was honor's listed for the 2007 James Tiptree, Jr. Prize in SF. His criticism is published internationally by magazines and institutions like *Parkett*, *The Rambler*, the Whitney Museum and LA MOCA. *Realometer*, a collection of literary essays, is forthcoming Spring '09 from Merve Verlag, Berlin.